Meet Me Under the Lights

CASSIE MILLER

VIKING

VIKING
An imprint of Penguin Random House LLC
1745 Broadway, New York, NY 10019
penguinrandomhouse.com

Edited by Dana Leydig
Design by Anabeth Bostrup
Text set in Perpetua MT Pro

Library of Congress Cataloging-in-Publication Data is available.

First published in the United States of America by Viking, 2026

Manufactured in the United States of America
LSCC

ISBN 9798217038923
1st Printing

The authorized representative in the EU for product safety and compliance is Penguin Random House Ireland, Morrison Chambers, 32 Nassau Street, Dublin D02 YH68, Ireland, https://eu-contact.penguin.ie.

For my mom, who surrounded my childhood with books, and for my dad, who introduced me to the greatest sport there is: baseball

"It's supposed to be hard.
If it wasn't hard, everyone would do it.
The hard is what makes it great."

—*A League of Their Own*

Chapter One

ELIZA

"When we are born, we cry that we are come to this great stage of fools." —William Shakespeare, *King Lear*

I had hoped that if I showed up to a party dressed head to toe in black and feathers, a gothic fairy from *A Midsummer Night's Dream*, I could hide in plain sight.

I was wrong.

It only took thirty minutes after my walking inside for one of my exes, dressed as Mario, to appear at my side and ask if he could "jump me to level up."

He earned a swift heel to his clunky plumber boot.

And minutes later, someone nameless dressed as Frodo hissed "My precious" into my ear.

Frodo's journey to Mount Doom would take him a bit longer now with a bruised kneecap.

God, I hated big parties.

My best friend, Lauryn, however, lived for them. She waved

and flashed a beaming smile while swaying with the bass in a haze of smoke. Her platinum-blond hair with lavender highlights bounced off her shoulders as her diamond nose stud sparkled under a chandelier.

"Elizaaaa!" she called out to the tune of "The Schuyler Sisters" before she wove through the crowd toward me.

Well, if anyone hasn't noticed me yet, they sure as hell know who I am now.

My watch glittered under the string of neon lights above me, and I scowled. Barely 10:30 p.m. and she's made a *Hamilton* reference.

It was Tracey's—the most popular and fakest girl in school—annual Beginning of Summer Party, and after what happened last year, I couldn't let Lauryn go alone to this one. If she had more than three Jell-O shooters, she was a hot mess of cabaret. Our friends still talked about last June's performance of "Lovely Ladies" and her . . . dancing.

"Would you please stop sulking? You're getting forehead wrinkles." Lauryn grabbed my arm and dragged me toward a bar covered with white twinkle lights. "It's a party! Lighten up! We're going to be seniors in a couple months!"

Don't remind me. I still had so much to do before school started again. "I'm not sulking. And I don't have forehead wrinkles."

"Maybe not yet, but you will." She picked and plucked at my tank top. "Then again, it's hard to tell anything about you underneath all those black feathers. Why'd you wear this, again?"

"I'm a dark fairy." I flicked away her hand. "Plus, it helps me blend in."

"You couldn't blend in if you tried, girl."

Fair.

It was hard enough having people fawn over me during the school year—the rich Crowley girl, daughter of the man who practically owned the town. But was it too much to ask to blend in for just one night? To not be a Crowley?

Lauryn hiccupped, her breath reeking of cherry syrup mixed with vodka.

"How many have you had?" I yelled over the music.

Lauryn snagged a pen from the bar and began doodling a necklace design on a small white napkin.

"Lauryn?" I nudged her. "How many?"

"What? Oh. Just a couple." She tossed the pen aside. "So how do I look?"

I scanned her over. "Like a cute bunny."

"I'm a cat."

Oh. "Right. A really *cute* cat."

I fixed my sequin-and-feather-covered mask so I could see better and gave a once-around to Tracey's house. Her parents always traveled at the beginning of summer, giving Tracey and her older brother dibs on the first official party of summer vacation for the last several years. Warm beer or horribly sweet mixed drinks sloshed around in everyone's cups, and phones were out or close by because something always went down at Tracey's.

Lauryn adjusted her gray-and-pink pointed ears. "Okay, serious question. How's my tail? Too poufy?" She whirled around and bumped into two girls who were all over each other.

One of them whined and flipped her mermaid wig. "Hey!"

"*Please.* Get a room." As the girls staggered away, she wiggled her butt at me. "So?"

"The tail is perfect. Go get 'em."

The front storm door opened, and a group of costumed boys stood beneath its frame. The entire room slowed down to watch these outsiders make an entrance as the music changed. One looked a little familiar, but getting a clear glimpse of him through this crowd? Impossible.

Not that it mattered.

In our small town, a group of strangers this time of year could mean only one thing: Diamond Boys.

When new crews of ballplayers came in from all over the state to play for Dad's baseball team hoping to impress college scouts and earn extra conditioning over the summer, the locals threw out all the stops—discounts to anyone holding a ball game ticket or program, closed businesses on game days, free ice cream to the winning team.

Going to a baseball game was as common and routine in this town as going to church, maybe even more so. Just like the opening pitch signaled spring, the Legion League signaled summer. Dad had a good reputation for his players going D1, getting invited to showcases, sometimes to the minors after a summer season. His boys were the best of the best, so the town treated them like homegrown celebrities.

Still . . . I had met most of Dad's team already. These boys didn't look like any of them.

Tracey hurried dutifully over to the newbies, her poufy cotton tail bouncing over black leggings, with a few of her friends, dressed as various animals, scurrying behind her.

It was like the costume designer from *Chicago* dressed Snow White's woodland posse.

"Who are those guys?" Lauryn stood on her tiptoes.

I shrugged. "Who knows . . ."

"I'll tell you who they are," a voice slurred next to my ear.

I cringed at the overpowering and familiar smell of whiskey and ginger ale.

Truth: My cousin TJ was equally annoying whether he was drunk or sober.

Lauryn flicked the front of TJ's pirate hat, which was too small to go over his blond, curly mohawk. "What are you supposed to be, Teej?" she asked. "A biker pirate? Oh! A birate? Or maybe a pirker . . . piraker . . ."

"I won the hat from some idiot freshman who bet me I wouldn't walk across the peak of Tracey's roof." He took a quick swig from his cup and set it down.

"So you're drinking *and* scaling roofs. Wow." I quickly swapped his cup out for my can of Coke.

"You know me. I never back down from a bet."

"Yeah, we know." Lauryn crossed her arms. "My mom says the other nurses in the ER still talk about that stunt you pulled last summer at the railyard."

TJ beamed. "That backflip was one of my best. It's not my fault the others decided to try it." He paused and leaned against the wall, his hat sliding down over one of his eyebrows. "We can go for a walk outside, Lauryn. Talk about it some more if you want."

TJ had been crushing on my best friend since we were kids. But Lauryn was the queen of playing hard to get.

"No, thanks." She pointed across the room. "I've got my eye on something better."

TJ followed her gaze and cursed. "Those guys? Ha. They're nothing but farmer trash trying to take away my family's trophies. Bunch of low-life hicks . . ."

My ears buzzed. "Wait. What do you mean, take away our family's trophies?"

TJ gawked at me like I came from another planet, an alien blip on his baseball radar. And then his eyes changed to his common mischievous-daredevil expression. I called it "the TJ."

"Haven't you heard, Princess? Old Man Fulton put together his own team this year, and he and your stubborn-ass father made a bet on the side. Our team has to have a better record than theirs or . . ." He took a swig of soda then looked at the can in confusion.

I smacked his arm. "Or what?"

"Or it's bye-bye, stadium."

"WHAT? Why would he—"

"I still can't believe he put it up for grabs. And for what? A dumbass feud from thirty years ago? Freaking Fultons always know how to weasel their way in . . ." He rambled off a string of curse words and disappeared into the haze of smoke and bass.

What the actual hell? Dad made a bet with the stadium as a prize?

I whipped out my phone and started texting him a flurry of angry, all-caps messages, but Lauryn took it away and closed the message out.

"I don't buy it. There's no way." Lauryn gave my phone back to me but held my hand and squeezed it. "TJ probably exaggerated. You know how he is when he's been drinking."

"Right." The room started pushing in on me from all sides. "Exaggerated."

But my gut told me TJ wasn't making this up. It was too big of a story to craft, even for him.

Lauryn crouched down a little so her face was directly in front of mine. "I'll see what I can find out, okay?"

"Okay."

True, I hated the way Diamond Boys invaded our town every summer, but baseball helped keep the town going. Small businesses were unpredictable, constantly having to adjust and change with the weather. Baseball wasn't. Was Dad really that prideful, to not only put our family at risk but the entire town too?

Or was it something else I had been too busy to notice?

A "nurse" sauntered by with a tray of shooters. I swiped one before I could think twice and squeezed the Jell-O out of the small Dixie cup into my mouth, immediately regretting it.

This crap tasted worse than cough syrup.

I hunted down a hard lemonade—one more drink wouldn't hurt, right?—and then scanned the house for a quiet place to hide. Opposite the dining room, two French doors stood open, and a small desk lamp illuminated an office. Keeping my back pressed to the wall, I inched my way around the awkward grinding, slinking into the office before anyone noticed.

It wasn't that I didn't like most of the people here; it was just easier to let only a few of them in at a time. My brother called it self-preservation, because with a last name like ours, we found that most people wanted to be our friends for the wrong reasons—popularity, favors, etc. I could count on one hand the number of real friends I'd had over the years, and that had always been enough for me. Like Grandma had taught me: quality over quantity.

Lauryn's laughter pealed across the house. She now danced with one of the new guys who currently twirled her around while singing—horribly off-key—at the top of his lungs. Lauryn was loud, but at least she wasn't on a table, so I took a slow sip of my hard lemonade, the tanginess numbing me all the way down as I settled into a high-backed armchair. Drawing my legs up underneath me, I pulled out my phone, then opened the PDF manual of the new light board for the community theater. The first tech rehearsal for *Romeo and Juliet* was in two days, and I needed to be ready.

I made notes with my ideas for how to light the stage for the opening sequences, the shading patterns I wanted to use for the two families. A brand-new ChamSys light board waited for me in the booth of the Lyric. With over twenty execute buttons and more color options than the paint swatches at Mom and Dad's hardware store, I couldn't wait to get my hands on it.

I added another note to check on the follow spot bulbs since they were notorious for being too weak when the noise outside the office grew louder. The new Diamond Boys, apparently Fulton's crew, yelled at some of the guys from my school. "Yankees" and "Red Sox" were dropped a couple of times.

Pathetic.

Couldn't they find something else to argue about?

And what was the point? The Yankees would always be better than the Red Sox.

The argument grew louder, and a dozen or so costumed players spilled into the office like a mosh pit at a concert.

Someone yelled from the opposite end of the room, and the crowd shifted. A tall boy with a golden crown over dark hair fell backward, one of his hands above his head, the other holding a spilling red Solo cup as he stumbled after something.

"I got it! I got it!" he yelled.

Oh crap. "Watch it!" I stuck out my leg to stop him from crashing into me. But it was too late.

He dropped the ball, tripped, and fell onto my lap, his beer splashing all over me.

Warm, pee-smelling liquid dripped off my chin. I shoved the idiot to the floor. "Are you freakin' kidding me?"

He picked up his crown and shook it dry. "My bad. Wild throw."

That voice.

Why did it sound so familiar?

The room erupted in laughter as my cheeks seared with heat. "I'm sure it was." I tucked my phone away and kicked the clumsy royal as I passed by.

"Eliza?" he called.

I turned around slowly, and my pulse raced faster than a rookie actor's with stage fright. "Reed? Reed Fulton?"

Great. Just great.

Of all the summers for the Reed Plague to hit, it had to hit this one. *What next? Locusts?*

Reed jumped up and straightened his fluffy white shirt. "What's it been, four, five years?"

"Four." My eye twitched.

He had grown at least a foot taller since I last saw him. The broad shoulders and stubble on his jaw were new, but he still had that same annoying smirk and that dimple . . .

"That's right," he said. "I was thirteen when—"

"You deserved it," I snapped.

He reached around me and grabbed my drink, taking a long sip. Whatever. I didn't like it anyway. "So what's Princess Crowley doing at a party? Shouldn't you be home letting your daddy tuck you in?"

"Shouldn't you be back on the farm milking cows?" The Fultons didn't have cows, but that was always my go-to.

His ears reddened. "Actually, I'm here to pitch against your dad's team this summer."

Crap, I forgot he pitched. And didn't I read somewhere that he was really good? Like really, really good? "So was this whole bet your granddad's foolish idea or yours?"

A hush fell over the room. Even the music grew softer.

"There's nothing foolish about claiming back what's always been rightfully ours." Reed stood up straighter. "But don't worry. I'm sure we won't embarrass the Crowley *dynasty* too badly."

I chuckled and stepped closer, kicking the baseball to the side. "The only one who should be worried about being embarrassed this season is you, Fulton."

Half the people at the party now watched us with unblinking eyes, most of them with their phones already recording our standoff. The town lived for this.

Crowley versus Fulton.

But as much as I loved torturing my childhood enemy, I hated the audience. I dealt with that enough when he wasn't here. "I don't have time for this," I mumbled, pushing him as I walked away.

Reed straightened up, sticking out his chest. "You know, you just shoved a prince. Most would treat me with a bit more respect."

"Oh, my apologies, Your Royal Assness. I'll just fly south now and be on my way." *Jerk.*

"Actually, it's Prince Charming," he yelled, like he was freakin' James Bond or something. "Although I do have a pretty royal ass if I do say so myself. Can't say the same for yours from this angle though, Crowley."

I stopped.

The baseball that started this whole nightmare encounter lay at my feet, its laces smiling at me. In an instant, I scooped it up, spun around, and hurled it at his crown, knocking it cleanly off his head. It dropped to the floor with a satisfying *thunk*, this time breaking off two of its arches.

"Your Majesty." I bowed to the applause of the room before leaving.

Chapter Two

REED

"I do what I've trained my whole life to do. I watch the ball. I keep my eye on the ball." —Barry Lyga, *Boy Toy*

Damn. That crown had cost me the earnings from half a yard's mowing.

Ben appeared in front of me and laughed. "Well, that's one way to make an entrance."

I bent down to pick up the crown and cursed.

"Don't worry." He snatched it from me and held it up to the light. "That's nothing a little duct tape can't fix."

I followed him through the swarm of people, several of whom snickered and bowed the way Eliza did as I passed, before we made it to the massive kitchen. Even with all the trash and open pizza boxes, the marble counters gleamed under the fancy pendant lights.

What Nana wouldn't give to be able to afford a kitchen like

this. Meanwhile, these people probably have enough money to pay someone else to clean it.

"You know, if we used last year's Halloween costumes, this wouldn't have happened," he said, rummaging through some drawers.

"Ben." I rubbed my face. "I was not about to come to this thing dressed up as Dusty—"

"But you would've had your trusty Steve the Babysitter with you, man."

Ben and I started watching *Stranger Things* after Dad's first deployment a few years ago. At first, it was a distraction, but after round three of Dad going overseas, it became tradition—something familiar to hold on to.

Eliza breezed into the room and grabbed a can of Coke from the fridge, oblivious to me scowling at her. Her arms flew around her wildly while she talked with someone dressed as a bunny . . . or maybe a cat. They all looked the same at these things.

Bunny-Cat Girl nodded in my direction, and then Eliza turned to me and flipped me off before grabbing Bunny Cat's hand and whisking her out of the room.

Right back at ya, darlin'.

"So *that's* the Crowley I've heard so much about?" Ben asked.

I nodded. In the flesh. Or in her case, feathers.

She should've come as a Dementor.

"She doesn't look like an annoying, evil rich girl with big

ears." Ben ripped off a piece of tape using his teeth. "Hold that arch there for me."

I did as he said. "That girl ruined my Transformers collection when I was eight years old."

"How'd she do that?" He rotated the crown around to the other broken piece and motioned for me to hold it still again as he got another strip of tape.

I tugged at the cuffs of my sleeves. "She stole them from me when I played at the library."

He stopped taping. "You used to go to the library?"

"Yeah, I used to go to the lib— That's not the point. The point is . . ." Jesus, my head hurt from this shit music. "The point—"

"The point is that she's hot." He craned his neck and stared at her. "Can't see her face with that mask on, but I'm kinda feelin' that whole dark and twisty vibe she's got goin' on."

I laughed. "Don't let the black feathers fool you. Her family's a bunch of rich snobs who act like they own the town. 'Dark and twisty' to them is a week without Starbucks."

Ben made a face and fell into the chair closest to me. "So what is it with you guys? Your families?"

"It's a long story." One I definitely didn't want to talk about right now. "We used to be friends, but then her family stole the stadium right out from under mine. Money talks here." *And they're the loudest people in Fairfield.*

"Well, for a rich girl, she's got a good arm." He held up my crown and smiled before pressing it onto my head. "There. Good as new."

Good as it'll ever get is more like it.

"You wanna get out of here?" I asked. My hand itched to hold a baseball.

Dad always said I had the imprints of baseball laces in my fingers the same way most kids had grooves on theirs from climbing monkey bars. I was born to pitch.

Or at least I thought I was, before last summer.

"Nah. This party is just now getting interesting." He smirked and pulled his mask back onto his face. "I think I'll go dance with Eliza's bunny friend again. Or cat . . . Whatever."

"Hey, now." I grabbed his shoulder. "Don't forget our pact. All baseball—"

"No girls, yeah, I know." He scratched his jaw. A long pink scar with faint stitch marks rested just above it. "I was the one to come up with it, remember?"

"I remember." When Ben's long-term girlfriend dumped him for a college guy days before our junior prom, he hit rock bottom and stayed there for a while. Lots of drinking. Lots of fighting. I hadn't seen him down that bad since his dad left a couple of years ago.

"But just one dance. What could go wrong?" Ben winked and grabbed a slice of pizza before walking away.

About a million and two things, actually. Not that me listing them would've stopped him.

I wove in and out of the crowd, making my way toward the back deck, and a few of my teammates gave me high fives with slurred comments.

"Fulton!"

"Ace, ace, baby!"

"It's your year, man!"

My year.

God, I hoped so.

I slid open the door to the deck and quickly closed it shut, falling against it hard enough to knock my crown to the fancy Trex flooring.

"Prince loses his crown a second time in one night," Eliza called from the railing across from me. She let out a low whistle. "Some prince you are, Fulton."

"Goth Bird comes to a party but sneaks away to play on her phone." I scooped up my crown and shoved it back on my head. "Pretty pathetic, Crowley."

"Bite me."

"No, thanks." I crossed the deck and leaned in toward her. "I don't wanna get fleas."

"God, you're annoying."

"You've missed it."

"Ha. 'Bout as much as I'd miss an ETC console." She bumped my arm as she walked down the steps and into the yard.

An ETC console?

When the hell did Eliza become a techie?

"Hey." A guy dressed in a cop uniform three sizes too small called to me from the opposite side of the deck near a bunch of people smoking pot. "Is it true your granddad made his own team this summer?"

"Yeah. It's true." I texted Ben to ask if we could head home yet.

"How the hell did a Fulton get the money to start up a team?" The guy snickered as he took a hit.

"Sponsors." And favors. Lots of favors I wasn't supposed to know about, but old farmhouses had thin walls. "What's it matter to you?"

He shrugged. "Just think it's funny that a farmer put together a team. What's he know about baseball, anyway?"

"A hell of a lot more than you. He and his brother helped build Crowley Park."

"Yeah?" He smacked his friend's shoulder to get his attention. "Then why's it not called Fulton Park?"

I didn't have time for this kind of shit.

I moved toward the sliding door, and he quickly hurried to block my path.

"Oh shit. I knew I recognized you. Weren't you the kid who blew it at the UNC showcase last year?"

I clenched my fists. A low ringing hissed through my ears.

Caveman, Cop Guy's friend, joined in. "I heard he didn't make it past the first round."

"You guys play?" I asked.

"Left field." Caveman straightened up and pointed to Cop Guy. "He plays first."

"Reed!" Ben yelled, throwing open the door. "What's good?"

I kept staring at the idiots in front of me.

"New friends?" Ben asked, getting in between us before he slapped the cop's gut. "You lost a few buttons there, officer."

Oil, meet my friend Fire. "These guys play for the Crowley team, Ben."

"No shit?" Ben lifted up his mask. At five-foot-ten, he stood a couple of inches shorter than me, but he towered over both of them. "You two can actually run the bases?"

"Better than you." Caveman took a step closer.

Ha. Ben had the fastest time in the sixty-yard dash last season back home.

"Bet." Ben smiled and grabbed Caveman's drink before he slowly poured the beer onto the deck.

Caveman grabbed Ben's collar.

Cop Guy and I stepped closer, fists out, but then a couple of girls called out to the Crowley crew. One of them hurried over and started to drag them both away. "You'll regret that," Caveman said.

"Nah, I won't." Ben waved at both of them before turning to me. "I'm gonna go grab one more drink and then we'll head out. You good?"

I watched Eliza ease into one of the swings, then said, "Yeah, I'm good. Thanks."

After Ben went inside, I shoved my hands into my pockets and strolled across the yard toward the swing set.

Eliza looked up from her phone and sighed. "Are you following me?"

"Nope. Just needed some air." I sat on the swing next to hers.

"Was the air not good enough on the deck?"

"Actually, no. I hate the smell of pot."

"Same." She went back to reading on her phone.

I twisted my swing back and forth. "If you're so bored, why not leave?"

"Can't."

"Why?"

She huffed. "Don't you have somewhere else to be?"

Of course I did. The ball field. The farm. Hell, I'd take Saturday detentions with Mr. Lederman again over this, and yet . . . irritating her was second nature. "Nope. My whole night is free just to bother you."

She kept her eyes down. "If I leave Lauryn alone at a party, she goes full on Lin-Manuel. Turns the party into her own performance."

Lauryn.

I thought Bunny-Cat Girl looked familiar.

"Isn't that more your angle?" I asked. A Crowley would never pass up the opportunity to take center stage.

"No. I don't like the spotlight," she said almost too softly for me to hear.

Ha. Sure. "I seem to remember you twirling your way up and down Main Street in a tutu. You used to say you'd be a principal in *Swan Lake* someday."

"I was seven."

"And?"

"That was also the year I said I wanted to be a professional ice cream scooper."

The same year I wanted to be Batman. Still mourning that one. "I heard someone say something about Rocky Road in the freezer a few minutes ago." I waved her on toward the house. "Don't let someone like me get in the way of your dreams, Crowley."

She started to laugh and then turned it into a cough. "News flash: I'm allowed to change my mind about what I want. Anyone is."

Fair enough. "I figured it was wired into your Crowley DNA or something. Craving attention—"

"Just because I'm a Crowley . . . ugh. Never mind." She twisted her swing away from me.

I could've gone inside then. Could've kept arguing with some dude dressed as Frodo about how much the Red Sox sucked, but annoying Eliza Crowley when I was in town was tradition.

Who was I to break with tradition?

Plus, this was a different side than I had seen before. Ms. Goody-Goody was now a puzzle. And I hated puzzles with missing pieces.

"What game are you playing on your phone that's so interesting?" I stood and leaned over her, but she pressed her phone against her chest.

"I'm reading a lighting manual."

"A lighting manual?" I dropped back into my swing.

Who was this girl?

She pinched her lips together before saying quickly, "For *Romeo and Juliet* at the Lyric."

"Seriously?" I laughed. "Of all the plays to pick, they picked that one? For this summer?"

"Meaning?" She twisted her swing to face me.

"It's pretty ironic. Our families facing off . . . 'Two households, both alike,' blah blah blah."

She rolled her eyes and went back to reading on her phone.

I dug my feet into the freshly cut grass. A few fireflies blinked nearby. "So . . . you're really in the booth and not on the stage?"

She kept her head down. "Is it really that surprising?"

This was the same girl who used to wear huge, fake pearls twenty-four seven, who pranced around in heels and oversized dresses when we were kids.

Uh, yeah. It was surprising.

"What would a pitcher know about stage lighting?" she mumbled.

"Gel changes. Tightening a frame. Follow spots. Underexposure?" I kicked a clump of dirt.

"Where did you—"

"I know movies."

The sound of glass shattering followed by cheers came from the house. *Christ, I hope Ben didn't break anything.*

"Movies?" she asked.

"Movies." I could've told her about my favorite directors, some of the classes I took online, the indie festivals I snuck into with Ben, but I stayed quiet. If she was allowed to be cryptic, so was I.

"Huh." She went back to reading on her phone.

There were a bunch of letters and numbers written on the back of her hand. Without thinking, I reached for it. "What's all that mean?"

She jumped when I touched her. "Nothing."

"Doesn't look like nothing."

"It'd take too long to explain."

Translation: I was too dense to understand.

"Cops!" voices yelled as everyone inside poured through the back door and over the deck.

"We gotta go, E!" Lauryn ran across the yard and nearly tripped over herself when she saw me standing next to her best friend. Her gaze darted back and forth between us. "Oh. Hi, Reed. Uh . . . here for the weekend?"

I stood. "For the summer, actually."

The tie on Eliza's mask snapped, causing the whole thing to fall to the ground. Both of us crouched for it and bumped heads.

"Ow. Dammit, Fulton," she hissed.

I stared at the girl I had known since I was a kid. Same dark hair that flipped out to the side when it was humid out. Same small line of freckles on her cheeks. Same tiny scar in the shape of a fingernail near her right eyebrow. Same irritated look she always saved just for me.

Or was it?

Something was . . . different.

"*Come on*, E," Lauryn whined. "Byeeee, Reed." She pulled Eliza to her feet, and the two disappeared into the mob.

"Did you catch that cat's name?" Ben appeared at my side.

I picked up the forgotten mask by my feet and raised an eyebrow. "Lauryn. Why?"

He held up his hands. "Just curious."

We ran toward my truck as the sounds of more police sirens drew nearer.

Ben opened the passenger door and pointed to my hand. "What's that?"

I still had Eliza's mask. Crap. *Why did I take it with me?*

Ben jumped in and closed his door. "You good?"

"Yeah, why?" I pulled away from the house.

"Dunno. You seem distracted."

Distracted? More like stressed the fuck out.

He would be too, if his granddad recruited him and most of his friends to win back a stadium from the family who practically owned the entire town.

"I'm good." I pulled off the main road onto a dirt one that would take me toward the creek, a good shortcut for home.

"Okay." Ben put his window down and propped his arm on the door. "Because we both know you need a better showing this season. Can't afford to repeat last June."

I gripped the steering wheel tighter. "I know."

"We're all baseball this summer."

I tucked Eliza's mask into my door. "All baseball."

Chapter Three

ELIZA

"Great theater is about challenging how we think and encouraging us to fantasize about a world we aspire to." –Willem Dafoe

Of course Reed Fulton had to be here this summer, of all summers.

A warm breeze blew across my face, lifting the flyaways off my forehead. Normally, standing on the balcony listening to crickets trilling in the grass brought me peace, but not tonight.

It's like I was twelve again, when he took my favorite set of pearls and draped them on Marvin the Bookworm, a big statue outside the local library, and totally ruined their luster. Or like the time he jumped out from Ms. Loretta's hydrangea bushes when I was balancing library books on my head. The books toppled over and into a muddy puddle, and all my piggy-bank money went to the library for damages.

"Eliza!" Lauryn called from behind.

I plucked and twirled one of the feathers from my costume before peering over my shoulder through the open door of my bedroom. "What's up?"

"You coming in anytime soon?"

"Probably not."

She groaned. "Come inside or I'll eat all these chips myself."

Truth: Lauryn was super terrified of heights and almost passed out the one time she visited me in the light booth. She wouldn't step foot onto my balcony even if I dared her to.

The light in the apartment above our garage turned on. TJ must've just gotten home. When he stayed with us for the summers, it always added drama, but at least he wasn't in my house all the time. With a full kitchen, bathroom, and a place to park his motorcycle in the garage below him, he'd hopefully keep to himself like usual.

Lauryn threw a chip at my head. "The bag's already half empty."

"Of course it is." I dropped the feather and watched it sway back and forth like a pendulum before it changed course, twirling and tumbling to a tune only it could hear.

Must be nice to float wherever you wanted. To come and go as you pleased.

I wouldn't know. Crowleys never floated. We steered.

I passed Lauryn and walked back into my room, its walls covered with posters of old plays and movie quotes, before slumping onto my bed and grabbing my favorite pillow.

Lauryn pored over the bulletin board above my desk, covered with tickets, college brochures, and old photos. After popping a Dorito in her mouth, she wiped her fingers on her T-shirt and unpinned a picture of my grandmother, who beamed as she held a spoon over her head in victory—one of many against the Fultons in the annual Battle of the Bolognese.

"That woman did it all, didn't she?" Lauryn said as she joined me at the foot of my bed.

I took the picture from her and rubbed my fingers over its soft edges. "She really did."

Theater superstar, queen of fundraisers, with the ability to name every person who passed by her in the street, Grandma Marguerite was in a class all on her own. Even after that crap went down with the stadium, she still called Reed's grandmother, Joyce, every Sunday for their usual catch-up.

Grandma died on a Saturday afternoon, and when Joyce called the day after, I assumed it was because she didn't know.

She did.

She had called to check on me.

I'd never forget that.

"She'd be proud of you for being in the production this summer." Lauryn offered me the open and now nearly empty bag of chips.

"Well, I'm not in it, really—"

"Hey." Lauryn smacked my leg. "Everyone who works and

helps with a play is *in* the play, Eliza. 'There are no small parts . . .'"

"'. . . only small actors,'" I finished, nudging her.

We let my cat-shaped clock on the wall speak for us for a few moments, its ticking only interrupted by Lauryn's hand going in and out of the chip bag until she finished it. "So . . . when do we get to talk about Reed Fulton being in town this summer?"

I fell back against my plush headboard.

"It's been a few years since I last saw him, but damn, girl." She fell backward next to me. "He's fire."

Please. I made a gagging noise. "No, he's not."

She smacked my arm. "I know your mask was covered in feathers but come on. Tall, dark eyes—"

"Arrogant, irritating . . ."

"But those arms and shoulders." She fake-swooned. "Did you see them?"

Yep. I saw them, all right.

Gah. Wait. What?

"His triceps pushing against that shirt . . ."

"Lauryn." I threw my pillow at her. "He's a *Fulton*. The same boy who stole my toys when I was six. Who told me there was no such thing as Santa Claus—"

"Didn't you say it was an accident about Santa—"

"I was five."

She laughed and hopped off my bed, grabbing my iPad off

the desk. I changed out of the rest of my costume, throwing on a pair of old lacrosse shorts and a big T-shirt of Dad's before peering over her shoulder.

Lauryn now scrolled through the new Fulton team page.

"Are you nuts?" I snatched it. "My dad uses this to make game videos sometimes."

Three loud knocks hammered on my door before it opened, and Dad stood under its frame holding a toothbrush. His reading glasses rested on the top of his salt-and-pepper hair, and a pen sat tucked behind his ear.

He must've been watching game tapes again.

"Eliza, your mother and I were worried when we didn't get a text from you. You know you're expected to text us when you go somewhere and when you're on your way back," he said.

Why not just put one of those GPS chips in my neck like a dog from the shelter? "I know. I'm sorry . . . I, uh, forgot." That, and running from the cops kinda got me all distracted. Not to mention running into the plague of my adolescence . . .

"You two getting ready for bed?" He leaned against the door frame.

"We're getting there," I said.

"You didn't drink at the party, did you?"

"No," we both blurted.

"Good." He waved his toothbrush at us. "You never know what people 'accidentally' drop into drinks. I watched a documentary about it once." He stepped into the room and sat in my desk chair. "It was part of a series on PBS about the realities of social cultures and norms. Remember when we used to watch PBS on Sunday nights, Eliza?"

Yep. Back when you and I actually had stuff in common. "Dad." I rubbed my temples. "We're tired."

"Oh. Right." He stood up and glanced around like he had forgotten something before moving toward the door. "You've got an early morning, anyway. I need you to help Mom get the stadium ready—"

"But we were at the stadium all day today." I grabbed a handful of gummy bears out of Lauryn's stash in her duffle. "Banners are hung up for the new season. Locker rooms are ready to go. The concession stand is stocked."

"That stadium needs to be pristine. The Fultons have a Family Day set up at the B Field to raise money for their team in a couple days, and I want our field to be a thousand times better than theirs."

I coughed, almost choking on one of the green ones. "They're on the B Field?"

"Yeah."

"The sandlot?"

He nodded.

"Dad, that field sucks." I laughed. "Ours already looks a million times better."

"She's totally right, Pops." Lauryn grabbed the remaining gummies out of my hand and shoved them into her mouth matter-of-factly.

Lauryn had been calling my dad Pops for forever. When she lost her dad in a freak accident years ago, Dad swooped in and picked her up as if she were a baby bird who fell from her nest. Dad was known for doing that kind of thing—reaching out to others and bringing them in.

He did that with my brother's boyfriend.

With TJ.

I used to think he got that trait from Grandma, but she'd never be as reckless as he apparently had been lately.

"Dad." I rubbed my hands together. "Why'd you put the stadium up for grabs this summer? Isn't that a bit . . . risky?"

"TJ told you, eh?" Dad moved his glasses into the front pocket of his shirt.

"It should've come from you," I said, moving toward him. "What if we lose? The hardware store has been down in sales for years, and Mom said Grandpa's money is almost gone—"

"Easy, kiddo." Dad held up his hand. "Small businesses everywhere are down right now, and most of Grandpa's money is safe and sound in the bank."

"I thought most of it was drawn out in cash when you took the stadium."

Lauryn coughed.

The cat clock ticked five times.

Dad cleared his throat. “We didn’t *take* the stadium. We *bought* it, fair and square, and we’re not going to lose it this summer.”

“But the Fultons have Reed pitching. Isn’t he supposed to be pretty good?” Crap. Did I just compliment a Fulton out loud?

Dad’s mouth morphed into a tight, thin line. His nose crinkled, and his face paled. “Who told you that?”

My head blanked. “I . . . uh . . . well—”

“I did,” Lauryn chimed in. Thank God. “I Googled the team.” She picked up the iPad and showed him their team page. “Sorry.”

“Don’t worry about it.” He swatted away her apology with his toothbrush like it was a meaningless fly. “If, by some miraculous turn of events for the Fultons, we do lose the stadium, it’s not like I can’t manage another one somewhere else.”

Excuse me?

“What do you mean ‘manage another one’?” Lauryn sat up straighter.

“Nothing to worry about right now, girls. It’s late. Get some sleep.” He smiled. “I’ll make waffles in the morning.”

“Oh, you don’t have to do that.” Lauryn gave me her “Oh shit” look. Dad’s version of breakfast was usually too charred to be edible.

“Of course I do.” He stepped into the hallway. “Lights out

soon. Oh, and Eliza, please stop driving that piece of junk around town. It's a wonder it still runs, and you already have a perfectly good car, one that definitely suits you better too."

Suits me better?

"And can you update the hardware store's website with some new pictures and a revised work schedule?" he asked.

"Sure, Dad. Just shoot me an email."

"Not necessary. I've got it all downstairs on some notes and an SD card." His eyes shone with pride. "I even remembered how much you liked organizing with sticky notes, so I used some of those too."

"*Dad*, you raided my stickies again?" The last time he did I spent hours reorganizing them.

He winked and closed the door. "Goodnight, girls."

"Night, Pops." Lauryn took out her earrings, a rectangular hammered sterling-silver pair with pink coral stones through the middle. She made those a few weeks ago and already had orders for two more pairs. Lauryn was incredible at making jewelry—really, she was incredible at everything she did.

"I think your dad needs to be more worried about Reed." Lauryn's face glowed from the light of the screen. "He's got a fastball that was clocked at eighty-nine miles per hour, you know."

Great. "Can we please drop it?"

"Guess that's why he's called an ace, huh?"

Sadly, yes.

Having him here during my first big shot with the infamous summer theater troupe was like saying "Good luck" and greasing the stage before a performance, but having an ace pitcher going against Dad's team during *their* most important season? Might as well stomp all over the foul line.

"Don't worry." Lauryn closed the iPad. "Your dad has one of the best records for summer baseball leagues in the state, maybe even on the East Coast."

"True." I fell backward and let my hair spill around me. "But did you hear him when he said he could always manage another stadium elsewhere?"

"I did." She reached across the bed toward my nightstand and grabbed my lotion. "You don't think that means . . . he wouldn't make you move your senior year, would he?"

"No. No way. He would never."

Right?

I grabbed my new bottle of face wash off my dresser and strolled into my bathroom. "I still can't believe he's going to ruin my summer though."

"Who? Your dad?" Lauryn appeared at my side in front of the mirror.

"No. Reed." I turned on the water and splashed my face. "I've never been able to focus with him around."

"Yes, I know." She nudged me. "Your brother and I have been telling you for years—"

"Lauryn . . ."

"Sooner or later, you'll accept it."

Ha.

Me and Fulton?

That's about as likely as a TV musical being better than Broadway.

Although, I'll admit . . . Grease Live! *wasn't half bad.*

She did a twirl out of the bathroom and began rummaging through the pieces of my costume on the floor. "Before I forget, can I have the mask back? Mom doesn't exactly know I borrowed it."

"Sure. I think I left it near the balcony."

Twenty minutes later, though, neither of us could find the crow mask anywhere in my room, on the balcony, or even in the back of my Jeep.

"I don't understand." Lauryn threw her hair up into a messy bun. "It didn't just disappear. So where is it?"

And then I remembered.

The swing set.

The cops.

I jumped.

It fell.

We bumped heads.

Dang it.

"It's not a 'where.'" I sank into my bean bag. "It's a 'who.'"

Chapter Four

REED

"I know there are a lot of expectations of me, and
I will do the best I can." –Carlos Beltrán

Early mornings were the best time to be at a ballpark. No groundskeepers cutting grass in the outfield. No obnoxious music blasting from the booth or noon-high sun burning the back of your neck. It had only been a few days since I came back to Fairfield, but it had already been one day too many away from the mound.

This was what I needed. Just a blank scoreboard, an empty field, and a ball in my hand.

"I hate you," Ben muttered.

"What?" I grinned at him as he walked toward home plate like a hungover zombie. "It's a beautiful day."

"No one gets up this early during the summer." He pulled his hat lower and hissed at the morning sun. Or maybe at me.

"My family does."

"They're farmers." He stopped at the fence behind home plate and flopped against it.

"You could try it, you know. Farming. Helping out. You might actually like it."

He made a face. "I don't do farming, Reed, and honestly, I can't believe you can just pick it up again after being away for four years."

I flipped a rosin bag back and forth in my right hand. "It's like Granddad always said: You can take the kid out of the farm but you can't take the farm out of the kid."

"I'd like to take the farm and replace it with suburbs. Get the old Reed, who would sleep in till at least ten, back." He dropped his glove near home plate. "So why are we here again?"

"To get an early start before the guys come at noon." I dug the toe of my cleat into the damp clay on the mound and gave a once-over to the infield.

Damn, this place really needs a good screen drag.

"We played a game yesterday. Everything still hurts."

"Everything hurts because you got loaded with Brett last night."

He groaned and stretched his arms behind his back. "You should've been there. Brett had to hold me back from kicking the shit out of a couple of Crowley guys."

"What'd they do?"

"Does it matter?" Ben picked up his glove. "Still could've used you though." Somehow, I doubted that. Ben and I may have done everything together for the last few years, but his temper was far worse than mine. Throwing a fist was second nature to him.

"Sorry," I said. "My phone died, and my watch stopped working again." I smacked the old digital face on my wrist until it started blinking to life.

"Why do you wear that thing if it's broken ninety percent of the time?"

"I've had it for forever—just used to wearing it." My life had had enough unexpected turns over the years, thanks to the military. So yeah, if I had to deal with an old watch, I'd do it. It was too special to get rid of and at least I could count on it to always work 10 percent of the time. Couldn't say that for much else.

"So what did you get into last night?" Ben asked.

"Granddad took me on a tour of the fields." I dug my toe into the dirt.

He chuckled. "It's a bunch of corn. What's there to see . . . in the dark?"

"You can see a lot even in the dark. The fields are quieter at night too. Helps with focus." I soft-tossed the ball to him. "He also wanted to explain how all the numbers worked. Which field went to which market. And he kinda wanted my opinion about adding an orchard to the northern end of the property too."

"Your opinion?"

"Guess he wanted someone else to talk to about it other than Nana. It's not like Dad's here to chat with him." I pressed my fingers against a pair of dog tags hanging around my neck, the other thing I'd grown used to wearing. A deep ache spread across my chest. When Dad had these made before he was deployed again eight months ago, he said they'd bring me luck. Could've used them last summer, but something told me I'd definitely need them for this one. "Granddad's just proud of how far the farm's come over the years. Nothing wrong with that," I said.

"I know, I know." Ben threw the ball back to me. "But he needs to remember he asked us here to win the season for him. Can't do that if you're busy talkin' about fruit trees."

"Trust me. He remembers why we're here."

Yesterday's Family Day brought in a lot of money and support, but we played horribly. While we hadn't played for a few weeks after our spring season back home in Fayetteville, half the team acted like they hadn't picked up a ball in years. Dropped fly balls, shitty batting, and even a couple of missed grounders through the legs.

We had made Bill Buckner look good.

Ben hit his glove a few times before crouching behind the mound. "Did you see the Crowleys spying on us yesterday?"

"Which ones?" I still hadn't figured out what to do about Eliza's mask or how to return it. Honestly, I wasn't sure I wanted to return it. She did melt my Optimus Prime and Hot Rod—my favorites.

"Daddy and Princess were above the press box for half the game with some of the other players." Ben held open his glove. "That's probably her favorite spot, right? Someone like her wouldn't want to get too close to the field. Might get dirty."

"Eliza's been around a ballpark her whole life." I lobbed a couple of pitches over the plate. "She's not afraid to get dirty."

"She sure keeps her BMW clean, I can tell you."

"She drives a BMW?" Why was I surprised? Of course she did.

Ben flipped his hat around backward and leaned back on his heels. "I saw her pull out of the stadium in it yesterday."

Huh. "Didn't take her for a BMW kinda girl, honestly."

"Yeah, the way you talked about her, I figured she was more of a Benz." He hit the inside of his glove. "Did you know she led a sit-in at the coffee place in town a couple years ago?"

"At the Brew?" I kicked a few stones away from the mound.

God, this infield really sucked.

Ben nodded. "Brett read about it on their bulletin board when he grabbed coffee the other morning. The town wouldn't let some poet read her stuff there. Eliza organized the protest. She also won the hitting derby contest last year."

I almost dropped the baseball. "She won Fairfield's Hit and Run Derby?" Holy hell.

"Right?" Ben laughed. "How shitty of a town do you gotta have for a *girl* to win that?"

Seriously, Ben?

"Eri Yoshida was drafted by the Japanese men's league when she was only sixteen. Remember her sick knuckleball?" I propped my gloved hand on my hip. "Mo'ne Davis pitched a freaking shutout in the Little League World Series in 2014. Melissa Mayeux, Marti Sementelli—"

"Okay, okay." He held up his hand. "I got it."

Would've been cool to see Eliza put her dad's best players in their place though.

Not that I'd ever admit that out loud.

"Come on." Ben waved for the ball. "You dragged me out here. Show me whatcha got, Ace."

I leaned forward and stared at Ben's signals. The sun grew warmer on my neck.

He asked for a high-and-inside.

I shook it off.

Then he asked for a fastball.

I shook that off too.

He chuckled and brought up his middle finger before pointing it down and away.

My slider. Perfect.

I straightened my back, checked an imaginary base runner on second, brought my chin down, knee up, and arm out.

My cleat dug into the dry dirt as the ball zipped out of my hand. It crossed home plate with a perfect angle into his glove.

"Strike! That's what I'm talkin' about." He threw it back to me. "Now let's see that fastball, and make it a two-seamer."

Fuck. "I can't do my two-seamer yet."

"Dude. You gotta practice it again sooner or later."

Easy for him to say. He didn't hit three batters and send one to the hospital with a two-seamer last summer. He made it sound like it was nothing. "I dunno—"

"What did the coaches say when they came up to you after the first evaluation?"

"Control. Consistency," I muttered.

"Right. So focus on that." He moved back into position. "We won't win if you can't nail down those two things, and if we don't win, summer scouts won't even remember our names."

My stomach knotted up.

Scouts.

College scouts.

I had already fucked up once in front of them. If I did it a second time, they definitely wouldn't pay me a visit the spring of my senior year. I should have already been working on verbal commitments. Signing in November or December.

Now I'd be lucky to sign in April.

Ben was good enough to go at least D2, maybe D1 if he could get his GPA up and stay out of trouble. He was already in talks with UNC, his dream school, and I was happy for him.

Mostly.

The truth that I couldn't admit to him or anyone else was that I wasn't sure what I wanted most: to play college baseball or to not be left behind.

Later that day, I sat in the living room trying to read a copy of *Romeo and Juliet* from Nana's bookshelf. Why were people so obsessed with this depressing play? And the feud between the Capulets and Montagues? No one knew what started it.

At least our feud with the Crowleys made sense.

Nana called from the kitchen, "Reed, could you come help me with dinner?"

"Be right there." I stuck a receipt from the gas station into the book and stood. The sofa made a sticky ripping sound. Nana said that on a farm, plastic had to cover the furniture or everything would be ruined. I think I would've taken my chances without it.

Plastic on a sofa was as comfortable as Saran wrap on a toilet seat.

The old oaken floors creaked under my feet. Mickey, Granddad's old border collie, wagged his tail on the checkered tile near the sink, and Nana danced along to some music near the stove.

"Smells good in here." I rubbed Mickey's head before smiling at her.

She tossed me a head of lettuce from the counter and patted her side. "Did I tell you I got Lucille hooked up to my phone? Now I can read my levels without having to take her off my belt."

I smiled. "That's great." Lucille was Nana's insulin pump.

She had been a Type 1 diabetic for as long as I could remember. Mom and Dad helped pay for Lucille a couple of years ago when Nana's other pump kept malfunctioning. Nana fought tooth and nail against it, but after a couple of bad hypoglycemic episodes, she gave in.

Nana opened the fridge and took out some raw vegetables, placing them near the sink and a cutting board before staring at me. "Well, don't just stand there."

I brought the lettuce over and started shaving it off at the sides.

"What in the world are you doing, Reed?" she asked.

"Making a salad." I kept shaving the lettuce. Wasn't this how you did it?

"Honey, you keep cutting the lettuce like that and that salad won't be ready till next week." She laughed and smacked my arm with the spoon. "Don't you know how to make a salad?"

"Usually, we dump a bag of it in the bowl."

Nana placed a hand on her chest. "Dear Jesus. I'll have to have a chat with your mother—"

"No, no, no." I turned around. "She makes salad. But we don't have a garden like you. Remember? Plus, I'm not home for dinner a lot."

Nana raised an eyebrow. "A boy needs to make time to eat dinner with his family. You hear?"

"Loud and clear." What I didn't tell her was that I wasn't the only one who wasn't home a lot for dinner. Dad supervised a lot of the trainings at the base, and Mom, well, she didn't like coming home to an empty house. So she waited until one of us texted before she left the library where she worked.

Nana chopped the lettuce in half and then chunked the rest before tossing it all into the bowl. Next, she pulled out a peeler and a small knife. "Peel those carrots into the compost bucket near the back door."

"Wouldn't it be easier if you guys got a garbage disposal for your sink?"

She huffed. "Foolish to replace good composting with one of those fancy gadgets. You've been away from this farm for too long."

She showed me how she went away from her hand that held the carrot when she peeled. "Nice and slow. And then cut them into small pieces about the size of a nickel. Got it?"

I kissed her cheek right underneath one of her light brown age spots. "Got it."

She went back to stirring the sauce. The smells of garlic and some kind of herb made my stomach growl. "So did you see your dad's old rocking chair in the corner of the barn yet?"

Here we go. "I saw it."

"Think you can find some time to finish it?"

"I dunno, Nana. That B Field is a holy wreck. Needs a total overhaul. And we played like shit—sorry, crap—the other day."

"It's one chair, Reed. Would mean a lot to your granddad. And to me."

Ouch.

Never underestimate a nana's ability to throw a good gut punch.

"I'll take care of it," I said.

"Good." She went back to stirring as a trumpet solo began in the music. "You know your daddy played the trumpet."

He did? I swallowed over something hard. "I didn't know that."

"Mhmm . . . he was real good. Always wished he would play in college, but baseball took up a lot of time. Then the army called him up . . ."

And for the last eight months he fought in the city of Who-Knows-Where, Middle East, doing who-knows-what with zero weeks of contact.

I guess that's why they called it black ops. It put the families left behind in the dark.

Nana placed some bread in the oven and set a timer. The clock in the living room started to chime the hour. "He'd be so proud of you helping your granddad with this season. Walkin' in his footsteps."

Jesus. Between Nana and Ben's not-so-subtle pressure, I was going to need a ton of antacids this summer.

Suddenly, the sound of a tractor backfiring made us both jump, and a moment later, the kitchen door banged open.

Granddad went straight to the sink and wet a paper towel before wiping off his forehead and neck. "Smells good."

Ben stumbled in after him. Dirt covered his face, and he had grass stains on his pants and a ripped shirt sleeve.

I stifled a laugh. "Rough afternoon?"

He scowled and trudged over to the sink where he filled up a glass of water.

"Ben wanted to try to use the old tiller." Granddad winked. "It, uh, got away from him."

"How exactly does a tiller get away from you?" I asked, tossing Ben a towel.

"Don't ask," he replied.

Nana brushed some dirt off Granddad's hair. "The mail's on the hallway table, honey."

"What can I do to help?" Ben asked her.

Nana looked him over head to toe and pointed toward the hallway. "Shower."

The three of us laughed as Ben left. "Don't use all the hot water!" she yelled after him.

I started chopping the carrots when Granddad walked back into the kitchen a couple of minutes later with a frown. "I get so goddamned tired of reading about Will Crowley every other day in the paper. Is there no other news out there?"

"Language, Louis." Nana waved her spoon at him.

Granddad grumbled and dropped the mail next to me. The bright red lettering of "FINAL NOTICE" on one envelope. Final notice? I thought the farm was doing okay?

I stopped chopping. "Granddad, what's this—"

"That paper will start printing our names soon, you'll see." He smacked the refrigerator. "That tournament is the best answer to all our problems."

"Right, but did you really have to put forty percent of the farm sales on the table?" My eyes wandered to the overdue bills.

"First off, *he* didn't put that on the table, *we* both did," Nana said. "Secondly, if we can't afford it, then we'll figure it out, the same way we always do."

"But—"

"Will Crowley putting the stadium up for grabs is a blessing," Granddad added.

A blessing?

What about "Never trust a Crowley," the Fulton motto that had been drilled into my brain since I was ten?

Granddad patted me on the back. "Charlie would've been proud of the two of us, Reed. Putting a team together like this for the Legion League. The Fulton dynasty at it once again."

"Charlie sounded like a good guy. Wish I could've met him." I began chopping some cucumber.

"My brother was a lot like you. Tall as a tree, proud, focused." Granddad rolled up his newspaper and tossed it into the recycling. "Honestly, it was a good thing he wasn't around to see us lose that stadium years ago after all the work we did to get it up and running."

He marched over to the junk drawer near the fridge and

took out a case of darts. Newspaper clippings with "Crowley" in their headings were tacked onto the top half of the laundry room door.

He started throwing darts.

Nana groaned. "Honestly. Must you do that *every* day?"

"The doctor said I need to find better ways to de-stress, Joyce. Drinking beer doesn't count—apparently—so that leaves darts. Or would you rather I shoot my rifle off the back deck?" He tossed two more and hit the eyes of a black-and-white photograph of Will Crowley.

"Darts it is," Nana mumbled, running a hand through her curls. "You're bringing my wisdom tinsel out in full force. I'll be all silver soon."

"I've always said I liked your hair more silver than brown anyway." Granddad turned to me. "Wanna have a go, Reed? It's been a while, but you probably still got a decent throw, right?"

Uh. "Sure. Why not?"

A few minutes later, all my darts framed the outside edges of the photographs. Apparently, even though I could throw a mean fastball, I sucked at darts. As I plucked them out, I noticed a smaller headline and article underneath the latest picture of Will Crowley: "THE LYRIC'S SUMMER PRODUCTION OF 'ROMEO & JULIET' BEGINS ITS REHARSALS."

Eliza.

"Let me know when you need me to set the table, okay?" I said, leaving the kitchen. "I'll be out front."

The old porch creaked under my weight as the South Five's corn moved with the humid wind. Yesterday, Granddad had me feel a couple of husks to remind me of the color and texture I should hope for.

Mickey barked at the screen door. I opened it and then sat on the front steps, where he placed his head on my lap. That article said the first tech rehearsal was tomorrow, which meant Eliza would definitely be there.

I still had her mask, so that gave me two clear options.

Option one: I could burn it. Call it retribution for what she did to my Autobots.

Option two: I could take it to her and stick around just long enough to ruffle her prim Crowley feathers.

By my math, I had hundreds of days of Operation Reed Bothers Eliza to make up for.

Raking the infield could wait.

Chapter Five

Eliza

"The theater is so endlessly fascinating because it's so accidental." —Arthur Miller

I repeated the order of the catwalk lights in my head while waiting for rehearsal to begin, hoping it'd calm my nerves. R1, R2, R3, E1, E2, E3 . . . chained together in groups of three . . .

But nothing helped.

As the auditorium continued to fill with the production crew, my stomach squirmed, feeling hollower by the minute. I studied each face that passed me, recognizing only a handful of them. The ones I did know were by reputation. The regulars, whose drama club pictures and trophies still dominated the bookshelves in the theater classroom at Fairfield High, were famous not only in our town but also in the tri-county area. Shows were picked every summer based off which of them would be returning home.

I wanted this opportunity so badly, I almost cried in front of Ms. Sparrow when she offered it to me last spring—my first "job" with the prestigious summer troupe. But did I really belong with this elite group of thespians?

"Hey." Lauryn squeezed my hand. "You've got this."

I smiled and immediately my jitters calmed.

Thank God for Lauryn.

Sometimes I swore she had a sixth sense about me, knowing exactly what to say and how to say it the moment I needed it the most. While I loved that my best friend and I got to do this show together this summer, I loved the fact that she got the lead over a handful of hungry, crazy-talented college girls even more.

Lauryn was a total badass.

The murmurs around me hushed when Ms. Sparrow, our director, flitted across the empty stage, weaving around as if crowds of people were in her way. She wore square red-rimmed glasses and fiery lipstick to match. Around her neck lay one of her infamous scarves—black with white polka dots. Her white flowy blouse billowed behind her, the sleeves rolled up to her elbows. Once she hit center stage where the light burned brightest (thanks to me), she stopped and clapped twice.

"Welcome, tech and set crew, costuming and makeup, to this season's production of the classic Shakespearean tragedy *Romeo and Juliet*," her voice trilled. "I am Ms. Sparrow, your director, and the cast and I are thrilled that you chose to spend your summer vacation with us here in the *theater*."

In the three years I've worked with her at the high school, she always said "theater" with a slight British accent. She was a piece of work. But her shows always sold out weeks ahead of opening night, and even though she was known for working a cast till they collapsed, everyone still respected the heck out of her.

I know I did.

"Do you really think she's related to Kristin Chenoweth?" Lauryn whispered.

I leaned back, propping my knees on the back of the seat in front of me. "Who knows."

Ms. Sparrow walked around the stage, motioning to empty spots while sharing her vision of what the sets would look like once they were completed.

Lauryn kept her voice low. "Did you hear what happened to Tracey?"

"No. What?" I asked.

"After the party got busted by the cops, she was sentenced to community service. At the library. Can you imagine Tracey McInnis working at the library?"

I snickered. "Ms. Jackson is going to eat her alive."

Lauryn snorted loudly, and Ms. Sparrow gave a sharp clap. "And there you have it. Now, where is Eliza Crowley?"

Crap. Was that center spot too bright?

Lauryn pushed and poked me before she pointed at my head. "She's right here."

Gee, thanks. I tugged my Crowley Cardinals ball cap lower.

"For those of you who don't know her, this is Eliza Crowley, granddaughter to Fairfield's Lady of the Stage, Marguerite Crowley." Ms. Sparrow waved her hand toward me, smiling.

Dozens of heads whipped around and sized me up like I was an invader.

An outsider.

Not one of them.

Thespians were in a league of their own when it came to loyalty. Sure, I did great lighting shows at the high school, but most of those students and my peers weren't sitting in this auditorium.

"But today," Ms. Sparrow continued, "I'd like you to think of Eliza as our very own Lighting Goddess Extraordinaire."

Oh, dear God.

"I'm tweeting that," Lauryn mumbled.

I smacked her. "Don't you dare."

"Too late." She smiled at her phone. "Ah, already three retweets. You'll be trending in no time, *Goddess*."

"I hate you—"

"Welcome aboard, Rookie," a smooth voice spoke from behind us.

"*Rookie*"?

Lauryn kicked my ankle as I turned around and came face-to-face with none other than Raul Ramirez, aka Romeo. Raul starred in every play and musical at Fairfield High. He graduated last year, and his subsequent year at Duke definitely hadn't hurt him. His dark curly hair still framed his sun-kissed copper skin, and his blue eyes reminded me of a deep ocean.

Truth: I had a mad crush on him two years ago when he played Curly in *Oklahoma*.

Dreaminess aside though—"Rookie"?

I may have been new to *this* group, but not to the theater.

"E's going to blow the lighting design out of the water this summer, Raul. Just you wait," Lauryn said before mumbling another "Just you wait" under her breath. If there was an opportunity to quote *Hamilton*, she seized it.

"Thanks," I mumbled, my cheeks burning.

Raul fell into his seat as Lauryn and I turned back around.

Lauryn leaned close to my ear. "Can you believe I get to kiss him?" She fanned herself with her script. "He's so pretty, it's almost not fair."

I laughed into my shirt.

Lauryn sighed. "He reminds me of that one guy from the newer Star Wars movies . . . The pilot . . ."

"Poe?" I asked.

"Yes. A younger Poe. I'd let him take me in the cockpit of his plane—"

"Actually, it's called an X-wing." Raul's face appeared again between both of our heads, making us jump and burst into giggles.

I missed the laughter of that moment a few minutes later, when we were dismissed and told to get to work.

The work, I was ready for.

The hissing and whispering of my last name, I was not.

It apparently didn't matter that a plaque with Grandma Marguerite's name decorated the lobby of this theater, surrounded by dozens of other pictures of her charity work for the arts, or that it was her work that saved this theater from bankruptcy more than once.

The name Crowley didn't hold weight here like it did the other parts of town. Not anymore.

After spending some time backstage with the tech and set design crew, I did a once-over of the tormentor spotlights in the alcoves and moved up to the catwalk, which was, hands down, the scariest place to be in an auditorium. Dropping out of the ceiling, the old grille floor angled downward. What wires weren't haphazardly tied to the railings were crossed over the walkway like tree roots. One wrong step and I could find myself falling over a can to a certain death below.

Too bad I couldn't start setting cues until I cleaned up this mess and angled the lights correctly.

I slowly climbed along from stage left toward stage right

with my laminated map tucked under my arm, adjusting the lights that had been moved during the last performance here. If I moved too quickly or bumped into one of the daisy chains, I'd knock a can out of place, or worse, knock a bulb loose and have it shatter below.

I was almost done with everything when the ladder creaked behind me. "Don't come up! There's only enough room for one of us up here."

The ladder kept creaking.

I whirled around. "I'm almost done—"

"Eliza?" A head popped up out of the floor like one of those moles in a carnival game—a mole I'd very much like to hit with a hammer right now.

"What the hell are you doing here?" I asked. Then again, was I really that surprised?

Reed Fulton *would* come to the place that had one escape route and block that route with his big head.

"You left your mask at the party." He held it out and took another step up, making the suspended floor wobble.

"Stop!" I grabbed the railing. "It's really tight up here. One of us could fall."

Wait. Was that part of his plan?

He paused and sat on the edge of the hole, his long legs dangling against the ladder. "This is cool. I always wondered what the catwalk looked like."

"Well, now you've seen it. So just leave the mask by the ladder on your way out." I put a new gel into the second to last PAR can.

"I recognize those." He pointed to the can then clicked his tongue a few times.

Ugh. Why wouldn't he leave?

Was this the contingency part of his plan? *If Eliza doesn't fall off the catwalk when I come up, annoy her until she thinks about jumping off of it?*

"I learned about gels in a film-appreciation class last year," he said.

"Fascinating," I said. "Bye, now."

Loud hammering came from the stage. Some of the set guys finished another piece while small groups of the cast did team-building exercises around the auditorium.

Reed drummed on the ladder. "Busy around here, huh?"

I wedged my clipboard under my arm. "So this has been *super fun*, but remind me again: Why are you here?"

Other than to make me mess up bad enough on day one that Ms. Sparrow fires me.

Crap. *Could* she fire me?

"I told you. To bring you your mask."

I jumped, startled by another loud *thwack* of a hammer. "You could've left it down below."

"I like climbing things."

"I remember." Trees, barns, old railcars. We used to climb a lot of those together. But that was a long time ago.

He rubbed the back of his neck, revealing the long tendons of muscles in his arm.

Oh.

Those are new.

I snapped my head down and made notes about the new positions.

"Didn't think you wore ball caps, Crowley." He cocked his head to the side. "Won't it mess up your perfect hair?"

Ha. Perfect hair doesn't exist on a catwalk, where it's a million degrees. "I've been wearing this ball cap for years, Fulton." I scowled at him.

"Crowley Cardinals," he mumbled. "Saw the new statues all around town too. Bet they threw a parade for it."

They did. Dad made me ride in a convertible with him and Mom. I hated those damn statues—not that I'd admit it to him. "Jealous?" I asked.

He pulled up his legs and stood.

Geez, he *was* a lot taller.

"Ha. No. Just surprised your dad couldn't come up with a better mascot. Weren't you the Robins before that?" He laughed.

"The Blue Jays," I hissed. "And what's the Fulton mascot? A gnat?"

His jaw twitched. "The Hawks."

Crud. That's actually pretty good.

Lauryn yelled from below. "Hey, E! You about done up

there? Sparrow has some questions and said you forgot to wear your radio."

Dammit. Not the way I wanted to start. "Be right there!"

Reed peered over the edge. "Is Lauryn in the play?"

"She's the lead."

Reed nodded, looking impressed. "Badass."

Well, that's one thing we agree on.

"I really need to get going now." I moved to pass him, but he turned around too quickly and bumped into me. My clipboard dropped and clattered down the ladder, and I stumbled forward. For the longest second, I was weightless.

I opened my mouth to scream, but Reed grabbed both my arms and pulled me against him, knocking us into R1.

My ear pressed against his hard chest, the hammering of his heart reminding me of the bass drums warming up outside of a stadium before a football game. His strong shoulders and heavy arms radiated heat.

This is . . . new.

I had stumbled into Reed once before, many years ago, when we raced down Main Street. The winner had to buy the other a milkshake at Scoops. Reed had tripped on his shoelaces, and both of us crashed into the mulch pile outside of Mrs. Brown's Thrift Store. A mess of gangly limbs and scratched from neck to knee, we hurried away to our separate parts of town before we were forced to clean up the mess.

One malted milkshake sat on my front porch an hour later.

But this?

This felt . . . different.

That's because you almost just died, genius. "Tha . . . thanks."

"Don't mention it." His breath warmed my forehead. He smelled like sun-warmed metal and the oil of a glove. Not that I smelled him or anything.

I pulled away, still feeling as dizzy as—if not more so than—when I stumbled. He held out my mask, and my hand shook as I took it.

"Oh, I get it." His thumb brushed over the writing on the back of my hand. "Those letters and numbers are the order of lights, right?"

Right.

Lauryn yelled from below. "Eliza! You okay?"

I quickly pulled my hand away. "I'm fine! Heading down now."

Reed shoved his hand into a pocket. "Well . . . this was fun."

I snorted and started climbing down the ladder. "Highlight of my day."

"So does your family own this theater now too? I saw your grandmother's pictures all over the lobby." He climbed down after me.

"No. The hardware store and the stadium. That's it." I flipped my hat around after I stepped off the last rung.

"And soon, it'll *only* be the hardware store." Reed reached the floor with a loud *thump.*

Psh. "Whatever."

He took a couple of steps closer to me and patted the top of my hat. "You've shrunk a bit, Crowley."

"And you're stealing too much of my air, Fulton." I rammed my heel into his left foot before spinning around and hurrying away, smiling as he swore under his breath.

Point: me.

Chapter Six

REED

"Baseball is a game of inches." –Branch Rickey

My shins were on fire.

Coach should've let me keep my shoulder warm by throwing with Ben. Instead, I ran bleachers with the rest of the guys at the A Field in the scorching sun.

"Pick it up, Fulton!" Coach Monaco yelled. "Even pitchers need to be in shape."

I was a thousand times more in shape than most of these guys.

"Who put a stick up his ass?" Ben asked between breaths as we ran back down a set of metal stairs.

I groaned as I reached the bottom. "I never thought I'd say I missed the hills from our high school, but fuck, I do now."

"It's not our fault we were pranked by those Crowleys. If you could even call it a prank. Amateurs." Ben panted and cursed under his breath. "They obviously don't know who they're messing with."

Ha. True.

Ben and I also bonded over our love of pranks. After his dad left, everyone treated him differently, so he spent his time creating elaborate setups. The same went for me. When one of Ben's traps strung me upside down in a tree, I knew he and I would hit it off. Only, while I was fine keeping the mischief purely funny, he recently started moving toward vandalism, tagging the back walls of buildings or schools.

Hope he didn't plan to go that far here.

As for the Crowleys' idiotic prank, all that hay would take forever to clean up. It went almost to the roof of the dugouts in the sandlot and poked through the rusted chain-link fence in each.

Where the hell did they get it all?

It was almost as much as what I helped Granddad move into the loft of the barn years ago before Thanksgiving.

Finally, Coach blew his whistle twice. None of us made it to the field. We all dropped on the warm metal. Two of our guys rolled over and puked, but my arms and legs spread out around me like a body at a crime scene.

"You were up late last night." Ben's chest heaved. "What were you doing?"

"Nothing." I sat up slowly. "Just watching some pitching videos on YouTube."

And spending far too long scrolling through Eliza's Instagram, and then maybe falling down a rabbit hole of her and Lauryn's TikTok videos.

Neither of which I could share with him.

No girls. All baseball.

Ben sat up and motioned for me to help him stretch. We spread and straightened our legs so our feet touched, leaned in, and pulled each other across the space between us. "Did your grandparents tell you I took the combine harvester out yesterday?" he asked.

I laughed. "Yeah, Nana mentioned it. How many rows of corn did you take down before you could stop it?"

"A few." He stretched forward. "Your granddad showed me his antique lighters collection too. Makes mine look like crap."

"When do you get yours back?"

He smirked. "Already got it back."

Translation: *stole it back.*

Ben's mom had taken his lighter away the week before we came to Fairfield, to "prevent him from causing any trouble with it."

True, he had gotten caught multiple times smoking on the campus of our high school while skipping classes, but he would've found a way to smoke with or without his own lighter.

The lighter wasn't the root of his problems.

He had the literal scars to prove it.

Maybe if Mrs. Talbot spent more time talking to her son instead of working herself to death, she would've noticed that.

Later, after a short intrasquad scrimmage, everyone trudged back to the sandlot to clean up the shit-tons of hay. Using a couple of infield rakes and our bare hands, we managed to move it to the edge of the woods. I had been around hay all my life, but it was clear the others hadn't. They sneezed nonstop.

Once Coach gave us his second speech of the day about "growing up" and "taking the higher road," we hauled our gear toward the parking lot.

"You heading home now?" Ben tossed his duffle into the back of my truck. "Or you wanna grab a quick burger at the diner?"

"I think I'm gonna go for a walk. Can you take the truck home?" I dropped my bag next to his and tossed him the keys.

"A walk?"

"Yeah. Just wanna see how much the town's changed."

Ben took a long drink of water. "Cornfields. Main Street. A tiny-ass creek. What's there to see?"

I tugged my hat lower. "Let Nana know I'll be home in time for dinner, okay?"

"Whatever."

“And don’t take any more equipment out of the barn.”

“Yes, Mom.” He climbed in my truck and started it up while rolling the window down. “Brett’s got some decent ideas about how to get the Crowleys back later tonight.”

“What if Coach finds out?” I could think of a hundred things I’d rather do than run bleachers again.

But Ben ignored my question and started backing out of the parking spot. “Hey, let me know if you hear the voice of Shoeless Joe Jackson out there.”

I whispered loudly, “If you build it, he will come.”

“Go the distance, my friend.”

Ben wasn’t wrong when he said there wasn’t much to Fairfield. But it had a past, and whether I liked it or not, I was a part of it. Where he saw cornfields, I saw acres and acres of hiding spots and the mere minutes it took Mickey—that dog had a nose like no other—to find me.

Where he saw a run-down Wade’s Grocery near a shadowed alley, I saw the perfect brick wall for tossing a ball back when I had no one to play catch with. The same alley where I accidentally broke Granddad’s radio after it fell off my bike. Where moments later, Eliza appeared out of nowhere with a paper tiara on her head, crouched down, and fixed the radio in a matter of seconds.

He saw a creek. I saw a place where I dug around for crawdads. The same creek where I tripped and fell into a fallen beehive. Where Eliza, again, had appeared out of thin air and helped me up, never mentioning my crying while she quickly slapped mud on my stings.

But that was a lifetime ago—six years, to be exact.

Before her family cheated my family out of the stadium.

Before her father and my granddad forbade us to hang out together—the one thing they truly agreed upon.

Walking through this town with my glove and ball made me feel like a kid again, and for the first time since I had come back, I felt like myself.

After a half an hour of wandering and counting over five bougie cardinal statues around town, I reached the old train station. Its red paint had peeled, and it leaned a bit. A few abandoned, rusty railcars shone burnt orange in the sunlight. Tall grass and weeds covered the tracks.

Dad had taken me here sometimes after we hit a few balls at the elementary school field. "You can tell a lot about a town by what it keeps and what it throws away," he had said. "Fairfield keeps everything. Remembers everything. Do good things here, and they'll love you forever. Screw up, and it'll follow you to your tombstone."

They may have kept the train station and the old barbershop on Maple Drive, but he had been wrong about the doing-good part. All Granddad and his farm did was good for this community. And they repaid him by taking a cash offer from the wealthiest family in town.

Fast money always made people look the other way.

I tucked my glove and ball under my arm before picking up a couple of rocks. Winding up slowly, I tossed them at one of the already broken windows of the station. Dirty glass shattered loudly to the ground.

"Do you mind?" a familiar voice snapped.

Well, damn. Of course she'd be here.

Chapter Seven

ELIZA

"A theater is the most important sort of house in the world, because that's where people are shown what they could be if they wanted, and what they'd like to be if they dared to, and what they really are." —Tove Jansson

Dear God, if you could please strike down Reed Fulton with a mighty lightning bolt right now, I promise I'll curse less and go to church more. Amen.

Reed waved to me from the railyard parking lot, and the skies stayed clear.

So much for the power of prayer.

Was there nowhere in this freaking small town for a girl to find some peace?

I closed my script and glared down at his tall shadow. "So what, are you following me now?" *First the catwalk, now here . . . What's next, my favorite booth at Jenny's?*

He scooped up another couple of rocks, tossing them into

one of the empty trash cans near the boarded-up entrance of the station. "Can't a guy just walk home?"

I pointed toward the Fulton farm behind him, the town limits a literal stone's throw from one of their fields. "Home's that way."

He cupped his hands around his mouth and shouted toward the cornfields. "'It's okay, honey! I was just talking to the corn.'"

"Excuse me?"

He faced me. "'This is my corn. You people are guests in my corn.'"

Still loved quoting movies, I guess.

"'Is this heaven? . . . No, it's Iowa!'" He tossed his baseball up and caught it in his glove. "You seriously haven't seen that movie?"

I pinched the bridge of my nose. All I wanted was a quiet place to get away, and now here I was in the million-degree humidity listening to Reed speak *Field of Dreams* quotes to his corn.

Then again, while he continued pretending to be Ray Kinsella, maybe I could escape?

The closest ladder was only a few feet away, but it was right behind him, and this railcar was notorious for squeaking.

I guess I could go with the classic plan B: ignore him until he got bored enough to leave.

"Are you giving me the silent treatment hoping I'll give up and go home?" he asked.

Damn.

"Crowley, I thought you were smarter than that."

I *was* smarter than that. My SAT scores may have sucked, but I wasn't stupid.

"So the question remains." He tossed the ball up again, higher this time, and caught it while still looking at me. "Does the daughter of one of the best baseball coaches on the East Coast know one of the greatest baseball movies of all time? Survey says no."

Ha. He couldn't be more wrong.

I had memorized James Earl Jones's baseball monologue from *Field of Dreams* years ago when I auditioned for the role of Fiona in *Shrek Jr.* for our middle school spring musical. I nailed the audition but had to drop out before the callback because I had gotten mono. At the time, I was devastated, but in the end it all worked out.

Lauryn got the lead—she slayed it—and I shadowed a college student who ran lighting and sound, thus beginning my love of the technical side of theater.

Reed threw the ball up again and caught it behind his back.

Show-off.

"Who am I kidding," he continued. "You probably don't know that movie any more than you do *The Sandlot*."

I rolled my eyes. "Whatever."

There goes the silent treatment. But how could I stay silent? Anyone who claimed to be a fan of baseball but not of those movies could not be trusted any more than a theater "fan" who claimed *CATS* was Andrew Lloyd Webber's greatest musical.

Reed grinned like he won whatever standoff we were having, and his annoying dimple made an appearance.

Could I hit it with my pencil?

The wind did feel just right for such a throw.

He stepped closer to the railcar. "Can I come up?"

"No." I opened my script to where I'd left off.

"Why not?"

"Because some of us have work to do this summer." I flicked my ponytail off my neck, which was damp with sweat.

"What if I *promised* to leave"—he stepped onto the first rung of the ladder and paused—"*if* you let me sit up there with you for . . . twenty minutes?"

Twenty minutes? Had he lost his mind?

Then again, I might if he stayed for longer.

"Crowley?"

"I'm thinking," I snapped.

He did say the word "promise," but could I really trust him to keep his word? I needed leverage. Something he'd hate to lose . . .

"I'll give you ten," I conceded, "but you'll have to surrender your ball and glove."

He took another step up, his head appearing over the edge of the railcar. "Seriously?"

"Ball and glove or it's no deal." Dad might've been a fool putting the stadium up for grabs this summer, but I wasn't one.

"Fifteen."

"Twelve."

"Do you always have to have the last word?" he asked.

With you? Yes. "Twelve or it's no deal."

He sighed and slapped his glove with the ball in it onto the railcar before climbing up, his T-shirt lifting just high enough to show a hard, toned stomach.

But abs didn't change anything, no matter how sharp those lines were. Nope.

After he reached the top, I snatched his glove and scooted a couple of feet away, letting out a loud yelp when my thighs hit the scorching metal.

Perfect. Less than, what, a minute, and already he was making me burn myself?

I whipped out my phone and set an alarm for twelve minutes.

Twelve minutes.

I could last for that long if it gave me another sixty or so of peace before I had to head home.

But then he grabbed my play from my lap.

"Hey, give that back," I yelled.

He set it down behind him. "If you get my glove, I get your play."

Ugh. "Fine."

He could have it, but *I* wouldn't be the first one to speak.

"Man, it's really hot today," he said after a long seventy-five seconds. "I had forgotten how bad the humidity gets here."

Grandma had always said the humidity kept her skin healthy, but I still hated it.

The high-pitched music of the ice cream truck sounded from Main Street. The kids in Fairfield were probably jumping on their bikes, racing one another to Mr. Lee before he ran out of his famous homemade shaved ice.

"Man, I'd kill for a strawberry-mango right now," Reed said, turning toward the sound.

"Blue raspberry is still top tier." I crossed my legs.

"False." Reed drummed a rhythm on the metal. "Honestly? I'm craving a burger."

He glanced my way, but I checked my phone. Ten minutes and seventeen seconds to go.

"How'd you get here?" He looked around the parking lot, completely unfazed by my Jeep.

"That's mine." I pointed to the Jeep. "It used to be my grandmother's. TJ fixed it up for me."

He took off his hat and scratched his head. "I thought you drove a BMW?"

"Who told you that?"

"Heard it somewhere."

With the way this town fawned over my family, I wasn't surprised. "The Jeep just feels more like me," I whispered.

"Bet your grandmother would've loved to see you drive it." He cleared his throat. "I'm sorry, by the way, about her passing. We didn't hear about it till after the funeral, or we—"

"Would've come? Yeah, sure." I fake laughed and turned away.

It had been three years but I could still feel that sharp, burning pain in my throat and that stabbing ache in my chest. Grandma's funeral was, hands down, the worst day of my life, and yet I couldn't make myself leave her side. I had waited by her grave site till the streetlamps turned on, and then Lauryn came and walked me home.

"I should've been there," he whispered.

She would've liked that.

Maybe a small part of me would've too.

Neither of us spoke for a few moments until a warm breeze moved over the railyard, making the building moan and the broken shutters shake. "Do you still believe in ghosts?" he asked.

I snorted. "I've never believed in ghosts."

"Yes, you did."

"No, I didn't."

Truth: I 100 percent did and still kinda do.

"Then why did you refuse to touch the station when we were kids?" He drummed his fingers against the empty railcar, the sound echoing underneath us. "You always made up excuses when I dared you."

"Maybe I didn't trust you not to shove me inside and lock the door."

His finger drumming stopped. "That was your brother's idea the first time, and you know it."

Another railcar groaned when a stronger breeze moved in and around its broken windows and open doors. A small animal—a rabbit, maybe—scurried into the tall grass and bushes nearby, sending a cloud of gnats skyward.

Reed shuddered.

"Is the big, tough Reed Fulton afraid of ghosts?" I smirked.

"Only of your breath, Crowley."

"Please. I chew gum like it's my job."

"Oh yeah?" He scooted closer.

He leaned across the now smaller space between us and inhaled slowly. The corner of his mouth turned up into a surprised smile, the same smile he had when I fell into him on the catwalk the other day. "Cinnamon?" he asked.

Why did his voice suddenly drop and sound all gravelly?

And why the hell was I once again close enough to feel the stubble framing his jawline?

"Big Red," I blurted, scooting back. "Dad keeps a lot of it in the garage."

Something backfired near the Fulton farm, sending a bunch of crows squawking into a row of trees.

Reed ran a hand over his face and groaned. "That'll be Ben, screwing around in the barn. Again."

From what Lauryn had already learned about him, I wasn't surprised. Who would leave someone that reckless alone in a barn? We didn't stock a lot of replacement parts for heavy farm equipment at the hardware store, but I knew enough about tools to recognize that farming stuff was expensive.

Maybe that was why Mr. Fulton wanted a team and agreed to the bet this summer? The earnings from the stadium would definitely help with running a farm as big as theirs.

Be that as it may, I wasn't ready to throw in the towel and leave my entire life behind either. Go Cardinals.

The chimes from the Methodist Church on Main Street dinged the time. Seven o'clock. Five minutes left.

"So were you in on the Crowley prank last night?" he asked.

Ah, there it was. The real and oldest reason why a Fulton would ever want to sit down with a Crowley. It always came back to blame.

And I stupidly thought Reed was actually interested in catching up on lost time.

"No. Sounds like something TJ would do though." I picked at some dirt under my fingernail. "Besides, I was busy."

"Ha. I'm sure you were." He *harrumph*ed.

"What the hell does that mean?"

"Nothing." He drew one of his knees up to his chest. "I just never would've guessed the Eliza I knew, who used to spend days reading in her room, would want to spend all of her time out shopping."

"Who said I liked shopping?" I scoffed. I hated shopping. "And anyways, who are you to talk? At least I don't spend every waking moment with all the other pathetic Diamond Boys."

"What are Diamond Boys?"

Oh, please. Like he didn't know. "Ballplayers like you who swoop into town hoping to get noticed by scouts. You guys waltz in here and act like you own the place, getting everyone all spun up, but it's all an act. You don't know Fairfield."

He gawked. "*I* know Fairfield, Crowley. My family knows it a hell of a lot better than yours."

"Being born here doesn't make you an expert." I spun to face him, crossing my legs. "You left, remember?"

"I didn't want to leave. We had no choice." He scooted closer to me, shaking the car as he moved. "Dad and Granddad's deal with the stadium went under, thanks to your family—"

"My family bought it fair—"

"—and then Dad decided it would be easier if we lived closer to the base. You think I wanted to move? I moved three times before second grade, before we came here."

I opened my mouth to say something, to argue, but I couldn't.

I'd never moved, never dealt with being the new kid. And while part of me always wished I could be, wished to get away and start over, a much bigger part of me would be terrified to do so.

"So you're here only to help your granddad? No other reason?" I pressed my hands against my bouncing knees.

Reed raised his eyebrows. "Should I have another reason?"

"Never mind." Honestly, I wasn't sure why I asked it.

Reed pulled off his hat, making his hair stick out in every direction. "My granddad's farm is going under, so he agreed to a ridiculous bet and needed my help. Families help one another. That's what they do."

Once again, I couldn't think of anything to say.

I didn't know his family was having money trouble.

But I did know about families helping one another. Or at least I used to know what that was like. We didn't help one another anymore though. Not really. Not like we used to when Grandma was still alive.

She was the thread that bound us all together.

Now we were all a bunch of knots too tangled up in ourselves to notice anyone else.

"So were you in on the prank against my team or not?" he asked, his voice sharp and low.

"Not." How pathetic did he think I was? "What'd they do?"

"Your team—"

"They're not *my* team."

"Fine." He tugged his hat back on, keeping it lower than before, which shadowed his eyes. "Your *father's* team dumped hay all over the damn dugouts at the sandlot. Took us forever to clean that shit up." He picked off a piece of hay I hadn't seen on his shorts and flicked it at me. "But they'll be sorry."

Oh, give me a break. "Can't you guys just, you know, play some baseball?"

He made a face. "If someone stuffed hay in *your* light booth, wouldn't you want to get them back?"

Yes. I'd destroy anyone who went after my light booth with the power of a thousand PAR lights.

Laughter sounded from the tracks below. I whirled around and crouched low to the railcar, feeling Reed do the same behind me before I craned my neck over the edge to see the ground. Trevon and Marcus, grandkids to the Browns, one of the oldest families in Fairfield and the ones who owned the thrift store, carried fishing poles on their shoulders and tackle boxes in their hands.

If they saw us, they'd definitely tell their grandparents. And Mr. Brown would then tell my dad who would totally blow a fuse and ground me for life. I'd have to quit the show. Ms. Sparrow would never let me work with her again or ever consider writing me a recommendation for college. My life would be over, and all because I sat on a railcar with a frenemy.

This was not good. Nope.

My heart pounded so loudly I swore it echoed off the metal. Could they hear heartbeats from down there? Reed exhaled near my neck, making me shiver. Did he have to do that so loudly? And why was he so close to me? He had like twenty feet of open railcar to use.

Everything was still. Even the air didn't make a sound, so naturally, in that moment, my phone alarm went off like a failed nuclear power plant.

"Shit, shit, shit," I hissed, fumbling with the thing until I could turn it off.

"Should've given me twenty minutes, Crowley," Reed whispered, chuckling.

"Shut up," I whispered.

He army-crawled toward me and tried to touch my wrist. "Wait. Is that a tattoo? When in the hell did you—"

I elbowed him quickly, smiling when he grunted.

Trevon and Marcus stopped walking. I crouched lower.

Had they seen us?

If they did, would they tell someone?

The two boys below set down their tackle boxes and opened them, sifting through the lures and bobbers as they chatted. I fought back a groan. As if it wasn't bad enough being stuck here in the stifling heat with Reed Fulton, now I'd be here even longer with him *and* two kids who would pass the time debating crappies versus perches?

Thankfully, though, the two boys didn't hover over their tackle boxes for too long, and after a few—painfully leg-cramping—minutes, they picked up their gear and edged down the bank on the other side of the tracks. The tall grass and wildflowers reached their waists as they plodded away.

"Must be heading toward Potter's Creek," Reed whispered in my ear.

I jumped and started sliding off the side before he grabbed me around my arms and pulled me backward. We were now only inches from each other. I had a ladder behind me and one on the other side behind Reed, but I couldn't force my legs to move toward an escape. My heart pounded the same way it did on the catwalk.

In the theater, we were surrounded by an entire cast and crew. But here, we were alone.

And definitely closer.

If he had let me fall, no one would have known but the two of us.

Yet he chose to save me.

Again.

"Jesus, Crowley. Do you make it a habit of falling off high places?" He smelled of sawdust, sunblock, and infield dirt, and it took me far too long to answer him.

"Only when you're around, apparently."

"You hurt?" One of his hands moved to my knee, where I had a new scrape. The pads of his fingers were rough, calloused—the way I always imagined fingers that were used to hard outside work felt. It was . . . nice.

Nice? Whoa, whoa, whoa, Eliza.

I scooted backward. "I'm . . . uh, fine."

"You sure? You're kinda pale."

From my brief brush with mortality.

Obviously.

I huffed and stood. "You're like a black hole, you know that? Sucking all the gravity and stable footing out from under me."

He smiled, and there was that damned dimple again, glaring at me.

My pencil could've taken it down. I was sure of it.

His phone started chiming. He took it out of his pocket and waved it at me, grinning even wider. "Would you look at that? Twenty minutes on the dot."

Chapter Eight

REED

"I would have liked to have had that chance. Just once. To stare down a big-league pitcher. To stare him down, and just as he goes into his windup, wink." —Moonlight Graham, *Field of Dreams*

Had I known my walk home yesterday would end up in a full-on locking-horns rumble with the Princess of Fairfield followed by having to rescue her—again—I would've skipped it and driven.

At least it wasn't a total waste of time. I had climbed up that railcar to learn more about this "new Eliza" and if she really had changed or if it was all an act.

Jury was still out.

She had the newest iPhone but chose an old Jeep over a new Beemer. She mapped out lighting cues for fun and preferred to sit on top of railcars instead of hanging out at her own house or in town.

Strange.

But one thing that really gave me pause was her tattoo: a small one on her wrist—a baseball in the shape of a heart with letters spelling out something in the stitching. Crowleys definitely didn't have tattoos, and not knowing what it said had gnawed at me for the rest of the day.

Ex-boyfriend?

Current boyfriend?

Lucky stock numbers?

Why. Did. I. Care?

So what if she had a boyfriend or owned stock in Microsoft or Apple?

And then there was the way she looked at me after I pulled her from the edge of that railcar. That same look she gave kid Reed a long time ago when she pulled me out of that creek. Like she was really seeing me as Reed and not the enemy, Fulton.

I had forgotten that look. That feeling.

I stepped outside onto the back porch of the farmhouse and stretched. Nana's wind chimes stayed quiet in the still air, and the sun already sat hazy in the sky despite it being early. It would be a hot one at Crowley Park later today for our game, but for now, I needed to pay a visit to the barn.

Next to a baseball field, there was nothing better than the smell of dry hay mixed with chainsaw dust and gasoline. Rusty metal blended with fresh-stained wood. I could see why Granddad loved it.

Just stepping over the threshold made me feel almost as calm as taking the mound. It had been ages since I walked in here, yet nothing had changed except the sheet over Dad's unfinished rocking chair in the corner.

My fingers shook as I pulled off the thin fabric. A cloud of dust puffed into the humid air. The chair looked better than I remembered. The arm rails and spindles felt smooth and firm, and the runners appeared sturdy enough too.

"Need something to connect them across the chair and from the front to the back," I said to no one. A stretcher? Is that what Dad had called those?

He had started this project on our last visit, Christmas two years ago. But we weren't here for long before the arguing began between Dad and Granddad, like it always did.

Granddad had yelled his usual, something like, "I'm proud of you for fighting for our country, son, but I need someone else here to help me."

Then Dad had given his typical response: "There are plenty of good workers in Fairfield looking for a job. Hire one of them."

Granddad would never do that though. He didn't trust 90 percent of the people in this town. Claimed they were too loyal to the Crowleys.

He may have had a point.

Dad had called it quits on that argument and stormed into the barn, where he worked on this chair until the next morning. In the afternoon, we drove home and left the chair behind. I figured we'd go back for it at some point, finish it, but a couple of months later, Dad got word he'd be in one of the special-ops divisions, and everything changed after that.

I sighed and rocked the chair back and forth. I didn't want to finish this. Didn't want the pressure of this season riding on every damn pitch I threw.

Dad should be here to do it. To help Granddad with this season. To help with the farm. With the money problems.

Between the bank statements and all the whispers about them, I didn't have to be a psychic to know that Granddad and Nana were behind with payments. But what could I do to help?

Winning the tournament for them was one thing, but then I'd leave at the end of the summer. Who would help them after that?

Running a stadium and a farm would be next to impossible for them to do alone, but Granddad would do it, or try to. Because he was so damned stubborn.

Maybe I could put up some "Help Wanted" posters around town while I was here? The library did have a good color printer.

Ben leaned against the open doorway. His hair stood up in every direction, and his eyes had bags under them. What had kept him up all night?

Doubt it was a small wrist tattoo.

"What's that?" He motioned toward the chair.

"My dad's. He didn't finish it before . . ."

"Before he was deployed?"

I nodded.

Ben rolled his shoulders and walked over to where I stood before he ran his hands over the smooth wood. "So let's finish it."

I scoffed. "I don't know anything about finishing a rocking chair."

He picked up a couple of small pieces of wood near our feet and held them near the runners. "How hard could it be?"

Ha. I grabbed the small pieces and placed them over the top of the chair where they belonged. "Harder than you think."

Ben took out his phone and started typing and swiping. Less than a minute later, he had a YouTube video pulled up with instructions. "Easy."

Easy. Right.

Ben's solution to almost every problem was to YouTube it. I didn't want YouTube to fix this, but before I could say no, Ben had already grabbed one of Granddad's chisels.

"Okay," I mumbled.

He smiled and started separating the pieces on the floor.

I knew Ben was doing what he always did when I got sad about Dad's deployments—distracting me. But maybe this time, I didn't want Ben to be the one to help me fix this.

I wanted my dad. And yeah, maybe a small—hell, foolish—

part of me hoped that if I left it incomplete, maybe it would bring Dad home sooner, faster.

Nana walked into the opened doors with pruning shears tucked under her arm and a big, floppy straw hat on her head. "Mornin'." She placed a couple of protein bars and two bottles of water on one of the tractor seats. "Big game today, eh, boys?"

"We're ready." Ben opened one of the bars and took a big bite. "Thanks."

"Your daddy would be so happy to see you working on that, Reed." She grabbed a pair of gardening gloves off the shelf. "Be sure you hydrate. Gonna be a scorcher today."

"We will." I crossed the space and gave her a kiss on the cheek. "You sure it's okay that we finish this?"

"Absolutely." She ruffled my hair. "I'd like to think there are a few things we can finish this summer. The chair is one. The feud is another. Get a win today, boys."

Ben pointed his water bottle before downing half of it. "Don't worry, we will. We got the ace on our side. He's ready."

I hope so.

Later that afternoon, I warmed up in one of my least favorite places: the enemy bullpen on a game day. Although I loved the pressure, the dare of it, this wasn't just any enemy bullpen.

Plus, I had my coach from Fayetteville, Coach Roeper—a dude more ripped than the Rock—staring down every single one of my pitches.

I threw a slider. He crossed his arms and leaned against the wall.

Translation: *I'm not sure.*

I switched to a curveball. He spat twice to his right.

Translation: *Eh. Maybe.*

If he spat to the left, though, I might as well put on an extra pair of pants to keep my ass from getting splinters. They'd bench me for at least three-quarters of the game. The local paper may have titled me the Ace, but Roeper didn't give two shits about that article. He only read the paper for *Calvin and Hobbes.*

I took a deep breath and forced myself to show him my changeup. Remembering Ben's advice, I fixed my footing before the throw. Perfect release with a beautiful slowdown right before it smacked Ben's glove directly over our make-believe plate.

Hell yes.

Coach cleared his throat, pulled a toothpick from his pocket, and put it in his mouth.

Damn. I got the throat and a toothpick?

"You gonna throw another one of those, Fulton?" Coach asked. "Or just stand there like a toothy moron?"

A laugh drifted from above. Eliza peered down, her blue

eyes shadowed by her Crowley Cardinals hat. Lauryn stood next to her, dressed as a cardinal and holding her costumed head in her hands. My ears burned.

'Course they heard that.

"Fulton?" Coach Roeper yelled. "You ready now, or should I come back later?"

I snapped my head back and tried to only worry about the ball in my hand and not the ones that Coach just kicked the shit out of.

Ben signaled his pointer finger down and away.

Slider. Got it.

I took my stance and pressed the glove to the bridge of my nose before winding back and releasing.

Low and true.

Coach gave a quick nod before moving over to watch Cameron Carter, a lefty from my hometown.

Eliza let out a low whistle. "Not bad, Fulton."

Ben stood. "Don't you have something better to do, Crowley? Sitting above the press box or posing for pictures?"

"I did." She leaned over the railing. "But I had to help pick up all the Mardi Gras beads and toilet paper *someone* put on the cardinal statues. You wouldn't know anything about that, though, would you, boys?"

Ben and I gave each other a look before shaking our heads.

Eliza rolled her eyes as Lauryn tugged on the cardinal head, and then the two of them walked away.

Coach walked over to the phone in the bullpen. "Fulton, good arm. Keep it up." He picked up the phone and turned around.

"Can you believe that?" Ben kicked the ground.

"I know. Coach actually gave me a compliment." Maybe the heat was getting to me already?

"No, I meant the princess paying us a visit." He scoffed. "God, she's so much like Erin. Snooping around and flaunting her—"

"Hey." I hit his arm. "She who will not be named, remember?" After what Erin did to Ben, we agreed not to speak her name out loud.

Ever.

"Shit. Right." Ben grabbed a bottle of water from nearby and took a long swig. "What's she doing here, anyway?"

"Well, it *is* Crowley field. And we're playing her dad's team today."

"Yeah, but she didn't need to come to the pen. Unless . . ."

"Unless what?" I took the ball from him.

He raised his eyebrows and batted his eyelashes.

"Ha!" I opened the gate, and the two of us started walking across the blazing hot outfield toward our dugout. "Eliza Crowley hates me."

Granted, neither of us killed the other one yesterday, but she *did* look like she wanted to punch me more than once while I was there.

"The way you two are with each other . . ." Ben mumbled. "Seems like the opposite of enemies."

"Trust me, it's not." I mean, she practically threw herself off a catwalk and a railcar just to avoid me, for Christ's sake.

"Wonder if she wore her pearls when she cleaned the statues." Ben chuckled.

"She doesn't dress like that anymore."

Ben stopped walking and made a face.

I rolled my eyes. "I didn't mean it like that."

"Uh-huh . . ."

"What I meant is that she doesn't need the pearls to play the part of a princess." Then again, princesses didn't work in light booths or sit on railcars.

Maybe I was wrong before.

Maybe she wasn't the princess I thought she was.

An hour later, I stood on the mound surrounded by a sold-out crowd and a scalding sun. Whoever thought it was a good idea to have a summer league play games in the middle of the day needed to choke on my fastball.

Even with sweat in my eyes, I knew when TJ Crowley took the plate before he was announced. He'd gained a good fifty to seventy pounds in muscle, but he still had the same strut and same dumbass smirk. For years, I'd waited for this—to face him on the field. To be the one in control.

Here, he couldn't shove me down the bank at Potter's Creek. Or let the air out of my bike tires. Or add salt to my frozen lemonade (couldn't get the taste of that out of my mouth for days).

On the mound, I called the shots.

The one running away with his tail between his legs today would be him.

It turned out he was just as predictable as any other asshat who took the plate.

He kicked some dirt.

Spat.

Swung the bat a few times.

A second after he looked ready, he asked the ump for a last-minute time-out and stepped outside the box.

In the end, though, it didn't matter. Five pitches later, I struck him out with my fastball.

Payback's a bitch, Crowley.

Ben laughed and waved at TJ as he stomped across the plate and chucked his bat into the dugout. Coach Crowley yelled something at him before pulling his hat lower and staring at me. I smiled.

Worried, King Crowley?

The heat continued to bear down on me like a twenty-pound wet blanket for the next few innings. By the bottom of the sixth, my jersey was soaked through. Every muscle hurt, and I needed an oxygen mask since the air around me weighed as much as soup.

TJ took the plate for the third time, and despite feeling like hell, I smiled because he looked pissed.

I'd be too if I were 0–2.

Ben signaled my fastball. A good call. So far, TJ couldn't touch it. I shook my sweaty hand loose and prayed my shoulder would hold out for one more inning, maybe two. After a deep and difficult breath in, I released the ball.

TJ swung and missed.

But he wasn't done with me yet.

Two minutes later, he had me backed into a corner with a full count. And as the smart-ass stepped into the box for the sixth pitch, he winked. My ears pounded in anger, and the memory of the last time he'd done that swarmed around my head.

I was twelve, and it was one of the hottest days in July on record, so Mom had taken me to the pool at the rec center. Half the town was there and swimming, including TJ. I had kept my distance and my eyes on him, but when Mom called me over to the wall to grab a quick drink, I lost him.

Two minutes later, while I swam underwater, he appeared out of nowhere and yanked off my trunks. Before I could get them back, he tossed them out of the pool and onto the umbrella where the lifeguard sat. She blew her whistle and yelled at me.

Me!

She chucked my suit at me, and everyone laughed as I slid them back on under the water. I wanted to kill TJ, but he was twice my size back then. And he knew it.

Because TJ didn't laugh when I was humiliated.

He winked.

"Reed!" Ben yelled. He now stood with his mask tipped back.

Shit. How long had he been standing there calling me?

"You good, man?" he asked.

I motioned for him to get back into position.

I hated throwing high and away, but TJ kept crowding the damn plate. He might've been a Crowley, but I couldn't hit another batter. Not after last summer.

Hitting one meant I could hit more.

I couldn't lose control.

I wouldn't lose control.

Not again.

Ben called the next pitch, and I did what Dad had taught me years ago—made the crowd fade away in the background, underexposed. *Put them in shadow. Out of sight*, his voice whispered inside my head. *Focus your breathing. Slow and steady, Reed.*

Slow and steady. Slow and . . .

But one person still stayed bright when everyone else went dark.

Eliza stood alone outside the press box. Her arms crossed in front of her. Ponytail fluttering in the breeze. Eyes staring directly at me.

Did she have nothing better to do?

TJ stepped back out of the box—of course—so I used the quick break to turn around and take off my hat. Sweat beaded on my eyebrows. My arm throbbed.

"Do not pay attention to her," I mumbled. "That's what she wants. To distract you. Get you back for bothering her yesterday. Don't let her."

I rolled my shoulders. After another deep breath in, I faced home plate again and ignored Eliza, who still stood by the press box. I leaned forward and focused solely on Ben's glove.

"You got this, Fulton!" Brent yelled from second.

I straightened up and pulled my arm back to throw what should've been my slider.

But it went right to TJ's left shin.

Oh, fuck.

Ben jumped up and ripped off his mask.

TJ threw down his bat, hopped around a few times, and charged me. Coach Crowley ran out of the dugout and yelled at him to stop.

Ha. TJ Crowley never stopped for anything or anyone.

Ben dropped his glove and sprinted after him, reaching him a second before he could throw a punch.

My heart hammered so loudly that my teeth numbed. I took a few steps toward him with clenched fists, but Brett's arms wound around me and tugged me backward toward the mound.

None of them understood. This was about so much more than baseball.

I wanted TJ to hit me. If he did, I could finally push back like I should've all those years ago. I wasn't a scrawny coward anymore.

TJ shrugged off Ben and stormed away to first. Coach Monaco then called a time and jogged out to the mound.

My stomach clenched, and my mouth tasted grittier than the dirt under my cleats. It was embarrassing enough to know when you were done. But having a coach come out to tell you so in front of hundreds of people only made it worse.

"You tryin' to get your teeth knocked in, Fulton?" he asked me with a glint in his eye.

I rubbed the back of my now sunburned neck. "Just trying to finish out the game."

He spat a sunflower shell to his left.

Coach Monaco translation: I was done.

Dammit.

"You threw a great game," he said.

Must've been a really great game if I'm out after one mistake.

Coach spat another seed. "Tom's ready to come in and finish it."

I sighed and handed Coach the ball. Dad always told me to never drop my head when a coach took me out, so I kept my eyes on him and said what Dad always told me to say in this situation: "Thank you, sir."

When I was on the mound, the cheers, boos, and heckling blended into white noise most of the time. But the jog from the mound to the dugout made that white noise sharper. Clearer.

"He had it comin', Fulton!" one kid yelled.

Damn right, he did.

"Why don't you go back to the farm you came from?" another cackled.

Screw you.

"Another summer, another year of Fultons losing to Crowleys!" a third one spat.

We're winning, you moron.

I threw my glove against the wall behind the bench and sat next to it, fumbling with Dad's tags under my jersey. Several minutes later, Tom finished the inning. We'd probably pull out a win today, but it still felt like I lost.

Ben took off his hat as he joined me in the dugout. "Did you mean to hit him?"

"What do you think?" I said.

But even as I sat next to him on the bench, I wasn't so sure.

Yes, I wanted to hurt and humiliate him for all the times he had done so to me, but that wasn't the way I'd wanted it to happen. I was better than that. I had to be—especially this summer.

Ben dumped some sunflower seeds into his hand. "You were on point all game, dude. You could've taken him."

I know. I took a long drink of Gatorade.

"You can't afford to have a repeat of last summer." He put a hand on my arm. "You gotta keep your shit together—"

"I know!" Who the hell was he? My warden? I shook him off and walked to the other end of the dugout.

I had played the game for over ten years, worked my ass off to become as close to the ace pitcher my father was—did his workouts, learned his tricks, his pitches, all of it.

This summer was supposed to be all baseball. But playing against *that* family, with a bet that could save or sink my granddad's farm, gave this season a hell of a lot more complications than I expected.

Granddad had a lot of sayings when it came to the Crowleys and this town. I usually rolled my eyes and chuckled at most of them, but one always struck true:

Nothing was fair in Fairfield.

Chapter Nine

ELIZA

"Theater is a mirror, a sharp reflection of society."
—Yasmina Reza

After a normal game, Dad-the-Coach-Crowley was completely unbearable when the team lost.

But losing to the Fulton Hawks in our first home game brought out a whole new kind of fury. On the surface, Dad looked like the eye of a storm—eerily calm, quiet, calculating. But behind closed doors—or in our case, concessions—the verbal wrath surfaced. Our own personal hurricane.

A slew of creative curse words swirled around the sinks, and the ice machine received another dent on its face. When I was eight, I named it Miss Hannigan after one of the most horrible humans created for the stage. Not a good start of the season for her.

Dad kept muttering under his breath as he counted the

money at the register. "I'm callin' Ed in the morning about those umps. Lousy, no good, biased . . ."

"Save it for home, Will," Mom warned, her gaze down as she mopped. "Too many people will hear—"

"I don't give a damn about the people."

"Well, maybe you should." She plopped the mop in the sudsy bucket that smelled of lemons and bleach. "Because even if your team takes the title at the end of the season, it won't matter. No one will want to work for our stadium and Cyclone Crowley."

The tower of plastic cups I carried toppled to the ground.

Truth: Mom and I—and quite possibly the entire town—had been calling Dad that for years during any season he coached . . . behind his back. Obviously.

Dad stopped counting the money and faced me, cheeks blotchy.

Yikes. Definitely a Category Three now. Make a clear path for the inevitable pacing.

"Cyclone . . . Crowley?" The vein above his right eyebrow pulsed.

"Well, have you seen your face when you lose?" Mom continued mopping and shaking her head. "You make a volcanic explosion look like a hiccup."

I held back my laughter.

"Hey, it could be worse." I bent down to pick up the cups

that fell. "What if you were . . . Cutesy Crowley? Then everyone would want hugs, and Lauryn would be out of the job as our mascot because they'd want it to be you."

The popcorn machine stopped popping.

The back prep sink dripped three times.

And then Dad did something I hadn't heard in forever. He laughed.

It bellowed around the kitchen, rich and full, while my feet stuck to the floor. I wanted to record this moment, take a picture, a video, something so I could visit it or play it back later, during another moment when he was caught in the eye of his own storm.

I'd forgotten how much I liked that sound, how much I'd missed it.

This was the same laugh from when he used to pitch to me at the ballpark, when he taught me to ride a bike and watched my dance recitals. Mom used to say he only laughed that way with me. But then I outgrew my bike and dance shoes and started enjoying being behind the scenes more than standing center stage. Dad stopped asking me to play catch, and I stopped missing it.

Yet here he was, laughing like he used to, and I had no idea what to think or how to respond. I couldn't open myself up to disappointment. I wouldn't allow myself to believe he changed courses that quickly.

He was a cyclone, after all.

Mom tiptoed over to him and kissed his chin. She whispered something in his ear, and he cackled before smacking her butt.

Bleh. "Come on, guys." I covered my eyes.

Mom shushed me and went back to her mopping. "I can't help but wonder if maybe you wouldn't be this tense if you hadn't made such a foolish bet, Will."

Oh boy.

"Maybe I did what I thought would be best for our family, Maggie," Dad snapped.

"Without talking to your family first?"

Point: Mom.

"If you didn't notice, we had a sold-out crowd tonight," he added, his voice tense. "First time in years we had that on a season opener. Drama draws crowds."

Point: Dad. Much as I hated to admit it.

"I noticed," Mom mumbled. "But we also lost."

Whoa. Mom with the game changer.

Dad slammed the register shut before storming out of the concession building, rattling the walls and making an old framed team picture clatter to the floor.

I picked it up and gently placed it back on the small peg.

Mom swished the mop near her feet. "Maybe I shouldn't have brought it up."

"You had every right to bring it up." Last time I checked,

our house wasn't a dictatorship—or it didn't used to be. I tied off the top of one of the trash bags and scooped it up, pausing at the door to grab my book bag. "I'll see you later."

"Text us when you're on your way home. Remember you have a curfew," Mom warned.

Did anyone else have a curfew in the summer? Doubtful.

My body immediately relaxed when I stepped into the fresh, humid air. On these kinds of nights, you could almost taste summer. Sweet and salty mixed with earth.

I tossed the bags into the dumpster before kicking it to make the lid drop. All I wanted after all this drama was a cold lemonade from the Brew and a slow drive home with the windows down, far from here, far from baseball and all the hell it had already brought us this season.

Unfortunately, baseball had other plans, in the form of an ace pitcher.

"Have you lost your mind?" I hurried across the parking lot, peering in every direction to make sure we were alone. We were.

For now.

"It's a nice night." Reed leaned against my Jeep, looking like he owned it.

If he scratched it, I'd kill him. "Do you have a death wish, Fulton?"

"Do you always have to be so dramatic, Crowley?" He crossed his arms. "Relax. We're not surrounded by a cast and crew. No kids walking by with fishing poles this time. All the cars have left."

Yeah, except Dad's truck.

The concession door was closed, and I didn't see any sign of him, but we were in a parking lot.

With no other cars nearby.

Dad would definitely turn into a Category Five if he caught me out here with the pitcher who just destroyed his team.

"I wasn't ready to go home yet." Reed stared across the lot at the darkened baseball field.

I almost asked him how that was my problem, but curiosity—or maybe heat exhaustion—got the best of me. "Why?" I propped my arm against the roll bar. "You won, remember?"

"I know," he said.

I waved him on. "So . . ."

"So . . . going home means a lecture from Granddad. I'm not in the mood." He turned his hat backward. "It wasn't my best game."

For a moment, all I could do was blink at him. He was a Fulton, and I was a Crowley, so why the hell would he be saying this to me, of all people? Regardless, I stepped up to the plate.

"No, it wasn't," I said.

His eyebrows shot up.

If you're looking for sympathy, you've come to the wrong place.

"Your curveball needs some work." I shrugged.

"Does it, now?"

I unzipped the front of my backpack and took out a bag of peanuts, but Reed made no motion to speak or move. He just stared at me like I had grown two heads or something. I hated that look. "What do you really want, Fulton? And don't give me that crap excuse about not wanting to go home." I cracked open a shell. "You could've gone to Scoops or the Brew. I'm sure your team is already out celebrating."

"Is it so hard to believe that *maybe* I just wanted to talk?" He picked at his fingernails.

To me? Um, yeah.

I tossed a shell at his shoulder, and the door to the concession building opened, my father standing in its frame.

I gulped. "Oh—"

"Shit," Reed said.

"Eliza?" Dad raised a hand above his eyebrows and squinted under the bright light above the back door. "You still out there?"

"Quick! Get in!" I shoved Reed's head down near the roll bar. Had TJ not taken out the back seats last year, there was no way Reed's tall frame would've fit inside.

Without a word to Dad, I jumped into the driver's seat, started the engine and gunned it out of the parking lot. Reed's head popped up behind me, and I smacked it. "Get back down until we're in the clear," I yelled over the wind whipping around us. My mind raced a mile a minute.

Reed Fulton was in my Jeep.

I helped Reed Fulton escape from my father, and he was now in my Jeep.

With *me*.

In the dark.

Alone.

What the hell are you doing, Eliza?

By some miracle, I made it down Main Street without having to stop at any traffic light and without seeing anyone I knew on the road or on the sidewalks. Only when I passed the faded green sign that said "Leaving Fairfield: Come Again Soon!" did I ease up.

Reed's head slowly came into focus in my rearview mirror. Hat off, his wavy hair fluttered in the wind. "Is it okay to sit up now?"

I nodded.

"Can I come up to the front seat?" he asked.

"No. Not after the last time and that stupid bet—"

"What bet?"

Sure, pretend like you don't remember.

I must've inhaled some gas while manning the hot dog grill—the only explanation for my brief trip down Lunacy Lane.

"Where are we going, Crowley?"

"No idea." I just had to keep driving. Maybe the longer I drove, the more this insane idea would start to make sense?

A *THUMP* sounded from the back, followed by a loud flapping noise.

Oh no. No, no, no . . .

Reed leaned out of the back on the passenger side. "I think you've got a flat."

"Of course I do." God had a seriously twisted sense of humor.

"Bet this wouldn't have happened if you had just driven your shiny Beemer."

"I told you already: I hate that car."

Reed mumbled something close to "Must be nice to have a choice," but I ignored it.

Yes, I knew I was lucky to have a choice with a lot of things in my life, but I never asked for it. I didn't want it. Maybe if he had been around over the last few years, he would've seen the charity events I helped with for our local scouts, or how I had convinced Dad to do a couple of benefit games for the Clairview Women's Shelter the last two spring seasons.

But would it have mattered?

Probably not.

Because no matter what I did, Reed Fulton would always see me as a selfish princess.

I drove on, the back side of the Jeep now vibrating, until I found a pull-off near the woods and turned off the car, letting my head fall against the steering wheel.

I'm stuck in the middle of nowhere with a flat tire and Reed Fulton.

All that was missing was a hailstorm. And maybe a ravenous bear.

Reed jumped out and walked around the side toward the flat. "Looks like you must've had a slow leak. I don't see anything sticking out. Does your tire pressure light not work?"

"Mary Elizabeth is practically an antique." I lifted my head. "She doesn't have one." I sent my parents a text letting them know I might be a little late for curfew.

"Mary Elizabeth?"

"What, is the name not good enough?"

He held up his hands. "Actually, I was going to ask if it was the same Mary Elizabeth who was the first woman to play pro baseball?"

Hold the freakin' phone.

He knows about Mary Elizabeth Murphy? "It . . . is."

"Good name, then." A tense silence settled between us for what felt like hours, until he drummed his hands on the flat's fender liner. "So you calling Triple A?" he asked.

And wait hours for someone to come, making me miss curfew? No thanks.

I grabbed my Yankees hat from the passenger seat and tugged it on, threading my ponytail through it before heading to the back of the Jeep.

A moment later, I had the spare on the ground along with

the jack, lug wrench, and the owner's manual—not that I'd need it. TJ and I had changed many tires on this old girl even before it was mine.

I got to work and used the lug wrench, turning the nuts on the hubcap but not enough that they came off completely. TJ had taught me only to do that once I was ready to remove the tire.

"Eliza Crowley can change a flat tire." Reed crouched down and slid the jack underneath the Jeep. He began pushing down on the handle till the flat tire rose a few inches off the ground. "Now I've seen it all."

I smiled, facing away from him so he couldn't see, and began unscrewing the lug nuts.

Reed knelt down and held his hand open for them. Once he'd put them in his pocket, he helped me pull the flat tire free and carried it to the back of the Jeep.

"How did you learn to do this?" he asked as he rolled the new tire toward me.

"TJ." I helped him lift the new tire onto the lug bolts before we both pushed it forward till the bolts showed through the rim. "Dad was too busy." 'Course he wasn't ever too busy for my brother, Robbie, but I wasn't about to open that can of worms.

Reed set to work putting the nuts back onto the bolts. "Not too busy to buy you a fancy car though—"

"Oh my God." *What is it with you and the Beemer?* I adjusted my hat. "For the millionth time, Dad knew I didn't want that car. And for your information, I tried to return it, but the dealer and my dad go way back, so he wouldn't have it." Sometimes it really was annoying when your dad knew every freaking person in the tri-county area.

Reed stayed quiet as he finished working with the bolts and didn't speak again till the last one was done. "I get it."

"Having your dad buy you a car you don't want?"

He laughed. "No. Having a dad who's too busy."

I knew Reed's dad was in the army, but the Mr. Fulton I remembered smiled a lot more than my dad, and he used to hang out with Reed all the time when we were kids.

I reached forward to start tightening one of the lug nuts by hand, but he had the same idea. Our fingers brushed, my skin tingled, and we both drew them away just as quickly as we had placed them there.

"Um, s-s-sorry," he stuttered.

What was he nervous about? I was the one who was going to be grounded for an eternity for being out past my stupid curfew.

"You . . ." He swallowed, hard. "Go ahead." He stood and moved his phone flashlight over the tire.

Maybe I had breathed in some kind of fumes? I mean, why else would the same boy who spent the majority of sixth and seventh grade bothering the hell out of me help me change a tire and then apologize? I'd definitely have to talk to Mom about what kind of gas we used for that grill in the concession kitchen.

I continued tightening the lug nuts by hand while night came to life around us. Crickets chirped in the tall grass near the woods, an owl hooted in the distance, and fireflies dotted the darkness in between the trees. Last time it was this quiet, I was alone with Reed at the railyard. I had hated the tense awkwardness of it all.

But tonight? It was anything but.

It felt strangely peaceful.

Reed lowered the Jeep back to the ground and then put the jack away before handing me the lug wrench.

"You sink into your front leg too much," I blurted.

"What?" he asked as he rubbed the back of his neck.

What are you doing, Eliza?

But I couldn't stop now. "Your curveball. It's not bad, really . . . but it could be better if you didn't ease into it so much." *Sweet Jesus. Shut up. He doesn't want to hear your opinion about his pitching.*

His toe turned back and forth into the gravel. "That's a good point, actually."

Wait. Seriously?

"My dad used to say that throwing a good curveball starts with keeping a clear head. You have to think about throwing it as hard, if not harder, than your fastball if you want to confuse the batter." He crouched down and offered to take a turn with the wrench.

And I didn't hesitate to let him. For some reason.

"I, um . . . well, I had a hard time keeping my head clear tonight," he said.

Same. "Baseball has that effect on people."

His eyes met mine. "Maybe it's not just baseball," he whispered.

Chapter Ten

REED

"Life is hard. Life is humbling. I do all I can to keep it simple."
—Mariano Rivera

The theater was Eliza's turf. The catwalk, the railyard, the stadium—those had all been ballsy moves just to get a good read on her. Which I still wasn't sure I had.

I mean, the girl changed a flat tire like she worked with NASCAR on the weekends, for Christ's sake.

I shouldn't be here.

And yet here I was. On the actual stage of the Lyric. Might as well have painted a big-ass target on my chest, but I had promised Granddad over a week ago that I'd help out Thatcher Newcomb, an old friend of his, with setwork today, since we didn't have practice. And a Fulton always kept his word.

Would Eliza see it that way?

Or would she accuse me of following her and deliberately trying to ruin her summer again?

My gut told me she wouldn't. That things were different . . . were changing. Hell, she hadn't blamed the flat tire on me or knocked me out with the wrench.

Then again, she did make me ride in the back of the Jeep with my head down on the way home and dropped me off a mile outside of town.

Flat tire or not, this "new" Eliza didn't stop me from eyeing every exit in this theater and keeping my head down.

At least Thatcher had me working backstage.

"Reed," he called from the opposite side of the stage.

Jesus, just announce me to the whole crew.

He pointed behind me. "Go downstage center to where I left my toolbox and grab me one of my drill bits, will ya? The high-speed ones, kinda twisty looking."

"Kinda twisty looking." Right.

I turned around and looked left and right, scratching the back of my neck. Downstage? Where the hell was downstage? Was that theater-talk for a basement?

One of the actors running lines nearby, a young kid with a cool sword on his belt, pointed toward the front of the stage where an old red toolbox sat.

"Thanks," I said, hurrying toward it.

Thatcher's toolbox would make Granddad break out in hives. His Allen wrenches and random-sized nails sat sprinkled throughout the top compartment. Wing nuts were mixed up with hex nuts, and scrap pieces of paper littered the entire container.

How does he find anything in here?

More voices entered the auditorium, so I crouched lower and kept rummaging through the toolbox till I finally found the drill bit. I hurried back across the stage and gave it to Thatcher, who smiled in approval.

"Now, hold up this frame here for me while I mark a couple of spots," he said. We both grunted as we lifted the piece. "Ah, darn," he muttered. "Should've had you get the brad-point bit. Wood's too thick for this kind. Don't go anywhere. Be right back."

He hobbled away toward his toolbox and left me alone with the frame. If I tried to lower this beast, it'd slip out from under me and bash me in the freakin' head.

Sweat beaded up on my eyebrows, and my elbows began to twitch.

Hurry up, Thatch. Hurry your ass up.

I swallowed over a dry rock in my throat and cursed under my breath. If I hurt myself doing this, Coaches Monaco and Roeper would kill me.

The wood made a funny, squeaky sound as the bottom started sliding away from me. "Oh shit," I yelled, not caring anymore if I gave myself away.

But then another set of hands appeared and pulled the wood

upright again. "Too heavy for you, Fulton?" Eliza now stood smirking next to me. Her hands gripped the other side of the frame. She had several colored pens stuck into her ponytail, and she wore a gray shirt with big block letters that said "Though she be but little, she is fierce." I hadn't heard that quote before.

But I liked it.

"I'm surprised you didn't let it fall on me, Crowley." I winced as something pricked my palm. Splinter?

"Well, you did help me change a flat tire last night."

"Nah." I chuckled. "You had it covered."

Her cheeks turned pink.

Oh. Did I embarrass her?

Definitely wasn't my goal.

She grinned, and the scar above her eyebrow wrinkled. I remembered the time she got that very scar. We were nine or maybe ten years old. TJ and I had dared each other to jump off one of the railcars, and Eliza had tagged along. TJ and I had leaped at the same time, and we both rolled when we landed. Eliza laughed, and then TJ had challenged her to do better. I remembered shouting "No!" when she jumped—but it was too late.

She had landed harder than we did and instead of rolling to the side, she rolled forward and smacked her head on the gravel. TJ tried blaming me, but Eliza stepped in and asked him to take her home. The next day when I saw her outside

Scoops, she told me it was her first battle wound. I was proud of her, but I never told her so.

I should've told her so.

"Fulton?" Her voice sounded almost musical. "You good?"

I blinked a few times. Childhood Eliza vanished, and grown-up Eliza still holding the frame materialized in front of me.

Did she ever think back to the same memories I did?

"Sorry," I said. "I was thinking about the time you got that scar."

A guy I didn't know stepped out from the shadows. "I haven't heard that story, E." He looked like he came straight from a country club or golf course—polo tucked into khaki shorts above the knee, white, unstained shoes. "Maybe you should tell me sometime."

Maybe you should go find a sand trap.

Eliza nodded to Mr. Preppy. "Reed, this is Chad Dupont. He moved here a year after your family left. Chad, this is Reed Fulton."

Dupont? As in the mayor?

Chad stopped short. "The same Fultons who own the run-down farm off Birch?"

Heat flashed at the base of my neck. "Our farm—"

"The Fultons' farm is one of the biggest in the tri-county area, actually." Eliza stood up straighter, taking on more of the set piece's weight. "And how many times did your nana's 4H club have one of those Diamond— What's it called, Reed?"

"Diamond Clover Award," I said. The heat cooled a bit. "She had a kid win it three years in a row."

"Fascinating." Chad took out his phone and swiped a few times, looking bored. "Anyway, Eliza, your dad sent me to tell you not to be late for dinner."

She scoffed. "Why couldn't he just tell me himself?"

Chad shrugged. "He said you weren't answering your phone."

"Yeah, well, I'm working today. I'll be home when I'm done."

Shots fired. I looked down so neither of them could see my smirk.

"Relax, Princess. I'm just the messenger."

Call her Princess like that one more time. I dare you.

Chad started turning around and then added to me, "Good luck this season, Fulton. You'll need it."

Not as badly as you need bigger shorts, asshole.

Eliza shook her head as he walked away, making a call on his phone. "I cannot believe I dated him for five months. Worst decision of my life."

Clearly. "Bet *he* drives a Beemer."

She laughed, and something warm and unfamiliar stretched across the inside of my chest. Eliza Crowley had defended me.

Where had that come from?

Thatcher's hand appeared out of nowhere and clasped my shoulder. "Found it!" He held up the different drill bit and looked at Eliza with surprise. "Needed a break from the booth today, Ms. Crowley?"

She let go of the frame as Thatcher took it back and helped me lower it to the ground. "Actually, I came down to meet with our director and a couple lighting technicians, Mr. Newcomb." Her eyes moved around us both. "And I think they just got here, so I'll see you around."

Eliza walked toward the front of the stage and shook hands with two older guys in matching dress shirts as a tall woman with a peacock-colored scarf and bright framed glasses joined them. Eliza's gaze moved back to mine, and that unfamiliar warmth returned.

"Theater brings out some interesting characters, eh, Reed?" Thatcher commented.

"Yeah." I broke eye contact before the heat moved to my face. "It does."

Chapter Eleven

ELIZA

"When you feel like you've only got a bit part in your own life, write the script yourself." —Benny Bellamacina

Outside of a damn golf swing, Chad probably never worked with his hands a day in his life. He wouldn't know hard work if it hit him in the teeth.

Yet here was Reed, on his day off, helping one of this theater's oldest supporters. Grandma always said Thatcher Newcomb was a "good egg," giving a lot of time and his own money to different projects at the Lyric and never wanting any credit for it.

She used to say Reed was a "good egg" too.

I never told him that.

I should have told him that.

"Ms. Crowley?" Roy, one of the lighting technicians tapped my shoulder. "You were saying?"

Oh, right.

"Sorry. What I was going to say was that I double-checked

the board this morning, and it looks like I have a couple ERS bulbs out. I was told this theater always used them, but I'd like to see a quote for a Fresnel instead."

Roy and the other technician, who happened to be his brother, gawked at me. I beamed, feeling taller than the Yankees' best outfielder, Aaron Judge.

That's right, boys. All rise.

I may not have read the brochures from all the business programs Dad had dropped on my desk over the last year, but I did listen to *Girlboss Radio*.

Carl tugged on the belt of his jeans. "But the Fresnel won't be nearly as strong of a light—"

"I don't need it." *Hold eye contact.* "Everything else was updated last year and works great. We'll save money by going with a Fresnel too."

Roy *harrumph*ed. "Maybe Ms. Sparrow has different thoughts about it though?"

"It's like I already said on the phone, gentlemen." Ms. Sparrow propped her glasses on top of her head. "Eliza's opinions regarding lighting choices are my opinions."

"So go ahead and draw it up," I added.

Roy tapped his clipboard with a pencil that had a chewed top—gross. "We'll get a quote to you soon." He and Carl hurried away as Ms. Sparrow fist-bumped me.

"Men," she muttered. "And my mother still wonders why I've never been attracted to them."

I snorted and thanked her before turning around to where I had left Reed. The frame now stood alone, fastened to the floor. Reed was gone, and my heart sank a little.

I bet he would've liked seeing me put those two jerks in their place.

"So everything still on schedule with your cues?" Ms. Sparrow now faced upstage, taking notes.

On schedule? Um . . . "Yes." Total lie. "Yes, the cues are going well."

Truth: The board had frozen twice in the last few days.

I had lost dozens of cues and had to nearly start over each time. Now I saved my progress every two to three cues in case it happened again. It was painstakingly slow, and I was scared shitless it would happen during one of our live performances.

Ms. Sparrow bought my fake smile, though, and patted my shoulder before leaving the stage.

Later that afternoon, I pulled into the driveway to find Dad leaning on his truck with his arms crossed, staring at me.

I wasn't late for dinner, so what was this about?

Wait.

My stomach dropped.

Did he know about Reed being with me when I left the stadium last night? Shit. I was so about to be grounded.

I stepped out of the Jeep, swallowing over grittiness when he laughed. "Relax, Eliza," he said. "You look like you're walking to your doom."

"Am I?"

"I noticed your spare tire on the Jeep. How many times do I have to tell you to drive the BMW? When did you get the flat?" he asked.

Oh. "After the game."

"Well, I'm glad Triple A was able to help you. We'll take it in for a new tire this—"

"I changed it myself," I said, leaving out the part where Reed was there too.

He rubbed his chin. "Who taught you how to change a flat?"

"TJ." *Because you were too busy to show me, remember?*

He nodded approvingly before he pulled out his North Face backpack, the old hiking one, from the back of his truck. "I thought maybe we'd hit a couple trails today before dinner. You know . . . like we used to."

Dad and I hadn't hiked in over five years. What the heck brought this idea into his head? Maybe his therapist?

"Eliza?" Dad returned his backpack to the back of his truck. "Hike? Today?"

"Dad, I don't know if now's a good time. I came home for a snack, and then I wanted to go back to the theater for some cue work while the cast wasn't there." I flicked my keys back and forth in my hand.

"Come on. You can spare one afternoon for a walk with your old man." He made a pouting face—no one had a pout like his.

Dammit. "Okay, fine. Let me go get my old sneakers."

A half an hour later, Dad parked the truck at the Chestnut Oak and Swift Creek Loop Trail. We used to walk this every Sunday evening together, just the two of us. Mulched, shaded pathways looped around the tall trees, and in areas where the overgrowth was too thick or where the ground sank too low, wooden planks turned the path into more of a boardwalk. The trail even had benches and lookout posts. I used to love coming here in the late spring and summer when everything was in bloom, but my favorite time to visit was always the winter, when it was still.

I felt as much reverence for winter in the woods as I did in church, maybe more so.

"Swift Creek or Beech Tree Trail?" Dad asked me as he tightened the straps of his pack on his shoulders.

"Swift Creek." I had forgotten to put on bug spray, so Swift Creek's boardwalk paths would be a safer bet.

The first half of our walk was taken by silence, but not an uncomfortable one, with Dad in front of me. I picked up a fallen branch and broke off the twigs to use as a walking stick. Dad had his binoculars out and stopped to scan the trees every so often. Chipmunks scurried under the ferns along the path and squirrels raced effortlessly up and down the trees. Sunlight filtered in through the leaves high above, tinting the path in different shades of green. With a bit more blue, this kind of lighting would be perfect for the balcony scene.

"So your mother tells me your show is going well," Dad said, pausing to lift his binoculars toward a tall oak.

Did she? Half the time I talked about it, I wasn't sure she heard me. "It is. Kinda."

"What do you mean, 'kinda'?"

I ran my stick back and forth over the boards. "It's nothing I can't handle. Just had a run in with a couple of chauvinistic jerks this morning—"

"Do I need to go down there?" Dad's binoculars smacked against his chest, his hands now resting on his hips.

"No." I smiled. It was nice to see him stand up for me like this. It had been a while. "I took care of it and set them straight."

He beamed and patted my shoulder. "That's my girl."

My heart squeezed. *My girl.*

It had been a while since he had said that too.

After stopping at an overlook, Dad spoke up again. "I know I made some pretty big decisions about this summer without talking to you or your mother"—*You got that right*—"but I stand by what I did." He took two bottles of water from his backpack and offered me one. "We needed the bigger crowds, and we've already gotten them."

"Yeah, but what if we lose, Dad?" I tossed my stick into the woods. "I don't wanna move my senior year. I've worked so hard—"

"I know you have. And you'll continue to work hard no matter where you are."

"Not helping . . ."

He rummaged through the pack and grabbed his Crowley Cardinals hat out of the main compartment. "We won't lose, Eliza."

"But what if we do?" Sweat beaded up at the base of my neck. "Reed Fulton is really good, and—"

"Reed Fulton is a loose cannon on and off that mound. Always has been. Always will be. Steer clear from him, you hear?"

Steer clear?

I literally steered out of the stadium with him yesterday and was fine.

Other than the flat tire.

I swallowed hard.

Dad patted my shoulder and smiled tensely. "Not that I need to tell you that. You know all about that family."

Did I though? "You know, we used to be friends before—"

"Besides, there's nothing wrong with starting somewhere new." He started walking again. "Sometimes it's good to leave behind the ghosts."

Ghosts? What ghosts?

Sure, our house made some creaky noises when the wind moved too hard against it, but—

And then it all clicked into place.

Grandma.

Grandpa.

Both had died unexpectedly in the last six years, Grandpa first followed by Grandma three years later. Is that what all of this was about? Running away from our memories?

A lump in my throat sharpened. "Dad, if this is about—"

"It's about baseball, Eliza," he snapped. "And what's best for our family."

I didn't push it after that. You can't argue with grief. I had lost my grandparents, but he had lost his parents. I couldn't imagine that kind of loss, and I didn't want to.

Too bad ghost lights were reserved only for the stage.

Chapter Twelve

REED

"I don't believe in curses. I think you make your own destination." —Manny Ramirez

After Eliza saved my ass from that frame falling on me yesterday and spoke up against her ex on my behalf, the least I could do was return something I took from her long ago.

I called it Operation Lost and Found.

Dad used to say there were two kinds of people: those who waited for change to come knocking and those who broke down the door.

I have never been a patient person, so I planned to do the latter. Not literally, of course—or her father would mount my head above their marble fireplace. No, if I was going to do this, I had to do it right and do it fast before I lost the nerve.

Granddad was keeping Ben busy with an oil change for one of the tractors, which gave me the perfect window of time before our afternoon away game. Ben would've ridden my ass if he knew I was going into enemy territory after I made such a big deal at the start of the summer about our "All baseball. No girls." pact. But that was mostly for his benefit, so he wouldn't spiral again. What he didn't know wouldn't hurt him, right?

After sneaking into the attic, I found what I needed and slipped the rainbow-haired ponies into a bag along with a note—which I spent way too long writing and rewriting—before hurrying toward Main Street on foot.

Other than new lampposts and the cardinal statues, Main Street in Fairfield looked exactly the same as it did when I was a kid. The grassy area between the courthouse and library still had dirt patches and dead grass where the locals set up tables for the weekly farmer's market. The fire department still announced birthdays on their roadside sign. And a small wooden plaque announcing the "Best Mint Chip Around" still hung in the window at Scoops.

I paused, though, when I reached the bank. My jaw clenched as I read the logo on a faded banner staked on their small lawn: "Fairfield Bank: We Are There for You."

What a load of shit.

Back in the early 2000s, Granddad and my great uncle Charlie finished building the stadium with Eliza's grandfather, Frank, and her father, Will. For a couple of years, they worked together to keep the stadium running. Then Frank took a job in New York for a few years to work in the stock market while Will went off to college. Apparently, they had verbally agreed to let my family take over the stadium. They already owned a couple of businesses in town, anyway.

Granddad and my dad kept the stadium running, but it was a lot on top of the farm and Dad's new enlistment in the army. Still, they made it work.

But just as Granddad had finally saved up enough to put a down payment on the stadium to own it free and clear, Frank Crowley returned with cash and bought it out from under him. With interest. How could the bank say no?

I rounded the corner of Oak Avenue and came face-to-face with Eliza's massive house. Tall and white with dark blue shutters, it stood exactly as I had remembered it. My feet felt weighed down with lead while I trudged along her perfectly paved driveway beneath the tall trees. The air grew heavier the closer I got. When I neared Eliza's Jeep, TJ stepped out from the garage.

Shit.

I ducked behind the closest maple tree and took off my hat. It wasn't that I was scared of him—far from it.

It was that I didn't want him to take what I had in my hands or twist my reasons for being here. Operation Lost and Found felt more like Operation Lost My Mind now.

Why did I think this was a good idea, again? Entering enemy territory during the most crucial season of my life?

I leaned against the tree, and the Ziploc bag crinkled in my hand.

If Eliza took these back, saw my number on the note and actually responded, then my gut would be right: She *had* changed after all these years. And maybe I had too.

But then what? What was next for her? For me?

For us?

Hell. Would there be an us?

Did I want there to be?

It's not like I lived here. I'd be gone at the end of the summer, and whatever went on between us would probably blow over faster than dirt on home plate.

Or would it?

Ever since the railyard, I couldn't shake the feeling that things were changing. And every time I tried to ignore it, the damn lump in my throat brought the thought right back.

Fuck it.

Dad's deployments may have sucked but they did teach me one thing: Never give yourself the opportunity to have regrets.

I pushed off the tree and headed toward her front porch. TJ worked underneath his bike, with music blaring inside the garage. A moment later, I set the bag down next to a big ceramic pot filled with umbrellas—who needed this many umbrellas?—and then headed back down the long driveway.

Operation Lost and Found was a go.

Later that day, we squeezed out a 3–2 win against the Burlington Bobcats. Since I pitched the opening game, Cameron pitched this time around. He had the nastiest curveball I'd ever seen, but after several innings, he started throwing grapefruits, so Tom was brought in to finish.

A misty rain fell on the drive home, which meant the rickety-ass bus the Crowleys "gifted" us now smelled like wet dog on top of sweat and chips.

My phone beeped an alert from inside my duffle by my feet. And my stomach did a weird flip as I read the message.

Unknown: Thanks for the bag.

Unknown: I can't believe you kept them after all these years.

I fell back against my seat. Holy shit. She got my note and actually used my number.

I smiled and started typing a response back when Ben's head popped over the seat. "Who you texting?" he asked.

"No one." I clicked off the screen. "Just Nana. Wanted to tell her and Granddad about that win."

He smacked my shoulder. "Did you hear the Cardinals lost? Ha! That stadium is ours. We should totally punk them again and rub their noses in it."

My eye twitched. "Why do you hate them so much?"

He scoffed. "Why *don't* you?"

Because maybe I've been wrong about them all these years. Maybe they're not all the same.

"I don't have to be from here to know what it's like. People like that swoop in and take whatever or whoever they want . . ."

And we're back to Erin again.

Ben leaned back in his seat as a heavier rain slapped against the bus's windows. "Did you see Eliza's Rolex? It's gold. Real gold."

"So what?" Mom had lots of gold jewelry from Dad. Plus, lots of kids had fancy watches. Just not kids like me. Which was fine. Because I had a watch that worked. Sort of.

Ben showed me his phone screen. "Dude, watches like hers cost close to twenty grand."

I pulled the screen closer. "Holy shit."

"Exactly." He sat back in his seat. "So the big question is: Why does a girl who wears that much money on her wrist choose to drive a beat-up old Jeep?"

I opened my mouth to argue, *Because she is more than just money.* But Ben had a point. It was hard to argue against twenty fucking grand.

And how did he know Eliza drove an old Jeep?

Was he keeping tabs on her?

If so, did he know I rode in the back of that Jeep a couple of nights ago?

"They're just a bunch of rich people runnin' all over everyone. Getting scholarships to top schools even though they could afford it." He hit his fist against the foggy window, hard. "Wake up and smell the hay, Fulton. Good guys like us never get to the top by playing fair."

Chapter Thirteen

ELIZA

"All the world's a stage . . ." –William Shakespeare, *As You Like It*

Summer may not have been my favorite season, but it was a solid second, thanks to the Fairfield Carnival that always came at the end of June. Rides, games, and amazing food—I adored all of it. But what I loved most of all was the way blurred neon colors from the rides spun and twirled, looking like Christmas lights when you lay under a tree.

Tonight, Lauryn and I worked an early shift at the Lyric's booth, where we sold cups of my grandmother's famous lemonade and snickerdoodle cookies as well as some beaded bracelets made by the cast and crew. Grandma had always had a booth at the carnival and gave everything to a local charity, church, or the theater. Every summer since she passed, I had asked the Lyric to keep the booth going in her honor. It felt good to finally be on the other side of the table working for a place that brought her so much joy, but I found myself wishing that she stood next to me, that she could tell me if I got the recipes right or notice how I fanned out the paper napkins the same way she would when she hosted tea parties.

After the sun finally went down, Ms. Sparrow and a couple of other techies relieved Lauryn and me, allowing us to wander around till Lauryn found the merry-go-round and tugged me on board. The carousel chimed and music began as it started spinning. Lauryn pretended her unicorn was a legit horse and bobbed up and down above the saddle while using a make-believe whip and shouting, "Giddyap!"

I laughed and looped my feet in the footholds, then leaned back and stared at the swirling colors above me while stretching out my arms.

But as the ride slowed down, I could feel someone staring at me from the nearby fence.

Reed stood alone, in a polo shirt that tightly hugged his biceps over a pair of khaki shorts. It was a very different look from his usual athletic shorts and a baseball tee, but it was a good look.

A really good one.

He gave me a small smile and wave, and without hesitating, I did the same.

"Excuse me." A small kid tapped my sandal strap. "Are you done?"

Oh.

The music had stopped, and new ride-goers were already weaving in between the animals, picking their favorite.

When did the ride stop? And where was Lauryn?

"Sorry." I swung my leg over and hopped down, sneaking a quick glance over my shoulder in what I hoped was the least obvious way possible, but the spot where Reed had stood a moment ago was now empty.

Some strange, new feeling settled into my stomach—a heaviness I couldn't explain, couldn't name.

Or one I wasn't ready to name yet.

"There you are!" Lauryn shouted as I made my way through the exit. "I got tired of waiting for you, so I snagged us a couple fried Oreos."

Bless.

I groaned after the first bite. "These are so good, they should be illegal."

The outside batter was fried to perfection, leaving the inside just warm enough to not be gooey. Pure heaven in a cookie.

"So where to next?" Lauryn asked. She took a sip of a large sweet tea she had bought before offering it to me.

"Hoops?"

She smiled and flicked her braided pigtails over her shoulders. "Hoops."

We took a quick detour near the fishbowl toss and lollipop tree, neither of us winning anything but we at least each walked away with a strawberry-flavored Dum-Dum.

The crowd grew heavier the closer we got to older games like hoops, the dunking booth, and the cup catapult toss. Thankfully, by the time we reached the basketball games, the lines weren't nearly as long as the others.

"Well, well, well, if it isn't the princess herself," a voice snickered from behind me.

Ben gave a fake smile and lifted his hat before taking a pack of cigarettes out of his back pocket. Reed pushed his hand down and said something I couldn't hear, but it made Ben roll his eyes and put the pack away.

"Eliza Crowley," I said, sticking out my hand.

"I know." He looked at it but kept his hands in his pockets. "Ben Talbot."

Charmed.

"Didn't realize you could play basketball too, Crowley," Reed said, a smile pulling at the corner of his mouth, where his damn dimple was already on display.

"She dominates this game every summer," Lauryn said, draping her arm around me.

"Does she?" Reed stepped out of line. "Wanna bet on it?"

Lauryn gave me a small shove toward him.

"Sure." Something tiny fluttered in my stomach. I tried to ignore it. "Five bucks."

Reed made a disappointed face and crossed his arms, daring me to look at the lines of muscles winding their way up toward his sleeves.

But I didn't.

Not for long, anyway.

"Slice of pie at Jenny's Diner?" he asked.

I stuck out my hand. "Done."

He shook it and broke eye contact for just a moment to stare at our joined hands before pulling his away. "Yeah . . . done."

Ben clapped. "Let's go!"

While we waited for two guys in front of us to finish their shots, Ben pulled Reed to the side and spoke quietly to him, probably some kind of pep-talk strategy thing. Lauryn leaned in and whispered, "So are you starting lefty or righty?"

I smiled. "What do you think?"

She laughed and rubbed her hands together. "I love it when you start lefty."

By the time it was our turn, the lines for the cup catapult and dunking booths had all but disappeared, making our audience three times larger than it was when we made the bet.

Lieutenant Rose of the Fairfield Fire Department gave me the ball first and flipped her hat around backward. "All right. You know the rules. You've got one minute to make as many shots as you can. Don't cross the line there by your feet, and no funny business." She shot Reed a hard glare.

He held up his free hand in defense. "That was six years ago!"

"It took me two days to fix that prize wall, Fulton."

"But I bet you made it twice as sturdy that second time,

right?" He smiled, and she finally caved, laughing as she tossed him his ball.

Reed bumped my shoulder. "Good luck, Crowley."

I smacked his arm and immediately regretted it. *Good Lord, he's all muscle there.*

I shook the thought out of my head, quickly changed my shooting stance to favor my left hand and said, "Won't need it, Fulton."

The lieutenant started the countdown timer, and five seconds later, a loud buzz rang through the air. Reed and I began to shoot.

He racked up the points, staying two to three ahead of me, laughing the entire time.

"Why are you smiling, Lauryn?" Ben shouted over the noise around us. "Doesn't look like she's 'dominating.'"

Lauryn called out, "That's because I know something you don't know."

"What's that?"

"She is not left-handed!" Lauryn said in a perfect Inigo Montoya voice.

And that's my cue.

I changed my footing and switched to my right hand. Reed stopped for a second to gawk and then laugh, a big, booming laugh that made me smile from ear to ear.

I made every shot after I switched hands, and he, clearly frazzled by my surprising changeup, missed one too many.

The buzzer sounded, and the crowd cheered.

"Eliza takes the win!" Lieutenant Rose said before she grabbed a huge green bear from the back wall.

Reed stepped forward to take it. Just as I was about to argue, he turned around and bowed his head to me, holding the bear out as a truce.

"Thank you," I said, smiling smugly.

But he held on as I pulled it closer and whispered, "It's a date, then, Crowley."

"*Date*"?

My stomach did that little fluttering tap dance again.

Oh, hell. This is not good.

As Lauryn got the crowd to chant my name, a scowling Ben dragged Reed away. Then, the air humidified, and the lights and noise pushed in on me from all sides.

"Hey, you good?" Lauryn guided me away from the game booths toward a bench that sat underneath a tall oak. I flopped down on it, my knees feeling less wobbly when I did.

Why did I have wobbly knees?

Lauryn put a hand on my shoulder. "E?"

"Yeah, I'm just . . ." Most of my words left me. The ones that stayed behind didn't make any freaking sense. I sighed. "I dunno what I am."

She sat down and faced me, tucking one of her legs under the other. "It's okay, you know."

"What's okay?"

"To like him."

"To like him"? Like him as what? A friend? A . . .

"You've known each other for forever. It was only a matter of time, really—"

"No." I pressed my fingers against the bridge of my nose, my cheeks now burning. "I've known a lot of people for forever, so . . . so why does it have to be him? Why Reed? Why now?"

She took my hand in both of hers. "I don't know. But I think you owe it to yourself to figure it out."

Do I?

She stood. "I'm going to go check on the Lyric booth, see if they need any help. Maybe you should go find those answers? Text me once you do—"

"I dunno—"

"*Go*, Eliza."

Ugh. "Fine." I stood. "Love you."

"Love you more."

Lauryn took the bear so I wouldn't look like an even bigger fool wandering the carnival looking for a boy, and not just any boy, but Reed freaking Fulton. Reed Fulton, who has now totally thrown a wrench in what should've been an all-theater summer for me.

You did literally give him the wrench though, Eliza.

I should've shut it down after the catwalk, not let him climb up that railcar, not texted him after he left his number on my front porch. And yet, I didn't. I couldn't silence the part of me that craved to know more about the person he had grown into over the last four years.

Was that really so bad?

Finally, after I did one complete circle around the swings, I found him about half a football field's length away. Reed Fulton. Head down, hands in pockets, and headed into the house of mirrors. Alone.

"No way," I said to no one before turning my back on the warped-looking building. Of all the places he had to disappear into.

Lauryn's voice danced around in my head. *Maybe you should go find those answers?*

Dammit.

Sometimes I really hated it when she was right.

I took a deep breath underneath the twisty lettering, then parted the thick curtains of the entrance and stepped inside.

The checkered black-and-white floor and walls, painted with drippy-looking clocks and funky symbols, reflected a rainbow of colors under a black light. From where I stood, rows upon rows of arches stretched in front of me and to my right and left, enticing guests to try a different path, but I knew better. This was not the first time I had been in this house.

A loud *thump* sounded somewhere to my left followed by a groan and a low "Shit."

I laughed, snuck around one of the corners, out of sight, and cupped my hands around my mouth. "You okay in there, Fulton?"

"Eliza? Is that you?"

"It's me." *In a dark house. Alone. With you.*

I must be losing my mind.

"Can you find me? I'm not sure which version of me is me anymore." He ran into another wall. "Hell, I think I may have a concussion now."

I giggled and peeked around the corner, spying where he was. I darted around the arches. "But this is too much fun."

He sighed. "How about a game of Marco Polo, then?"

I leaned against the mirror next to me and took a deep breath as more of Lauryn's words echoed in my head. *It's okay, you know. To like him.*

"Marco?" Reed called.

I stepped near another mirror, still out of sight. "Polo."

"Marco?"

This was too easy. I could walk through this place blindfolded. "Polo."

"Hmmm . . ." He patted the walls and walked more slowly. "Marco?"

He moved closer now. Much closer. The sweet pine smell of his cologne mixed with the smell of freshly cut grass made me dizzy. "Polo," I whispered.

"Marco."

The floor creaked on the opposite side of the mirrored wall nearest to me.

Was that my heart pounding so loudly? Or maybe it was the bass from the speakers inside the walls? My voice shook. "P-Polo—"

His hand reached around the corner and grabbed mine. Part of his face glowed from the neon lights while the rest was shadowy, but I could see his smile in both the dark and the light. He gently tucked one of the stray pieces of my hair behind my ear, lingering there for a moment too long.

I rolled out of reach. "What are we doing here, Reed?"

"We're . . . walking through a house of mirrors that's making me wonder if this is what it feels like to trip on acid." He propped his arm against an archway.

"No. What are *we* doing?" I flailed my arms between the two of us.

He stood up straight. "Eliza—"

"At the end of this summer, one of us will lose." Didn't he get that?

"But don't you think it'd be more of a loss if we didn't even try?" His eyes stared expectantly at me, and the energy, the buzz between us was so tangible that it hummed through me. Like Reed and I had our own kind of white noise. It was almost too much.

I backed up. "Just give me a second to think." I turned away from him only to realize he could still see me in the mirror.

Dang it.

He leaned to the side in plain view behind me. "Still thinking?"

"Trying to."

"About what?"

"About what"? "Well, for starters, how this is a recipe for disaster."

He ran a hand through his hair. "Look, I'm a Fulton. You're a Crowley. But we used to be friends, remember? And if we become more than that, I promise I'll still always be a pain in the ass who annoys you because I like making your nose crinkle."

"My nose does not crinkle—"

"And you'll always pretend to hate me because it's easier than the truth."

The weight on my chest squeezed a bit harder. "What truth?"

But I knew the answer before he spoke it.

Part of me may have always known it.

"The truth about how you feel about me." His fingers found mine, spreading a warmth throughout my arm. "And how I feel about you."

I turned around to face him, releasing his fingers. "How can you be so sure about this?"

Because right now, I wasn't.

Right now, this—"us"—scared the crap out of me.

And yet . . .

"I'm not." He swallowed.

"So then why should we try?"

"Because I'm running out of excuses not to. Aren't you?"

The weight on my chest grew wings, and the warmth in my arm spread to my cheeks. *Yes. Yes, I am.*

He smiled. "Do you remember the last time we came here?"

"I remember." I reached up and bopped his nose. "Sorry I made your nose bleed."

He laughed. "If . . . if I kiss you again, are you going to hit me like you did that night?"

I took a step backward again, my heart thumping wildly. "The only reason you kissed me was because you made a bet with my next-door neighbor, Drew—"

"I told you already a million times. The only bets I ever made with Drew were on Yankees games." He closed the space between us, and my breath caught in my throat. "I kissed you the summer after seventh grade because I wanted to. Because I knew we were moving, and I didn't know if I'd have another chance."

Oh.

"But you were right to hit me," he said.

"I was?"

He nodded. "I should've asked you first."

I smiled. *Yes, you should have.*

"So . . ." He bit his lip, which was kinda adorable. "Will you punch me again if I kiss you?"

"No." I ran my hands up his arms, over the outlines of tight muscles beneath his shirt, and finally admitted what I had kept hidden for a long time. "But I will if you don't."

He drew me against his chest and dropped his chin. Our warped, mirrored reflections blurred seconds before I closed my eyes and let his lips find mine, a small gasp escaping from both of us when he did.

Oh my God.

I had been kissed before, some good, most just meh. But this? This was what I always imagined a kiss should feel like.

Slow.

Curious.

But hungry. Like hearing a whisper of a secret that left you craving more.

Yes. More.

I parted his lips with my tongue, tasting sweet Nilla Wafers, and my fingers dug into his back, aching to feel closer to him. We stumbled through a few more arches until we bumped against a rounded mirror that opened into a room I didn't know existed. The mirror slammed shut behind us, leaving us alone in the dark, with only a sliver of light near our feet.

For a long moment, my forehead pressed against his chin. The rapid rise and fall of his chest under my hands told me he was just as breathless as I was.

But did he feel the same heat searing through his body?

The same weightlessness?

I let my fingers trail up his neck, let one of my thumbs brush over his swollen lips and that perfect dimple.

A second later, like two star-crossed, warped, confused comets, burning brightly to the point of a reckless explosion, we collided. He lifted me off the ground and spun me around. My legs crossed behind his back, pulling him against me as my back banged into another wall. Thankfully, this one didn't move.

But his mouth did. Leaving a trail of kisses along my jaw before he followed the freckles down my neck.

God dammit, Reed Fulton, you're good at this.

I moved my mouth down to where the stubble turned smooth on his warm, sunburned neck and flushed all over from the noise he made. Our hands reached everywhere for each other, searching, exploring, and Jesus, it felt so good.

Then voices drifted in from outside the secret room. He jumped, brushing his lips across my forehead before I unwound my legs and dropped—regretfully—back to the floor, which did nothing to help my wobbly knees.

"Eliza," he whispered into my hair.

He had said my name at least a hundred times in all the years I'd known him.

But it had never sounded like that.

Like a revelation.

A beat before his mouth met mine again, I echoed, "Reed," hoping it sounded the same.

Like someone who had left behind a part of themselves.

Someone who didn't quite believe that the unbelievable had just happened.

Someone who had floated away from the hall of mirrors and spun around as if on a carousel.

Chapter Fourteen

REED

"I love it when people doubt me. It makes me work harder to prove them wrong." —Derek Jeter

I had never pitched a no-hitter before, but kissing Eliza Crowley felt like what I imagined a no-no would.

I couldn't talk about it.

But I wanted to.

Couldn't think about it.

But I needed to.

Because thinking about it and reliving it in my head reminded me that it was real, that it actually happened, and that it was fucking amazing.

And yet I still couldn't keep another part of my head from screaming, *What the hell have you done, Fulton?*

This summer was already stressing me out to the max. Kissing Eliza and wanting to do it again and again would definitely not make it any easier.

"You're quiet this morning," Ben said from the passenger seat of my truck.

You would be too, if you had not only thrown our pact out the window but also lit it on fire.

To make up for it, I had packed up Granddad's fishing gear early this morning and taken Ben with me. Ironically, we were heading to the same area where Eliza got her flat tire. Couldn't escape the girl if I tried.

Not that I wanted to anymore.

"Just a lot on my mind. Sorry," I said.

"Brett's got some good ideas about new pranks, but I think you and I could do better—"

"Maybe we should just let it be for now. We've got a championship to focus on." Guilt snaked its way around my stomach and squeezed. I wasn't sure if I'd said that last part more for him or me.

A sign for Cattail Creek appeared on the right-hand side of the road. I slowed down and pulled the truck into a small gravel parking space.

Ben and I both moved around to the back of the truck for the gear. He opened the tackle box and rummaged through it. "Should we have picked up some crickets?"

"Nah," I said. "Trout here love PowerBait. We'll stick with that."

Ben held up the container of PowerBait balls and frowned. "Pink?"

"Don't ask me why, but Granddad has sworn by that color for years, and he always comes back with a bucket full of fish."

Several minutes after walking through the woods, we came to the creek. Fallen trees and moss-covered stones outlined most of the muddy brown water. Upstream, the water rushed around a half-finished dam of sticks and branches.

Ben stretched and groaned. "I should've taken your nana up on that extra cup of coffee before we left."

"Yeah, you should've." Nana's coffee was known for packing a punch. I only ever needed one cup to feel the jitters, but Ben was a caffeine junkie. He had to drink it all day.

I reached into the tackle box and handed him the container of bait. "No bobbers?" he asked.

"Nope. I mean, you could use them, but when you fish in a place where the water is always moving, like a creek or a river, it's not really needed. You can't see it much." I helped him put the bait on his hook, and then we separated by several yards, Ben upstream.

I stepped into the shallow water. The pebbles pressed through the thin soles of my old sneakers as I cast out. Ben stayed closer to the underbrush than the water. Neither of us spoke for a long while, until Ben yelped about his line.

"I think I got one," he said as he jumped.

I hurried over. "Did you set the hook?"

"Yeah, I tugged it good." He began reeling it in, but too fast.

"Slow down. If you go too fast"—the line grew still—"you'll lose it."

"Dammit." Ben finished reeling it in and trudged back to the tackle box for another ball of bait. "So where the hell did you go last night? Brett, Dominic, and I looked for you everywhere after we rode the Scrambler, but you just disappeared. And you didn't answer your phone."

Think fast. "The lemonade didn't sit well after all that spinning, so I called it an early night. Phone was dead, so I just passed out as soon as I got back to the farm."

"That's funny, because I called your grandparents and they said you weren't there." His eyes narrowed.

Shit.

Ben was the one person I told everything to. But this? How could I tell him I wanted to go back on a pact I insisted we create?

I shrugged. "Maybe they didn't hear me come in. It's not like I stopped to chat before hitting the shower."

"I thought you showered before the carnival."

"Jesus, Ben. Am I under investigation?" I stepped around a couple of moss-covered rocks, where I propped my pole. "I needed another one. It was humid as hell last night."

"Whatever."

"What does that mean?"

"Nothing." Ben slammed the tackle box lid shut and stomped

farther downstream now. If he kept that up, we'd never catch anything.

"Dominic apparently got a call from one of the UNC coaches last week." Ben kept his back to me as he cast his line out. "The guy said he was looking forward to coming out to a couple games."

"Good for Dom." I checked the bait on mine and tossed my line out as well.

Ben turned. "'Good for Dom'?" He shook his head and muttered something under his breath.

"What?" I asked, but I already knew where this was going.

"We both need those college scouts to come for *us*, Reed." He reeled his line in a little. "After last summer—"

"Would you stop fucking reminding me about last summer? I know I fucked up. Okay?" I tugged on my line a bit. "Want me to tattoo it on my face?"

A small flock of sparrows shot out of the trees across from us, and the air grew heavier.

Ben reeled his line all the way in and propped his pole on his shoulder. "Is this because of the princess?"

Seriously?

My jaw tensed. "Her name is Eliza. And no, this has nothing to do with her."

"Are you two hooking up?"

I opened my mouth but nothing came out.

"Are you?" he repeated.

Like a fucking coward, I just stared at my line floating in the water. "I met up with her at the carnival . . . after I told you and the guys I was going home. It wasn't planned, I swear. It just sort of happened."

"I knew it. I fucking knew it." He kicked the water.

"It doesn't change anything though. Really." I reeled my line in haphazardly. "She knows what's at stake. She knows why I came here—"

Ben cackled. "And you really think she won't get in your head? Screw you up like what happened last summer?"

"Last summer was on me. I . . ." I stopped, unsure of how to name what had really been twisting around in my gut since this tournament had started. "When I was at UNC, at the showcase, it just didn't feel right."

Ben frowned. "What didn't?"

"Pitching. All those eyes on me. The pressure."

"But you've played in tons of high-pressure situations before without issues."

I swallowed a huge lump in my throat. "I know. But I think that's why I fucked up so much. Why I hit those batters. It was like I . . . I forgot why I played the game."

"We play to win."

"No." I flipped my hat backward. "I mean, yeah, we do now, but that's not why I started."

The wind moved across the creek and through several redbuds. Their seedpods spun free and skidded over the water and stones.

"Look, Reed." Ben started walking toward me. "I don't know why you started, and honestly, it doesn't matter, because whether you like it or not, we were brought here to *win*."

"I know."

"And I think"—he paused and rubbed the back of his neck—"I think maybe if you spent a little less time worrying about what Erin—sorry—*Eliza* is doing, then maybe your head would be more in the game."

"I already told you, this has nothing to do with her—"

"You're wrong. You've been distracted since the moment she knocked that crown off your head." He ran a hand through his hair. "Don't make the same mistake I did."

"What the hell are you—"

"Girls like Eliza and Erin." He exhaled loudly through his nose and tapped his temple. "They get in here and screw with you and throw you away the moment something shinier comes along—"

"Oh my God, will you stop comparing her to Erin?" It was a good thing my hat was on, or I'd start pulling my hair out. "She is nothing like her. You have to let that shit go, Ben. Move on."

"'Move on'?" He chucked his pole toward the bank. "That's rich, coming from you."

"What—"

"Wake up, Fulton. Your family's farm is going under, and that stadium—this tournament—could be the one thing that saves them. But it's like you've already *moved on* from that. Like you don't give a shit that we all came here this summer for you. For them. Like I didn't give up everything to be here."

"*Give up everything*"? My head started to spin. "Ben, what the fuck are you talking about?"

He sighed, and his entire body sagged from the shoulders down. "I didn't know how to tell you."

"Tell me what?" Everything suddenly felt so heavy and tiring, like wet sand weighing me down.

"I was invited back to the UNC showcase this summer."

Wait. What?

He brought his head up, and his eyes were filled with sadness. "At first I thought it would be good to get away from everything with . . . after everything that had happened with *her*, but then your granddad called you up, and I knew you needed me more."

Shit.

I took my hat off. "Ben—"

"But seeing you here in this town with your family. With . . . her. You've changed. You're . . . different." He rubbed the back of his neck. "Maybe me going to Chapel Hill would've been better for both of us."

"Don't say that." My throat squeezed as I stepped out of the water. "*You're* my family."

"And you were mine. You're all I got left, man." He looked past me.

"That's not true. You've still got your mom, and . . ." Reality hit me like a line drive to the face.

Ben really didn't have much anymore. It had been the two of us and baseball for a long time. And I felt like I was losing both somehow.

"I think I should go." Ben started toward the shoreline.

"No, wait." I grabbed his arm. "You can't walk home from here."

"I'm not going home." He stopped. "This isn't my home. I don't belong here with these people."

"*These people*"?

He shook my hand loose. "Rubbing elbows and whatever else with the rich may be your thing now, but—"

"I don't rub elbows with the rich." I sighed. "I'm not like them. You know that."

"I'm not so sure anymore, man." He shook his head. "I'll text Brett and ask him if I can bunk with his host family for the rest of the season."

Something cold uncoiled itself in my chest. "No, come on, Ben. Don't do that."

"It's like you said. You've got enough on your plate this summer." He looked into the trees and ran a hand over his face.

"You clearly don't give a shit about the pact, so I won't either. But I will stick around to help your family win, because that promise wasn't just for you. It may not be a Rolex, but for some of us, a promise means a lot more." The water splashed as he left me and walked away toward the truck.

Chapter Fifteen

ELIZA

"We came into the world like brother and brother, and now let's go hand in hand, not one before the other."
—William Shakespeare, *The Comedy of Errors*

Two years ago, Lauryn and I started a summer tradition to visit the Gem and Mineral Show at the North Carolina State Fair grounds, and even though this year we had rehearsal in the afternoon, we weren't about to let it pass us by. To get there right when it opened, however, meant leaving at 7:00 a.m.

Thank God for ventis.

A couple of old carnival game tickets blew around in the back seat of the Jeep before flying out of my window, bringing me back to the insanely hot make-out session with Reed two nights ago. Naturally, I had told Lauryn all about it the very next day while I tried to focus on setting cues in the booth before rehearsal. But then the board had frozen up again and I lost an hour's worth of work, since I had been too distracted to save as I went along.

My confidence in getting back on schedule—or having the entire show set before Tech Week—was at an all-time low. It didn't help that Reed had stayed radio silent since that night. I figured it was to keep our families from getting suspicious, but as the hours dragged on, my nerves got the better of me and I wondered if he hadn't texted because he regretted it.

But how could you regret something that amazing?

Unless, of course, it wasn't amazing for him.

Oh God, what if it wasn't?

Was I a crappy kisser?

"You gonna eat that second croissant?" Lauryn asked me from the passenger seat. She wore her hair braided and tossed over her shoulder, the lavender and blond shining in the sunlight as her sundress ruffled around her knees from the swirling wind.

"It's all yours." I gestured to the to-go box in between us.

She laid her head back and breathed in deeply. "God, it's gorgeous out today. I love doing this play, but sometimes I miss just being outside, you know?"

I do. "Well, Dad needs a volunteer for the cardinal costume again later this week, if you're interested."

She cackled. "After wearing it on opening day, I couldn't get the smell of Fritos out of my nose. No thanks, Pops."

A little while later, we drove under the big "NC State Fair" banner and parked near Gate Two. I texted my parents that we arrived and grabbed my fanny pack out of the back. Why some people didn't like these, I'd never understand. They were amazing and a hell of a lot easier to carry than a clutch or purse.

"Why couldn't the expo center be on the other side of the fair?" Lauryn whined and waved her hand in front of her face while we paid for our tickets. "I hate that it's right next to all the livestock. No one wants to smell cows when looking at jewelry."

"I dunno. It's kinda growing on me." I took a sip of my coffee.

"I wonder why that is?" She winked at me.

But we weren't here to talk about that. Today was about my best friend. About tradition.

We hurried to the poultry tent and then to the Graham Building, where they kept the cows.

Cows!

Maybe I could convince Reed to convince his grandparents to start raising livestock? That could definitely help them with money. I took a quick pic with some cute ones and almost sent them to Reed before stopping myself.

The guy hasn't texted you in like forty-eight hours, Eliza. Now is not the time for freakin' cow selfies.

Lauryn pinched her nose the entire time—and to think, I was the one people called Princess—until we stood at the expo center's main entrance, where she finally breathed in deeply.

She smiled brightly as we entered, her eyes shining the same way they did when I helped her and her mom decorate their Christmas tree every year. "So where to first?" she asked me.

I linked my arm through hers. "You tell me, boss."

She tugged me over to a "Welcome" table where there were tons of brochures and picked up one of each. "Oh!" She pointed to the cover of one. "The Crabtree emerald. I've never seen one up close. Let's go there first."

Lauryn almost cried when she stepped in front of the dark green, black, and white stones. She touched their unpolished surfaces as if they might break under her fingers, like dried beach dollars. "They're so beautiful," she whispered.

I stepped away from her as my eye caught on two matching rings with an oval-cut emerald in the center. Both were set inside a white-gold band with a wave pattern winding around it. As Lauryn talked the ear off one of the associates, I paid for both the rings and hid them behind my back.

"What are you holding?" Lauryn asked as we left the table and headed toward the crystals section.

I smiled and reached into the large bag before pulling out both rings and handing her one. "Happy early birthday."

She gasped and slid it onto her middle finger. "Oh my God. I love it. And you've got one too?"

I nodded and pulled mine onto the same finger as hers.

"Friendship rings." Lauryn held hers up. "Puts our 'Friends Forever' bracelets to shame."

"Hey, I loved that bracelet. That was the first piece of jewelry you made for me." And then I had to go and lose it at Cape Hatteras in fourth grade. I still haven't forgiven the ocean for that.

"Well, these will definitely last us forever. Just like our friendship."

I hoped so.

But the way Dad so casually dropped that line about moving if we lost the stadium now made me wary of words like "forever."

We stopped at a table covered with wooden displays of black tourmaline bracelets and pendant necklaces. "Do you think these look too . . . rugged for my style?" she asked. "I've been thinking about using tourmaline, but I'm not sure."

"Oh, black tourmaline would be awesome to add to your collection!" I picked up one of the larger pieces. "Imagine this wrapped in silver, with maybe green accents. *Wicked* style."

"That's brilliant! I need to add that idea to my notes." She took out her phone and started typing furiously. "What about point pendants? Yay or nay?"

"Hmm." I scanned the table till I saw a size that I thought fit her vibe. "Yay, but I wouldn't go bigger than that one."

"Got it." Lauryn took a quick pic of the one I pointed to.

An announcement came over the PA system about a demo of the newest model of a cabbing machine happening in the demonstration zone close to the food vendors, and Lauryn all but sprinted in that direction. I followed close on her heels.

With some creative crowd-weaving and strong elbows, we

managed to squeeze our way to the front of the group packed around the large table that held a sparkling, impressive-looking machine with different colored wheels and an LED lamp on an adjustable neck.

An older man in an apron with the words "Schist Happens" printed on it waved to us and began talking about the new design. This one had eight diamond wheels, a splash guard, a submersible water pump, and a few pre- and post-polishing options. I wasn't an expert like Lauryn, but I knew enough to understand that this machine was amazing. It would cut down the time she spent doing all this manual work by hours.

"It's available on Amazon to preorder for a great deal of just twenty-five hundred bucks," the man said, beaming.

Lauryn coughed like she choked on something and quickly walked away from the display table.

"You good?" I asked her after we cleared the group.

"Yeah." She flipped her braids over her shoulder. "I knew it was going to be pricey, but over two grand? Jesus. I'll never have that kind of money."

"Sure you will." I put my arm around her shoulder. "You're going to make some new pieces, sell them at the Fourth of July Festival and on Marketplace and—"

"That money will barely cover the cost of my supplies, E."

"Oh." My stomach dropped.

I chewed the inside of my cheek while trying to think of what I could say to make it better, but everything I thought of made Lauryn sound like a charity case. And she was far from that.

Lauryn could turn any obstacle into something that drove her forward, fueling her fire. Her designs became more unique and creative every year, and I figured it was because she was determined to never let the money side of things take away her joy.

That was kind of how I felt about holding on to things that belonged to Grandma. Her Jeep and the ties she had to the Lyric reminded me that it wasn't about how much something costs. What mattered was how much love and care you put into it.

"Well, you've been doing amazing work without that stupidly expensive machine," I finally said. "But if you really want it, I'll help you find more vendor shows and places to sell everything."

She beamed. "Thanks, E."

My best friend looked taller in that moment, her face brighter, and I couldn't help but be in awe of her optimism and hope.

"I think you're amazing, you know that?" I looped my arm through hers.

"I do." She pulled me closer. "But you can still tell me so as often as you like."

I smiled. "Deal."

Chapter Sixteen

REED

"Baseball is also a game of balance."
—Stephen King, *Blockade Billy*

Bees buzzed around Nana's big hydrangea bush near the barn door. Mickey lay a few feet away with his paws propped on either side of a bone he busily chewed. I used Granddad's mortises to attach another seat support underneath Dad's rocking chair. After making sure each mortise fit the support, I grabbed a rag and wiped my forehead. The glue would have to set for the day.

I took a seat in one of the tractors outside of the barn and watched the sky turn from deep purple to pink to burnt orange as the sun rose over the tall corn. Amelia Earhart, Nana's dominant and confused hen, gave her usual gargled-sounding crow, stirring the rest of the chickens in the coop. Granddad was already up and had taken the Gator to the South Five this morning. When I came outside about an hour ago, Nana was busy fixing coffee and making biscuits in the kitchen. The guest bedroom where Ben used to sleep, however, still stayed dark and still. No sound came through his open window.

He didn't speak to me on the drive home after Cattail Creek, and he all but rolled out of the truck the moment I pulled into the driveway. Brett's host family called Nana and let them know Ben would be staying with them. I hadn't heard anything about him since.

"Shit," I mumbled under my breath. This was all my fault.

The guy practically picked me up off the ground time and time again after Dad's deployments, dropped everything, including an opportunity to play in the showcase again, to follow me to my grandparents' this summer, and this was how I repaid him?

What the fuck had gotten into me?

Way to go, Reed. You not only lost your best friend but you possibly also lost the championship and the farm.

"Reed? Can you grab the eggs from the coop for me?" Nana called from the open kitchen window.

I hopped off the tractor. "You got it."

I hated going into the coop for eggs. No matter how I sweet-talked the chickens, they didn't like me, and my ankles always got a few pecks before I escaped. But by some miracle, Marie Curie, Sojourner Truth, Queen Victoria, and Joan of Arc all let me check the nests without harming me, while Amelia Earhart watched from the corner. Granddad never wanted chickens, but Nana insisted, and once she named them all after notable women from history, they preferred her to any other guest in their coop.

Go figure.

The small wind chimes tinkled behind me as I entered the kitchen. "Here ya go."

"Thanks. And how were my girls this morning?" Nana asked.

I filled up a cup of water from the sink. "Fine. No fussing when I went in there either."

"Is that so?" She cracked the eggs into a large bowl. "Maybe they're getting soft in their old age, like me."

I laughed. "Maybe."

Nana reached for the wire whisk behind me but stopped and stared at her hands. They both trembled.

"Nana," I said, taking them in my own. "You okay?"

"Fine." She sighed. "Just a little shaky this morning."

"What's Lucille say?" I motioned to her insulin pump.

"She's been quiet lately, now that I think about it. Maybe I should check?"

I helped her hold up her shirt while she pulled the pump out of the band around her waist. "Huh. Battery's gettin' low again. That's the second time in a few months this has happened." She pointed to the junk drawer by the fridge. "Grab me a double-A from there, will ya?"

After replacing the battery, I convinced her to sit down and let me cook the eggs while she walked me through the process. My stomach growled. The biscuits dinged in the oven a moment before the eggs were ready.

I refilled her orange juice before pouring myself a cup of coffee and sitting across from her. My entire body relaxed with the first forkful of eggs. I should've put a little more salt and pepper on them, but damn. These were insanely good.

"Nothin' beats fresh eggs," Nana said with a wink.

You got that right.

"Heard from Ben yet?" she asked over her juice.

The eggs turned chalky in my mouth. "No."

Nana frowned. "Need to talk about it?"

Yes. "No." I pushed around the food on my plate.

"I'm sure y'all will fix this. You're too young to burn bridges."

And yet, here I was playing with fire, thinking about when I could be alone with Eliza again. That definitely wouldn't help any bridges between Ben and me.

"When was the last time you spoke to your mom?" she asked.

"Yesterday afternoon."

"Any news about your dad?"

A cold numbness spread across my chest. "No."

Nana reached across the table and placed her warm hand on mine. "Don't you worry a bit about it. Your daddy is as strong as an ox. We'll hear something soon."

I just hoped when we did, it would be good news.

Later that afternoon, the team ran foul poles six times before stretching. Foul poles were typical in practice, but today, in the humidity, it was hard as hell. Ben wasn't there. Brett said Ben had left in the middle of the night.

Left? For where?

Coach grilled all of us about it, but no one had heard from him. Guilt knotted up my stomach, twisting it tighter with every new stretch. Even after joining some of the others in center field, my secondary position, I still felt like I needed to puke.

The only thing that kept me somewhat grounded was the idea that maybe I could see Eliza later. I hadn't heard from her since the carnival, but I wouldn't allow myself to believe that was a bad sign. I had enough of those already.

Just as I was about to secretly send another text to Ben in the dugout, he finally showed up after Coach started batting practice.

Christ. He looked like hell.

His practice uniform was wrinkled, like he had slept in it, and his eyes were bloodshot, a bruise forming underneath one.

I cursed under my breath as he shuffled his feet into the dugout.

Coach Monaco left home plate and stomped over to Ben. I couldn't hear what he said, but from how his hands moved, I could tell he wasn't happy.

I should've gone over to Brett's last night. Brought Ben back home with me. Looked after him the way he'd looked after me time and time again.

A minute later, Ben chucked his glove toward the dugout, ripped off his chest protector and shin guards, and jogged out of the stadium.

"Bet coach has him runnin' the cross-country route," Cameron said from right field, which was his secondary position. "He needs to get his head on straight. We need him for PFPs later."

Coach hit a pop fly to left field. Nick caught it on a run and threw it to our cutoff man.

"He'll be okay," I said, more for myself than for Cameron. *He has to be.*

"He'd better be." Cameron hit his glove a few times. "After that close call with that bunt the last game, Coach will be pissed if he isn't back in time today."

Ben missed the PFPs.

He also didn't make it back to see Dominic nail a sweet backhanded catch and flip. Total Jeter moment.

When the turtle was rolled out and set up behind home plate, Ben walked back up to the field. He dripped with sweat and looked greener than I had ever seen him as he dropped onto the bench several feet away from me. He guzzled almost an entire bottle of water.

"You okay?" I asked.

He stared straight ahead.

Oh, come on. "Hello?" I waved my hand in front of his face.

He stood up and slid on his batting gloves. Coach Monaco began throwing from the mound toward the turtle. The top of our lineup and our first baseman, Alejandro, stood at the plate.

"So what, you gonna ignore me the rest of the season?" I asked.

He spat, stepped out of the dugout, and muttered a few things before he whirled around. "It would be easier for both of us if I did."

"No, it wouldn't." I hit the inside of my glove. "Come back to the farm. We've got season three of *Stranger Things* to start now—"

"I don't like season three."

I frowned. "But you said it's Hopper's best season . . ."

"I changed my mind." He sighed and rubbed the back of his neck.

Coach Roeper yelled from the outfield. "Let's go, Fulton! Footwork drills start in two."

"On my way!" I yelled back before turning to Ben. "Look, I'm sorry that you had to give up the showcase to be here, and I'm sorry about fucking up the pact."

"Let's be honest here, Fulton. This is about more than just the showcase and that damn pact."

"What?"

"You . . . you're different here. You never want to go out with me and the guys. You're letting your gramps take you into the fields for, like, farming lessons and shit." He tightened the Velcro on his batting gloves. "I came here to play baseball and hang out with my best friend."

"We've been winning, Ben. And we can still chill." I motioned to the field. "But I didn't come here this summer just to party with Brett and Dominic or tag some buildings or cardinal statues. There's too much at stake."

"I know that."

Coach Roeper yelled for me again.

"It's like you said. If Granddad loses this tournament, we lose the farm. I . . . I can't blow this. Not when it comes to family," I said.

"And yet you're still seeing *her.*" Ben stepped around me and started up the steps of the dugout. "You know, it's funny. You used to call me family once too."

Chapter Seventeen

ELIZA

"One man in his time plays many parts."
—William Shakespeare, *As You Like It*

The hardware store was unusually quiet for a Thursday morning. Thursdays were normally the days contractors came for supplies before taking on big weekend jobs. But judging by the sales reports Dad left open on the desktop computer in the back office (so careless . . . I can't even), Thursdays had been slow like this for a while now.

Maybe Dad wanting to leave Fairfield wasn't only about new stadium opportunities?

At the back of the store, Lauryn sang into the top of her broom handle like it was a microphone. She whirled around and belted the next few lines of "Waving Through a Window" from *Dear Evan Hansen* to the back wall of paintbrushes and tape.

I laughed and turned up the song from her playlist before I

grabbed the box of gloves and headed toward Aisle Four, straightening the hammers and band saws as I passed through Aisle Three. I sang too, but much softer than Lauryn. Her voice belonged on the stage. Mine stayed in the shower.

After adding the new gloves to the display and straightening up the cleaning products in the plumbing aisle, I headed back to the front counter. Lauryn now sat on it, legs swinging and head down, while her hand flew over a page in her sketchpad. She held it up while I grabbed another box behind the register. "So what do you think? I've been sketching like a madwoman since we got back from the Gem and Mineral Show."

I gawked at her newest design: earrings in the shape of a treble clef with stones framing the bottom. "Oh my God, they're gorgeous. How will you get the stones in place like that?"

"With a good set of needle-nosed pliers and a hell of a lot of patience." She laughed and closed the sketchpad. "So you wanna come over later? I'm in the mood to bake cookies."

I nearly dropped the box cutter on the floor. "Your mom is letting you bake again?"

She huffed. "Come on, E. That was a long time ago."

It wasn't, but I didn't correct her.

"Besides, Mom said I can bake again so long as I'm not home alone, so if you're there, I'm good!" She smiled.

Lauryn's mom put a heck of a lot more trust and faith in her than my parents did. The last time Lauryn tried baking, she almost burned down their apartment because of wax paper in a hot oven. It was . . . messy.

"I need to swing by the theater after work and set more cues. I'd really like to finish act one today. But I should be able to come over after dinner," I said. *With an extinguisher, just in case.*

My phone buzzed in my back pocket, and something fluttered in my stomach when I read the text.

Reed: You busy right now? Wanna meet me at the Fairfield town sign in maybe a half hour?

I did a little jig behind the counter and showed Lauryn the text.

Her eyes widened. "What are you waiting for?"

"I can't." I frowned and gestured to the empty store. "I've still got a few hours left for my shift. And I really need to set those cues—"

"You're ahead of schedule, right?"

Ahead? With a board I was still learning how to use? "I mean . . . not really, but . . ."

"I'll handle closing."

"You've never closed before, Lauryn."

"It's not like it's busy." She hopped off the counter and gestured to our one customer in the back, who was bobbing his head along to "What Baking Can Do" from *Waitress*. "I'll lock up at five and then count the money in the register and lock the drawer before I leave. Easy."

"*Easy*"? "I guess I could get up early and set cues in the morning since we don't have practice till later? Or wait, did we have something in the morning?"

"Eliza." She put her hands on my shoulders. "Go have fun for once."

Reed waited for me on the outskirts of town. Leaning against his truck, he smiled as I drove up and parked under a chestnut tree. He wore a white and dark-blue baseball tee over a pair of Nike shorts, and his Fulton Hawks hat sat backward on his head. Everything about him exuded confidence and comfort.

As for me, I never felt more nervous and excited in my entire life. My chest tightened. My hands shook the way they did when a curtain speech finished and I had to press my first cue. The difference was this: In the booth, I was in control. I set every mark, memorized each cue, and knew how each would affect the following moment. I knew the highs and lows of the story from the safety of the light board.

But here? Walking toward him? I was a principal on center stage delivering a monologue that I hadn't rehearsed on opening night.

"Hi," he said, his voice husky.

Maybe he was just as nervous as I was but better at faking it?

"Hi," I barked.

Smooth, Eliza. Smooth.

He swallowed hard and scratched the back of his neck. "So I believe I owe you a slice of pie."

"Yes, you do." I smiled.

"Great." He walked around to the passenger side of his truck and opened the door for me. His hand touched mine ever so lightly as I climbed inside. Warmth circled and coiled its way around my hand and wrist until he let go.

"How's practice going?" I pushed my sweaty hands against my shorts.

"Pretty good." He smiled at me, making my cheeks burn. "I'm getting more comfortable with my curveball. Gotta get used to throwing to Troy though—"

"Isn't Ben catching for you?" I tucked one of my legs under the other.

"He is, but . . ." He drummed on the steering wheel. "He hasn't really been himself lately. Coach wants to make sure Troy is ready."

"I'm sorry."

"You have nothing to be sorry about." He reached across the center console and squeezed my hand, sending little goose bumps up my arm. "This is between me and Ben. We'll be okay."

I opened my mouth and then closed it. Reed's face looked

sad. Pained. Whatever was going on between the two of them didn't sound okay or anywhere close to it. But I had never lost a best friend before. Who was I to give him advice about it?

A few minutes later, he pulled into Jenny's Diner, a place Robbie and I went to all the time when we were kids and old enough to ride bikes alone outside of town limits. Reed and I walked up together, and he looped his pointer finger through mine. It wasn't a big gesture, not full-on holding hands or leading me by the small of my back, but it was something. He was something.

And it felt right.

We found a booth near the far side and sat opposite each other. A waitress handed us laminated menus and said she'd be back in a moment to take our orders.

My leg bounced wildly under the table. I couldn't remember the last time I went on a date, but I don't remember ever feeling this excited about it.

Reed cleared his throat and flipped over his menu. "Apple or cherry, Crowley?"

"Yes," I said.

He laughed and lowered his menu. "Both it is, then." When he smiled, the dimple that I once wanted to punch but now desperately wanted to kiss appeared and made me flush all over. But just as I reached across the table to lay my hand on his, the door to the diner opened, and the universe threw us the worst possible curveball ever.

Chapter Eighteen

REED

"The harder you want to control something, the more it gets out of your control." —Clayton Kershaw

Eliza quickly pulled her hand back and slid down into her seat. She hid behind her menu and kicked me under the table.

"Ow!" I rubbed my shin. "What was that for?"

She lowered the menu just enough for her scared eyes to come into view and gave a short nod to something behind me. At six feet, I've never been able to be sneaky about looking over my shoulder, but that didn't stop me from trying right then.

I wished I hadn't.

Viola Gratton, Fairfield's nosiest church lady, walked over to the bar area of the diner. With her was none other than Eliza's father.

Busted.

I snapped my head forward and tried sinking down into the seat like Eliza had, but yeah, not possible. "What're they doing here?" I muttered from behind my menu.

"I have no idea. She's probably pressing Dad about fundraising for the church or something." Eliza now hid almost completely under the table. "He doesn't know I left work early either. Ugh. We are *so* dead."

Of all the diners the two of them could walk into.

Then again, this was the only one nearby . . .

Nana always said a good Christian didn't hate people but that it didn't count if it was directed at Viola "Greedy" Gratton. The woman was known for having dirt on everyone, and supposedly people paid her to keep quiet.

"We gotta get out of here," Eliza whispered.

Yeah, no shit.

It's not that I was afraid of Mr. Crowley. But if he or Ms. Gratton saw us, one of them would definitely tell my family or the rest of the town, and then what?

The team would lose every bit of trust they put in me to deliver them a championship win, and Granddad? Granddad would be furious.

He had been through enough, sacrificed enough, for this season and the chance to win back something that was his to begin with. If he found out I was hanging out with the daughter of his longtime enemy, it would destroy him.

I couldn't do that to him. Not like this.

If anyone was going to tell Mr. Crowley or Granddad about me and Eliza, it would be me or Eliza. Period.

I whispered around my menu (to the top of Eliza's head, since the rest of her body was still practically below the table), "There's an exit door behind you. I'll stand first and give you some cover. Maybe they won't recognize me from behind. Then you can sneak out, and I'll follow, okay?"

"Okay."

I stood and waved for her to move. The seat creaked loudly as she slid out of it, and she stayed hunched over until she reached the exit, stumbling down the steps into the parking lot. I tossed my menu to the table along with a twenty and quickly trailed her.

"That was close," she said after I pulled out of the parking lot. "Dad would've lost his mind."

"Ha. My granddad would've been worse." I opened our windows and was grateful for the low humidity tonight. "Nana would need to replace the door to the laundry after all the darts he would've thrown."

"Darts?"

"Never mind." I chewed on the inside of my cheek for a half a mile as the woods grew denser on the sides of the road. "So would your dad really have been that pissed if he saw you with me?"

She huffed. "Uh, yeah."

"Just because I'm a Fulton?" Granddad had a legit reason for not trusting her family. What was Mr. Crowley's excuse? What did we ever do to them?

"Yep."

Something sharp pressed against the inside of my throat. "But it's just my name. What's the real reason you guys hate us?"

"'Us'?"

Nana told me once that Viola Gratton spread some nasty lies about Charlie Fulton back in the day, but a Fulton would never do the shit that that horrible woman said he'd done. Would Eliza's dad really believe those kinds of stories? That I was the same fruit from the same poisoned family tree?

Or worse: Would Eliza?

The bright reflection from her Rolex caught my eye, and Ben's words swirled back into my head. *Dude, watches like hers cost close to twenty grand.*

My wrist prickled with sweat underneath my dingy watch when another possibility settled into my gut.

Maybe it didn't have anything to do with the past after all?

"Hold on a sec." She turned in her seat to face me. "Are you seriously saying *your* grandparents wouldn't flip out if they saw us together?" she asked.

"Yeah, but that's different."

"How?"

I turned my hat forward. "Because mine have a reason to be mad at yours. The stadium was theirs—"

"Reed, that was ages ago." She turned her face toward her window.

"Doesn't feel that way to them," I mumbled.

She crossed her arms and sighed. I thought about bringing up the fact that she still hadn't given me a real answer about why her dad would flip out over me being with her. Saying it was because of my name was an easy excuse. My name shouldn't have anything to do with it.

We drove on for a couple of miles in silence before thunder rumbled. Dark clouds filled the sky ahead of us.

I cleared my throat. "Should I just take us back to Fair-field?"

She started fidgeting with the bottom of her shirt. "Do you want to go back?"

My cell buzzed from inside my pocket. I let it go to voice-mail. It was probably just Nana asking me to pick something up on my way home, but I was thankful for the brief distraction. I knew the answer to Eliza's question.

But I wasn't entirely sure what she wanted me to say.

Did she want to go back? Is that why she asked? After a long, quiet minute, I reached across the seat and took her hand. "No. I don't want to go back."

"Me either." She smiled and then faced forward again. "Take a right where you see that turnoff up ahead. I wanna show you something."

I did as she said and wound around a few turns until the

road dead-ended at some kind of clearing lined with tall trees. The sky over us was dark with the promise of a storm.

Eliza opened the door and jumped down. "Follow me." She began running through the tall grass toward a large stage with an awning at the edge of the property.

I got out and followed as heavy raindrops started to fall. The clearing was ringed by large stones and angled down toward the stage in a horseshoe shape. Lightning flashed as I reached the stage where Eliza stood.

"What is this place?" I asked, shaking the rain out of my hair.

"The Clairview Amphitheater." She spun around one of the beams holding up the awning over us. "It hosts a ren faire every year in the fall and a few other events in the spring. My grandmother used to perform here back in the day."

Rain fell steadily now, but under the awning, we were kept dry except for the passing breeze that blew some of the rain sideways.

"It's pretty cool." I ran my hands over the pillar closest to me and breathed in the familiar scent of cedar. Tall trees outlined the outdoor theater but not close enough to block out natural light to the stage. Being here felt like I had stepped back in time. "Do you miss her a lot?"

Eliza stopped spinning. "Every day. But she was in a lot of pain—cancer—before she passed, so I like to think she's comfortable now. Plus, Grandpa had passed a couple years earlier, so I know he's with her too."

Jesus.

I know they can't live forever, but losing Nana or Granddad would be hard enough. I couldn't imagine, didn't want to imagine, losing them both. Someone would have to pull me out of the hole I would dig for myself in their cornfield.

"My dad's been having a harder time with it than I thought," she whispered, almost too softly for me to hear.

"Have you tried talking to him about it?" I crossed the stage toward her.

"Yeah. It, uh, didn't go over too well."

"I get that. Dads close themselves off a lot." If I tried to talk to Dad about his feelings, it'd probably go the same way.

Why was that? Why was it that older men felt like they had to keep all that shit bottled up inside?

Would I be the same way someday?

I hoped not.

The rain to fell more heavily now, and although the thunder quieted, heat lightning flashed in the sky over us. Fireflies started blinking in the clearing.

Eliza sat down and leaned against one of the wooden poles closest to her. "I don't want to move."

"Who said anything about moving?" I didn't plan on moving from this spot any time soon, unless a hurricane blew through. My knee touched hers, and I tried not to think about how charged I felt from it—like jumper cables hooked up to a battery.

She let her head fall back against the wood. "If we lose the stadium, Dad said we'll probably go somewhere else to manage another team. Leave Fairfield."

"Leave Fairfield? Like literally move?"

"Yep."

Shit. I didn't even know that was on the table. Sure, her family drove Granddad to throwing darts at a door and sneaking a beer every so often, but no Crowleys in Fairfield?

So if I led our team all the way to the championship and if we won, I was not only responsible for taking the stadium back but also taking away her home?

Guilt slid down my throat like sour syrup.

I brought my knees up. "I'm sorry. I . . . I didn't know you'd be moving."

"You don't have to be sorry." She placed her hand on mine. "It's my dad who decided all of this without talking to any of us about it."

Still.

"Lauryn said moving can be a good thing," she added. "That I can reinvent myself."

"That's true." I squeezed her hand. "Take it from someone who's moved around a few times. There are some perks." A lot of negatives too. But I didn't need to tell her about those.

"I'm not like you though, Reed." She dropped her head and lightning flashed across the dark purple and blue sky above us. "You walk into a room the way you take the mound. Like you own it. Like nothing can stop you—"

"It's an act." I laced my fingers through hers. "Most of the time I'm scared shitless. I've just learned how to channel it. All you have to remember is FAFI."

"Faa-fee?"

"F. A. F. I. The fine art of faking it." I grinned. "I use it all the time."

Except with you.

"I like that." She ran her thumb over the back of my hand. "I wish I didn't care so much about how other people saw me. I want to be more like my grandmother—leap first, think later. Or say what I believe instead of worrying about what other people think first." Her foot waved back and forth.

"When you're ready to take the big leap, you will."

"How do you know?"

I stood and opened one of my playlists on my phone, turning it up as "I'm with You" by Vance Joy started. "Because I watched you at the theater when you talked to those technicians. You're tougher than you give yourself credit for."

"It's so frustrating. All I want is for people to respect me for me and not because I'm a Crowley, you know? I want my own parents to see that." She held up her wrist. "Dad just thinks he can buy respect with watches or cars or whatever."

"Respect has nothing to do with money. Or it shouldn't." I opened my hand for her to take. "Not with my family."

"I like that about your family." Eliza smiled and took my

hand as I helped her to her feet. I spun her out and brought her back before we began dancing in a slow circle.

Buying respect with fancy watches and cars? She was right. Definitely backward. But would she expect that someday from me?

I frowned at the broken digital watch on my wrist as a hard truth settled into my shoulders.

What could I really stand to give her that she didn't already have?

She laid her head against my chest. "I didn't know you could dance."

"Your brother wasn't the only one who took cotillion. Mom wanted me to look presentable when we went to Dad's military balls." I twirled her out to where she wasn't protected by the awning. She squealed as the thunder rumbled and the rain touched her skin.

I laughed and tried to pull her back, but she yanked my arm, bringing me into the storm with her.

For the rest of the song, we spun around outside. Every part of me was soaked through, and I would've stayed out there with her forever if she'd let me.

But when lightning flashed a bit too close for comfort, we hurried back under the awning. Tendrils of Eliza's long hair stuck to her cheeks, but her eyes and smile had never looked brighter.

Damn, this girl was beautiful.

"When did I tell you about Robbie's cotillion classes?" she asked.

"First grade." I gently lifted her hair off her face and tucked it behind her ear. "You used to waltz around by yourself outside the post office."

"That's right. They had—"

"The best parking lot for dancing." I smiled. "Yeah, you told me that too."

"You remember all that?"

I gently wove my fingers through hers. "I remember everything."

We started dancing again but stayed quiet for a long moment. The thunder and lightning had stopped, but the rain poured on.

"You know what's the absolute worst? Thinking of exactly what you should've said twenty minutes after you should've said it." She stopped dancing but still had her arms around me. "Sorry. I ramble when I'm nervous. I'm totally ruining this first date, aren't I?"

Something like bubbles floated through my chest. "Is that what this is? A date?"

"Oh, I mean, it doesn't have to be. Not if you don't want it to—"

"I want it." I kissed her, and everything inside of me relaxed. Kissing Eliza Crowley felt like coming home. "And never apologize for being honest. I always want you to be honest with me."

Even if it hurts me in the end, which it probably will, because this already feels too good to be true.

She ran a hand across my jaw, making me shiver. "Reed?"

"Yeah?"

"I honestly want you to kiss me again."

The wind picked up and blew the rain under the awning, but neither of us moved as I kissed her slowly. Every wall that I spent years building up broke down.

Let them.

Let them all.

Let every single stone of mine lay at her feet.

She was worth it.

Chapter Nineteen

ELIZA

"O, teach me how I should forget to think!"
—William Shakespeare, *Romeo and Juliet*

My clothes stuck to me like I had swum in a river with them on, and my hair continued to drip down my back after Reed dropped me off at my Jeep. All the way home, I played the moment between us at the amphitheater over and over again, so distracted I almost ran the red light outside of the church.

Thankfully, my phone—still dry since I had left it in Reed's truck—kept buzzing with message reminders from Dad. For one panicked moment I thought maybe he messaged me because he saw Reed and me slip out of the diner. But it was pretty crowded at the time, and his back had been to us as we ducked out.

There was no way he saw us.

Right?

Either way, I didn't plan to read any of the missed texts from him until I got home. Nothing was going to ruin this moment and the bubbly giddiness I felt.

I pulled off Main Street and down our long driveway, absentmindedly counting the trees lining both sides, the same way kids often counted stairs while they climbed. Lauryn always said these trees creeped her out because they moved when she walked by them, like they followed her with their invisible tree eyes. It was strange to think that Reed had passed these trees not too long ago to drop off my bag of My Little Pony toys. So much had changed since that peace offering.

I stopped the Jeep short near the open garage, my smile disappearing faster than the makeup crew after touchups during intermission. Dad stood under the hickory tree near the old tire swing with his arms crossed and a frown on his face. An ice-cold rock dropped into my gut.

Oh God. He did see us at the diner.

What was he going to say? Would he ground me for the rest of the summer? Make me quit the play?

And what about Reed? What about us? Was this over just as quickly as it had begun because Jenny's had the best pie around?

My hands shook as I turned off the engine and stepped out of the Jeep. Dad gave my soaked clothes a quick once-over before he walked away from the tree, up the front porch steps, and inside the house, slamming the door behind him.

Truth: When Hurricane Dad gave you the silent treatment

first instead of yelling at you outright, that's when you were in the deepest of—

Mom swung open the door. "Eliza, inside. Now."

Shit.

I no sooner dropped my soaked Converse on the mat inside the front door than Dad started berating me with questions.

"Where the hell were you this afternoon? Why didn't you answer your phone?" His face changed to a deep red, almost purple. "And why in God's name did you leave Lauryn alone at the store on a Thursday? She doesn't work there, Eliza!"

I struggled to swallow. "She's . . . she's helped me before—"

"Helping you is a hell of a lot different than being in charge. A group of contractors from Dennis and Sons came by for their order, and she had no idea what to do. Finally, one of them had the sense to call me. I had to leave a very important meeting to handle it."

A meeting at a diner was "very important"?

He threw his hands up. "They were late to their jobsite, Eliza!"

"Will, calm down. You scream any louder and you'll shatter your mother's china." Mom entered the room with one of the bath towels from the guest bathroom and tossed it to me. I pushed it against my face, grateful for the brief escape from my father's heated stare, and relieved that he obviously hadn't seen us earlier.

"This behavior is not like you. Showing up late, forgetting to text us, leaving work without permission . . ." Dad pressed his hands together. "Help us understand what's going on here, Eliza."

"What's going on." Where can I even begin?

I had no more of an explanation than I would for why someone thought it was smart to put peanut butter and jelly in the same jar. "I was at the theater." It sounded believable. Kinda.

"I called the theater. They said you never came in today." Dad sat down on the arm of the couch.

Okay, maybe not so believable.

I tucked a piece of wet hair behind my ear. Now what? Did I have to tell them about Reed when I didn't really know what we actually were or if this was even going to be anything beyond this summer? "Okay, the truth is—"

"She was with me." TJ appeared from the kitchen, holding a sandwich with mustard oozing out of the side. "She needed an extra set of hands in the catwalk replacing some, um . . ."

"Cans," I blurted. "Couple of them blew out during our last rehearsal."

"Cans. Yeah, that's what they're called." TJ took a big bite and spoke with his mouth full. "She had the, um, the . . ."

"Presets on," I said, hurrying across the room. "So the stage was lit the whole time—"

"And no one probably knew she was even up there. You know how Eliza is, always quiet as a mouse."

Ha. I wish.

"Why is she soaking wet?" Mom asked, cocking an eyebrow.

"We had to help Ms. Sparrow move some sets inside once it started raining. I left earlier than her so I had time to change and dry off." TJ wiped his hands on the bottom of his shirt.

If they bought this, I owed him the best Christmas present ever.

Dad cleared his throat. "I still don't understand why you had to leave the hardware store to fix a . . . a can in the catwalk. Doesn't sound like an emergency to me but if something like that happens again, you need to call me or your mother first. You hear me?"

I nodded.

Mom took the towel from me and picked off a piece of pine from my shirtsleeve. "Go upstairs and clean up. We're going out to dinner tonight."

"'Out'?" TJ and I both said.

Dad stood and clapped his hands. "Yes, out. Gives us all time to chat some more about everything."

"'Everything'?" The rock in my stomach grew heavier.

"Couldn't we just order something to go like we've been doing all summer and eat in awkward silence?" TJ asked.

Yes, I vote for that.

Dad walked over to us and patted TJ's shoulder before nudging my wet head. "Meet us at my truck in twenty minutes, you two."

Angelo's had the best pizza across three towns, and they didn't take reservations, so it was rare to walk in and not wait. I had forgotten to eat since this morning and drooled just thinking about that Sicilian pie with crushed red pepper. Maybe if I kept shoveling food into my mouth, I wouldn't have to answer more questions about this afternoon.

"So anything you wanna tell me?" TJ slung his arm around my shoulders as we walked toward the front door of the restaurant.

"Nope." I flicked his hand.

"Because if this is going to be something you do all summer . . . sneaking away . . . we're gonna need to work on your lying skills."

Fair.

Dad opened the door for all of us, but I immediately bumped into TJ, who stopped short inside the entrance.

"Well, this won't be a silent meal, but it *will* be awkward," he said.

I peered around his big shoulders and gasped. Mr. and Mrs. Fulton sat next to the hostess stand holding their menus. As the door closed loudly, they looked up and gawked at all four of us. Mrs. Fulton smiled, but Mr. Fulton glared at Dad as if he were equal parts vermin and predator.

Reed approached from the back of the restaurant. "They redid the bathrooms, eh? Fancy automatic sinks—" He cut himself off as his eyes found mine before moving to TJ and then my parents. "Um . . . hello, Mr. and Mrs. Crowley."

He had changed too, but his hair was still damp like mine, wavy and messy in the sexiest way . . .

I blinked and looked down at my flip flops.

Get it together, Eliza. No more sexy-hair thoughts.

Until maybe later.

"Good evening, dear," Mom said, her voice tight. "How are your parents doing? I haven't seen them yet this summer."

"Mom's fine. Working hard at the library back home. Dad's deployed overseas right now." He shoved his hands—the same hands that had been deliciously all over me only hours ago—into his pockets, and eyed the exit behind us.

Maybe I could back out of it before Dad noticed?

"Please tell your dad we're all so thankful for our troops," Mom said, her face softening. "And maybe I can get your mom's number? Ms. Gratton could use some updates to her read-alouds—"

"No!" Reed and I both yelled at the same time.

My cheeks flushed so hot that my mascara might melt.

"'No'?" TJ's voice rose with his eyebrows as he looked back and forth between us. "Why not, you two?"

"My mom's, um . . . super busy with inventory right now. So

I'll, uh, have her call Ms. Gratton when she's finished." Reed rubbed the back of his neck.

"Of course," Mom said. "No rush."

Dad strolled up to the hostess. "Four, please. And we'd like a couple of menus while we wait."

"Sure thing, Mr. Crowley." She handed him some menus from behind her and made a note in her log. "It shouldn't be long."

"That's what you said to us thirty minutes ago," Mr. Fulton muttered.

The hostess—Rachel, on her name tag—turned redder than the checkered pattern of the tablecloths before hurrying away around the corner.

Mom, Dad, and I took a seat on the bench perpendicular to the Fultons with me, unfortunately, sandwiched in the middle. TJ chose to pace like an anxious cat. I hated when he did that.

Reed cleared his throat. "Congratulations on your winning record, Mr. Crowley."

I choked on my own spit, and TJ stopped pacing.

Mom elbowed Dad, who slowly lowered his menu and mumbled a barely audible, "Thank you, Reed. Same to you."

"Thank you." Reed smiled briefly until his granddad scowled at him.

What the heck was going on here? Was Reed buttering up Dad on purpose? For me? It was sweet, but it didn't stop sweat from dripping down my back.

"I think we've entered the Upside Down, Eliza," TJ said.

For real.

"What's the Upside Down?" Mom asked him.

Reed and I spoke at the same time: "From *Stranger Things*."

We smiled at each other before realizing we weren't the only ones in the room. I looked away first.

Dad closed his menu and narrowed his eyes at Reed's granddad. "Are you sure you'll be able to look after the stadium if you win this tournament, Louis?"

Oh, hell, here we go.

Mr. Fulton folded his menu and set it on his lap. "*When* we win the stadium, William, we'll be just fine. But your concern is noted. Perhaps with all your free time, you can volunteer your services there as needed."

Dad tensed next to me. "We'll be too busy managing another stadium elsewhere for that."

Thanks for the reminder.

The hostess appeared. "Mr. Crowley, your table is ready."

Wait. Our table?

Mr. Fulton slowly rose to his feet. "We were here first, young lady. We've been waiting for almost half an hour."

The hostess's eyes widened. "My manager had a table set aside for the Crowleys before they came—"

"But you don't take reservations," Reed said. "You never have."

Mr. Fulton put his hand on Reed's shoulder. "Never mind

that." His gaze went from my father, my mother, and then to me.

I shrunk a good four feet from that look.

"I've just remembered why we don't go out to eat here," Mr. Fulton said. "Let's go."

I jumped up. "You could have our table, if you like."

Everyone stopped and stared at me like I had grown three heads. I might've . . . I mean, anything was possible in the Upside Down.

"Thank you, sweetheart." Mrs. Fulton patted my shoulder. "But you go on and enjoy your meal." She looped her arm through her husband's and left, Reed following closely behind without a second glance at my family—or me.

Chapter Twenty

REED

"But baseball has marked the time. This field, this game, it's a part of our past . . . It reminds us of all that once was good and that could be again." –Terence Mann, *Field of Dreams*

Pitchers didn't have to report for practice Monday, and apparently Eliza didn't have rehearsal till later in the afternoon, so we met up at the old ball field at Clairview Elementary School. The one in Fairfield was in much better condition, but she had said it was too "risky."

I knew risky.

Risky was throwing too many games without enough rest time in between.

Or trying a forkball when the bases were loaded.

Or hoping a knuckleball could save your ass when you've all but ripped apart the tendons in your shoulder.

Hanging out at a ball field in the same town as your families shouldn't have been risky. Then again, eating at the same restaurant at the same time shouldn't force one family to have to leave either. After we left Angelo's, Granddad was angrier than I'd seen him in a long time.

But Eliza had offered her family's table to us.

Had he noticed? Had her father?

Did it really matter to either?

My gut told me Granddad wasn't the one to really worry about as far as "risks" go. But it also told me that, unfortunately, this was going to blow up in our faces sooner or later.

"You gonna start throwing, or should I come back later?" Eliza called from home plate.

"Sorry." I shook my head to focus. "Zoned out for a sec there."

She took her stance, and I grinned like a fool.

Damn. There was nothing hotter than a girl who knew how to play the game.

I brought my hand behind my back and rolled the ball around till the laces were perpendicular to my fingers for my four-seamer. I stared her down and imagined Dad behind the plate instead of Ben—because Ben would never play ball with a girl and we still weren't speaking—and threw it.

Crack!

The ball soared over my head and into center field, where it dropped with a soft thud. "Nice!" I yelled.

Eliza rested the bat on her shoulder. "You throwing slow for me, Fulton?"

"No."

Maybe.

Okay, just a little.

She arched an eyebrow and tugged her hat a little lower before tapping the bat on the plate. "Let's see your slider."

My slider?

You mean the slider that nearly took out your cousin in the season opener?

"Sure." My voice cracked. I grabbed another ball near the mound and rolled it around in my hand till my pointer and middle finger touched. When my palm started sweating, I closed my eyes for a second and slowed my breathing.

Relax. You've thrown this pitch hundreds of times.

But in the last second, I rolled the ball into a changeup before releasing it. It slowed too quickly.

Crack!

Eliza hammered it into right field. It plopped into the tall grass, and I turned around to face a scowling batter behind the plate.

"What was that?" she asked.

"A pitch." *Just not the one you asked for.*

She dropped the bat at the plate and closed the sixty-foot distance between us till her toes touched the edge of the mound. "Are you afraid of hitting me?"

"No." *Yes. Terrified, actually.*

"Reed." She took off her hat, and her hair spilled around her shoulders. "I wouldn't have come out here if I was afraid you'd hit me with a pitch."

"I know." My throat squeezed.

She made a face. "Do you feel this much doubt every time you take the mound?"

"No. But this is different—"

"Because I'm a girl?" Her hands went to her hips.

"Hell no. Girls kick ass at baseball. It's just . . . I don't want to hurt you." *Ever. At all. And especially not with a pitch.*

"I trust you." She picked up a ball and pressed it firmly in my glove. "But you're never going to be the pitcher you want to be unless you trust yourself. No one owns that mound but you."

No one owns the mound but me. I needed to save that for my next game.

After she walked back to home, she threaded her hair through her hat and picked up the bat. "Bring the heat, Fulton."

Lord, don't let me regret this.

I moved my fingers around for my four-seamer again, but this time, I threw it twice as hard. She swung and missed but smiled. "Hell yeah. Do that again."

And I did. I threw fastball after fastball. She didn't miss all of them, but she didn't hit them as well as the first two pitches of the day.

"Is that a four- or a two-seamer?" she asked after stepping outside the box for a break.

"Four. My two-seamer is a bit . . . rusty." I didn't elaborate.

Fairfield was a small town. The odds of her already knowing what had happened last summer at UNC were good.

"Let's see it."

Shit. "Eliza . . ."

"You're never going to throw it cleanly if you don't practice with a batter at the plate."

"But it's really not ready—"

"Reed, we're not going anywhere till you show me that two-seamer."

Fine. I kicked the old pitching rubber. "You know, I never would've thought it possible that you could get more stubborn than you were as a kid."

She stuck her tongue out at me and took some practice swings.

Dad's voice and old reminders about the pitch played through my head. His tags on my chest felt heavy. "Help me out here, Dad," I whispered to myself.

Eliza stepped into the box as I got into formation and threw up a prayer before the ball left my hand. The spin looked right, just enough off the center. It zipped across the plate and under her bat.

"That was awesome!" She beamed and threw the ball back to me. "Think you can do that again?"

Doubtful, but what the hell.

I rolled the seams around till my fingers aligned with them. This time, the ball didn't go as off-center as I wanted, but it moved just as fast. Eliza fouled it off and cursed before asking for another.

After five more pitches, we both called it quits. I waved her out to the mound where I lay down and rested my head on the rubber with my feet pointing toward center field. She put her head next to mine but faced her body toward home plate.

She stretched her arms out. "This is . . ."

"Weird?" I gulped. None of the guys ever liked lying down on the mound. Said it was too scratchy.

"Actually, I was going to say pretty cool." She sighed. "I've never looked at the ball field from this angle before. It's so different."

Finally, someone gets it.

I brought my hand to rest on my chest. "Dad and I used to lie down like this. We'd drive around and look for old ballparks, and when we found one, we always did this first to see if it felt like a good field."

"How could you tell?"

"It's kinda hard to explain. But he had me close my eyes and listen to the way the wind moved. I'd run my hands over the dirt too, just to get a feel for it. To understand how long it had been since someone had stood on it."

"Mine drives me crazy, but I can't imagine having him that far away." She sighed. "I bet you miss him a lot."

My chest tightened.

More than you know.

"When is he supposed to come back home?" she asked.

My fingers fumbled against the edges of the tags under my shirt. "I dunno. He's on some kind of special ops and has been radio silent for a while. Mom's really worried." *So am I.*

She rested her hand on my shoulder. "He went to UNC, right? Is that where you want to go too?"

"Yeah, he went to UNC. But I dunno where I'll go." I found a small stone and chucked it. "Doubtful I'll get any kind of a scholarship for baseball, anyway."

"What makes you say that?"

"You didn't hear about my showcase shitshow from last summer?"

"Oh, that." She laughed nervously. "Yeah, I heard about it. But who cares? That was almost a year ago."

"It set me back months of eligibility, of scouts coming to see me play my junior year."

She turned her head toward me. "Do you want to play college baseball?"

"Yes." *More than anything.*

"Then it'll happen."

It'll happen.

She had a gleam in her blue eyes when she said it. The shadow of her hat couldn't hide it or the trail of freckles across her nose. But it was the way her entire body seemed so relaxed about it all that got me. How easy it was to just believe in something I thought was unbelievable.

Eliza radiated a confidence I'd kill for.

Maybe, if I was lucky, being this close to her would help me get there.

I smiled, and the tightness in my chest vanished. "I've wanted it for such a long time. I love the way I feel on the mound. It's like coming home. You know what I mean?"

"I do," she said. "I feel that every time I turn on a light board and press the first cue for a show."

"Terrifying and exciting all at the same time."

"And in that moment, you know—"

"You're right where you're meant to be," we said together.

I laid my hand on top of Eliza's and squeezed it.

Right where I'm meant to be.

Chapter Twenty-One

ELIZA

"Theater was my first love. I can't take the theater out of me. And I wouldn't want to. To me, it's home." –Jim Parsons

Trying to sneak in backstage unseen was about as possible as maneuvering around a catwalk while blindfolded, ankle-tied to a penguin, and covered in sleigh bells.

I would've picked that Christmas-catwalk-penguin scene a million times over my late entrance to rehearsal Monday. I didn't mean to fall asleep with Reed earlier at the ball field in Clairview, but when the sun moved behind the clouds and the humidity dropped, we had let the quiet field speak for us.

I loved the peace of it all. I don't remember the last time I felt that calm during a show or baseball season.

The stage door slammed shut behind me, and half the cast glared and hissed. "You are so busted," Raul whispered, a sword belted to his waist. He and all the other Montagues frowned.

Right, because you've got all your lines and blocking memorized– Oh, wait . . . you don't.

I brushed by Cara, our stage manager, who wore her famous disappointed frown that she normally reserved for the freshmen theater students, and crept along the side of the auditorium till I reached the lobby. After shoving a dollar into the vending machine for a drink, I grabbed it and flew up the stairs to the booth.

I wedged my trusty wooden ruler in its place so the door wouldn't lock me in and started getting everything ready. The eyes of Andrew Lloyd Webber stared at me from his autographed picture on the wall. "Stop being so judgy," I whispered to him as I hurried to pull up the show file. "I'm not that late." I checked the time on my phone and winced.

Okay, maybe I was.

Cara barked orders at the other onstage crew members about how to properly set up act 3, scene 1. I missed the first cue waiting for the file to load but quickly caught up with the cast. I loved the lighting of this scene—lots of slow, creeping burnt oranges and deep reds curling in toward the center as the anger flared up between Tybalt and Mercutio during their duel. Everything was hitting perfectly.

I leaned back in my chair and stuck my tongue out at the framed face that had scolded me moments before. "See?" I said to him. "Just because I was late doesn't mean I wasn't prepa—"

A bright yellow box appeared on the computer screen over the display: "ERROR: SYSTEM SOFTWARE INCOMPATIBLE."

"Wait. What?" I rolled my chair closer, and a second later, the computer and the board shut down, putting the entire auditorium in the dark.

Everyone on the stage groaned, and the distinct click of Ms. Sparrow's heels sounded on the hardwood. "Ms. Crowley? Everything okay up there?"

I shot up out of my seat, sending it slamming into the door. The ruler snapped in half, the door closed, and the lock clicked. *Great.* "Everything's fine! I got an error warning before the entire system crashed, but I'll get it up and running in a sec."

"Define 'a sec'?" Cara asked over the radio.

My eye twitched. Since when was a stage manager also the director?

I switched on the house lights, which ran separately from the board, and grabbed the manual, flipping to the index till I found the section on troubleshooting errors.

"If an on-screen error warning has flashed, hold down numbers 7, 8, and 9 on your keypad and turn off the console . . ."

What? "It's already turned off!" I whisper-yelled at the book and shook it.

"Eliza?" Ms. Sparrow called again. "Would you like Cara to come up and give you a hand?"

I'd rather push my finger into a wall socket, thanks. "No, no. I've got it. Just a sec."

My stomach squirmed and soured as I read over the suggestions to fix the board. None of them had an answer for my board's problem.

Screw it.

I held the 7, 8, and 9 buttons, and then pressed the power button, waiting and praying for it to reboot while I took a another quick look at the framed picture of Andrew Lloyd Webber. "If you help me with this reboot, I promise never to make fun of *CATS* again."

Not out loud, at least.

The screen blinked twice, and the small yellow and red lights blinked on. *Yes!*

And then a new message appeared on the board: "INSTALLING UPDATES. THIS MAY TAKE A WHILE."

Oh my God, noooooo.

I swallowed over the rising bile in my throat and popped my head up into the window toward the stage. "Um, it says it's going to take a while to install updates. So I'll just turn on the presets. I'm so sorry."

"Maybe if you had been here earlier, you could've run the updates before rehearsal," Cara snapped from somewhere in the dark.

Maybe you should—

"Cara, that's enough." Ms. Sparrow's voice turned sharp, firm. "Eliza, please meet me in the kitchen after rehearsal."

"Yes, ma'am." I rattled the doorknob and cursed under my breath. I was locked in. "Ms. Sparrow?" I called out.

"What is it now?" she asked.

My cheeks flushed. "I, um . . . I'll need your master key to let me out. This door just locked me in. Again."

I had known about this stupid broken door for years and was told to always keep it propped open. According to Grandma, they had fixed it a few years ago, but the "fix" didn't last. Like most superstitious thespians, the locals all believed it was some kind of theater ghost.

I didn't believe anything evil haunted this place, but a big part of me hoped Grandma still visited it in some way.

The updates continued throughout the rest of the act and rehearsal. Nothing looked more pathetic than a dead Mercutio being dragged off the stage in plain sight, but the board was out of my control till it finished.

Theater kids were notoriously superstitious, but the way they pressed themselves against the wall as I passed them after rehearsal made me wonder if I had come down with a sudden case of theater plague.

By the time I reached the kitchen, the armpits on my T-shirt were soaked through. Ms. Sparrow sat alone at the old green-tinted table with two cups of coffee and two blueberry muffins in front of her. I choked back a gasp.

My brother told me once that you knew you were going to be fired if your boss wanted to speak to you alone *and* if that boss brought food. He had said food was meant for the immediate mourning process.

"Come in. Sit, sit." She waved to the empty chair opposite of her. "Have a muffin and some coffee."

Yep. I'm screwed.

The seat let out a squeak when I sat. The plastic, ripped in three places, pinched my bare thighs.

"I'm sorry about the board," I mumbled, my eyes focused on the muffin.

She drummed her fingernails on the sides of her plate. "Nothing you can do about a board that needs updates. But we can do something about that sticky door. I'll put another work order in today. Hopefully they take care of it before the end of the summer. Maintenance is hard to reach this time of year."

Ms. Sparrow unwrapped her muffin and continued. "I know it must be hard reading a new manual and dealing with a board that's entirely different from the one at the high school."

I took a sip of the coffee and winced as it burned the top of my mouth. "It is, but I do think I'm finally making some headway."

"I'm sure you are, but missing a cast and crew meeting before rehearsal and then arriving late—"

"There was a meeting?" I pulled out my phone and opened

to my Google Calendar. I could've sworn there wasn't one. I wouldn't have missed it . . .

Yet there it was, in the bright orange color I used for all things related to the show season.

"Cast Meeting: 10:00 AM."

"I . . ." My throat squeezed. "I'm so sorry. I didn't see that. Ms. Sparrow, I never miss meetings or run late. You know me—"

"I do, which is why I agreed to you running the lights for such a big show for this summer troupe." She broke off a piece of her muffin. "But to be honest, Eliza, you have seemed a bit . . . distracted over the last two weeks."

I sighed and took a big bite of my muffin, forcing it down.

She smiled sadly. "I know how much you have on your plate this summer, what with this show and then that big tournament with your father's team. It must be a lot to manage."

You forgot the part about a secret relationship with the grandson of the team trying to beat my father's, and the fact that if we lose, we also move, and then I'd have to start over with a new school, new friends, an entirely new theater program . . .

My head fell into my hands. "I don't know what I'm doing."

"With the board? Sure, you do."

"No, not with the board. With . . ." I swallowed over an achy lump. "With everything else."

She pushed the coffee closer to me. "Something tells me you'll figure it out in time."

"I'm not so sure." How do you choose between loyalty to your family and loyalty to something new that feels so right? Reed made me feel different, better than I had in a long time. I didn't know I needed that feeling, needed him, until this summer.

"Did I ever tell you that I had the privilege of watching your grandmother perform at the regional thespian conference a couple of times when I was younger?" she asked.

"Really?" I lifted my head. "I bet she was amazing."

I couldn't think of a time she hadn't been.

"Better than amazing." Ms. Sparrow leaned back into her chair. "When Marguerite took the stage, it was like the entire audience held their breath, waiting to be transformed."

My heart squeezed, and a familiar ache unraveled itself through my chest, a cold coil of rope winding and knotting and releasing, all at the same time. God, I missed her. "I wish I could've seen her on the stage," I whispered.

"She played Eliza in *My Fair Lady* when I saw her the second time. I haven't seen a better Eliza since." She cocked her head. "Is that how you got your name?"

"Yes. Grandma always said that Eliza was one of the best roles written for the stage." I took another bite of the muffin, but it had no taste now. I couldn't smell it anymore either. I had felt the same way for weeks after Grandma passed. Everything lost its color, flavor . . . even music sounded melancholy and flat.

"She was right." Ms. Sparrow scooted forward and took both of my hands in her own. "Do you know why?"

I knew.

Grandma used to sing me to sleep with "I Could've Danced All Night" when I was a little girl. She hummed "Without You" while she sewed. Thanks to her, I knew Eliza Doolittle's monologues long before I even knew what a monologue was.

I stared at the small tattoo on my wrist: the heart-shaped baseball with Grandma's name spelled out in the stitching. "Grandma said Eliza Doolittle never needed anyone to fix her. That she had it inside of her all along. She said once she realized she didn't have to choose between who she was and who she wanted to be that she was a force to be reckoned with."

"She was." Ms. Sparrow squeezed my hands. "This is an important production for you, for many of the cast and crew. They need a Doolittle in that booth, Ms. Crowley, and so do I. Are you ready to be that person?"

I prayed I was.

Chapter Twenty-Two

REED

"Baseball really is a glorified game of throw and catch. And if you don't have guys who throw it really well, you can't compete for long." –Tucker Elliot

On Wednesday afternoon, we played the Centerville Coyotes to a sold-out crowd in Crowley Park under a blistering ninety-four-degree heat. We had to win this game and the next one to officially clinch our spot in the championship, where we'd likely play the Crowley Cardinals.

So far, it didn't look promising.

Cameron pitched the first five innings and did really well, but he had no support behind the plate. Ben was all over the damn place. He botched what should've been an easy throw to second, which kept the tying run on base. He dropped a pop-fly near the third-base line in the bottom of the third, and he even got an official warning in the bottom of the fourth when he mouthed off to the ump.

Before I took the mound, Coach Roeper pulled me aside and asked me what was wrong with Ben. I shrugged, because I hadn't seen him or spoken to him since our last practice together when he all but said we weren't family anymore.

I could've told Coach about Ben's being pissed at me for losing focus and breaking our pact, but what the hell was the point? It wouldn't fix the errors from earlier in this game. Any good ballplayer knew you left your shit at home when it was game day.

Guess I'd have to pick up the slack myself.

But I didn't.

Instead, I had one error after another. I didn't cover first base fast enough with what should've been an easy out in the bottom of the sixth. Then, I missed a bunt that practically landed at my feet, but worst of all? I balked.

BALKED.

Who fails to step toward first when trying to throw out a base runner at this level?

I couldn't remember the last time I'd done something so careless. And because of me, that smug-ass base runner got a free pass to second base. Why the hell couldn't I get my head into this game?

What was wrong with me?

After a damn lucky strikeout with the first at bat in the bottom of the ninth, Coach Monaco called, "Time!" Ben lifted his mask before running out to the mound as Coach did.

I hated getting taken out in the last inning.

I needed to finish this one.

Please, let me finish this one.

Ben reached me a moment after Coach did and spoke first. "Ump's an ass, Coach. He's had it comin' for us the entire game."

"That's enough out of you." Coach pointed to Ben. "You're on thin ice already. Don't push it, Talbot."

Ouch.

I took off my hat and wiped my forehead with my glove. "I'm workin' with what I've got, Coach. I swear. His strike zone has been a hell of a lot smaller for us than it is any time Kominski takes the mound."

"Yeah, Coach," Ben added. "Kominski's throwing beach balls, for Christ's sake, and—"

"Enough!" Coach spat a sunflower seed to his left. Then to his right.

Mixed signals.

Was I out or would I finish this?

"Can you finish this game, Fulton?" Coach pulled down his Oakleys and stared at me from over the top of them.

My arm felt weighed down with irons, and my shoulder pricked with hundreds of needles, but I faked a stern smile. "I can do it."

Coach slid his sunglasses back up. "Then get to it. It's hot as balls out here."

As he hurried back to the dugout, Ben pressed the ball into my glove. "Let's end this already. The score is making me itch."

With us only being up by one run? Yeah, same.

"We good, man?" I asked him as he started turning around to go back to home plate.

Ben cracked his jaw and scratched the scruff on his chin before he lowered his mask. "Just bring the heat. Think you can do that?"

My fingers tightened around the ball. "Yeah, I can do that."

Ben ran back to home, and the crowd cheered as the next batter stepped into the box. He was three for three already this game, and he looked hungry for another.

I moved the ball around in my glove after Ben called for a fastball. He wanted me to bring the heat, so I'd do just that.

And I was gonna do it with my two-seamer.

I had tried it out on Granddad this morning, and he was thrilled. He had asked me what was different from the last time I had tried, and I replied with one word: "Focus." What he didn't know was that I meant I had to focus on a certain person.

So this time, when I blurred out the crowd, I also imagined that the base runner had changed to her.

Eliza.

If I pictured her, I felt calmer. My arm felt confident, and my head clear. Clearer than it had in years of being on the mound.

What was it she had said?

No one owns that mound but you.

I exhaled into my glove and took my stance. My knee drew up a second later, and I released the ball. It hit Ben's glove directly over the plate with a satisfying *thwack*.

The ump raised his arm and yelled, "Strike!"

Yes!

Ben clapped his hand against his glove before throwing the ball back. He gave me the signal for another fastball. I nodded and got into formation. A moment later, I threw another strike from my two-seamer. And a minute after that, I threw another one.

Three fastballs in a row for my fastest out of the game.

Eliza would've loved to see it.

Ben stood and held up two fingers to signify our outs and threw the ball to me. I couldn't see his face, but I liked to think maybe he was smiling. Ben and I had worked on my two-seamer off and on since last summer, but it was never consistent enough for me to really feel comfortable throwing it—till this week.

The next batter took the plate.

My last one of the game. My fastball would make sure of that. And maybe a good changeup to clench it.

But when Ben crouched down behind the plate, he used two fingers and tapped the inside of his right thigh.

A curveball?

I shook it away.

This same batter hit the shit out of my curveball earlier when I first took the mound. No. He needed my two-seamer and then a changeup. Ben must've known that.

But he smacked his glove and signaled for a curveball again.

I sighed, and my father's voice drifted into my head.

If you can't trust your catcher, you can't trust anyone, son.

Face hidden by my glove, I imagined Eliza at the plate again and reluctantly nodded to Ben. My knee drew up a second later before I released the ball. And then, everything slowed as the batter's eyes lit up.

CRACK!

Ben jumped to his feet and ripped off his mask. I whirled around and watched the ball sail deep into center field. Dominic sprinted after it.

"Catch it, catch it," I mumbled.

Dominic's glove shot up as he got closer to the wall. He leaped and reached over the top as the ball dropped.

I couldn't look.

But then the crowd went wild. Our team charged out of the dugout and threw their gloves into the air as the announcer called out our victory of 4–3 over the Centerville Coyotes.

Ben appeared next to me and scoffed. "That was your curveball?"

I flipped my hat up. "Why did you call for it? You know he hit the hell out of mine earlier."

"I didn't trust the two-seamer to happen again."

Seriously? All he'd wanted me to do at the beginning of this summer was master it, to force myself to throw it. Now he wanted me to hold back?

He scowled and walked away toward the guys who crowded around Coach Monaco near the dugout. I tucked my glove under my arm and followed.

Coach raised his hand, and the team quieted. "I know that scoreboard says we won, but we're damn lucky we did. We had far more errors than the Coyotes. Most of you played like your head was in the clouds instead of down here on the field. The only one who had half his shit together was Cameron. Nice game, son." He nodded to him, and my face prickled with heat.

"We've got almost a week till our next game, and I don't need to remind you how important a game it is," Coach continued. "Until then, rest up, be on time for our practices, and for God's sake, keep your head in the game, where it belongs. We got a lot riding on this one, and a family I don't wanna let down." His gaze moved across the group from each player and settled on me. "Have I made myself clear?"

Crystal.

Chapter Twenty-Three

ELIZA

"The world is a stage, but the play is badly cast."
—Oscar Wilde, *Lord Arthur Savile's Crime and Other Stories*

There were two holidays that Fairfield threw out all the stops for: Christmas and the Fourth of July. Judging by the piles of fireworks Dad loaded into his truck to take over to the fire station for later tonight, today's Fourth in Fairfield celebration would hold up to the hype.

Another favorite Fairfield tradition of mine was the annual spaghetti dinner on Main Street, which happened a few hours before the fireworks launched. Heaping bowls of pasta were passed down from the head of the table, from one plate to another, like the roast beast scene at the end of *How the Grinch Stole Christmas*. The garlic bread never ran out—unless TJ helped serve it—and Old Lady Gratton's famous creamy Italian dressing was in high demand for every garden salad. She may have been a gossiping nightmare, but the woman knew how to dress her mixed greens.

Unfortunately, since this year was the first that Fairfield had two baseball teams representing it in the Legion League, our horribly clueless mayor, Richard Dupont, thought it would show "great comradery" if members of both prepped and served the spaghetti meal this year.

Comradery?

At a spaghetti dinner?

Between the Fulton Hawks and the Crowley Cardinals?

Knives for the garlic bread, metal tongs heavier than my old AP Chem notebook for the spaghetti . . . What could go wrong?

I arrived early with Mom, Dad, and TJ to help lay out the plastic tablecloths and wrap the silverware. The local Boy and Girl Scouts helped their troop leaders hang paper lanterns across Main Street, from the post office to the thrift store, while we worked. After rolling what felt like my fiftieth fork, knife, and spoon together, TJ muttered, "Here they come."

My heart skipped as Reed and his grandparents walked toward us from the opposite side of the street, Reed carrying a big pot of what I assumed was sauce. He wore his hat backward and a gray Yankees jersey, with the silver chain I kept meaning to ask him about peeking out from underneath it. I hadn't seen him since our ball field date in Clairview. Between my needing to be in the booth every chance I could get and him having what sounded like hellish practice drills, neither of us had the time.

I hated it, but I needed to be a Doolittle for now.

Reed smiled at me from over the lid of the pot, and my ears burned.

"Dang, Fulton. Looks like you've been in the kitchen all day. Where's your apron?" TJ snickered, staring at some stains on Reed's shorts. I gripped my silverware to keep from smacking him.

"At home next to mine," Reed's grandmother—Nana, as he called her—said with a smile. "How's your mother doing, TJ?"

Now I knew why Grandma liked this woman.

TJ cleared his throat. "She's fine, um, thank you."

Reed's granddad rubbed his lower back and then pointed to the tables with the propane heaters. "You can set that pot over there, Reed. And then come help me get the other two from the truck."

"TJ can help him," I blurted.

"No, he can't," TJ said.

Reed looked like I had slapped him.

I smiled with a lot of teeth. I mean, if I could somehow get TJ and Reed to get along, then maybe there was hope for the rest of my family? Right?

"Actually, I think that's a fine idea," Mom said, appearing at my side. "TJ, go help Reed with the other pots of sauce, and then you can help Ms. Gratton prep the salads."

"Isn't there something else I can do?" TJ whined. "Run into traffic? Hold my hand over an open flame . . ."

"I vote for the running-into-traffic option," Reed said, wincing when his nana smacked him in the back of the head.

Yeah . . . this was going to be one interesting evening.

A couple of hours later, the spaghetti dinner was in full swing. The long tables sat in the middle of Main Street as they always did, but this time, instead of passing the pasta down, some of the Fulton Hawks and Crowley Cardinals acted as waiters and served the pasta to the guests, refilling the food and drinks as needed.

Lauryn and TJ scooped salad into bowls a couple of tables away from me. I stood alone at the sauce pots, ladling spoonfuls onto the pasta bowls to be delivered to the tables.

"You're cheating people out of the good stuff." Reed slid up next to me, his arm brushing against mine.

I smirked.

"The good stuff" was right next to me now.

Jesus, Eliza, chill. You'll start a fire.

But this was the closest we had been since our ball field date. So I tried to play it cool. "Excuse me?"

He pointed to the pot of sauce in front of me. "That's a Fulton secret family recipe, right there. You need to show it some respect and really spoon it on, Crowley. Here, let me show you." His fingers wrapped around my wrist, and he stepped closer till his chest touched my shoulder. My entire body hummed with energy as his breath moved the flyaway hairs near my ear.

It would be so very easy to turn my head just a little, to let his mouth brush my cheek, then maybe move lower down my neck.

"It's all in the wrist." His voice was low and a little scratchy—totally sexy. He moved my hand over the pot.

"Reed," I warned. His fingers caressed mine as he helped me stir. "Our families—"

"—are distracted right now." He slowly rotated my hand till the ladle dunked inside the sauce. "Don't be modest about the servings. These good people know what they want."

This one sure does.

I let my free hand slip behind me and slide through one of his belt loops, pulling his hips closer to my back.

His lips brushed the top of my earlobe, and I shivered.

Yes, more of that, please.

But we were too close.

Much too close.

Dad would definitely see this, and yet . . .

Screw it.

"So like this?" I eased back just enough to let my hips rub slightly below his and stretched my arm out over the sauce pot again.

"Mhmm." He stepped closer to me and ran his fingers down the left side of my shorts before brushing them against my thigh. "Just like that."

Holy sweet mother of–

"Eliza!" TJ's voice boomed from the other table.

Reed jumped back, and I dropped the ladle, sauce splattering the tablecloth. "Y-yeah?" I called back, my voice cracking.

"You spoon that stuff any slower and we'll be here all night." He waved a set of tongs at me and glared at Reed.

He held up his hands in an unfortunate surrender. "I should go see if my grandparents need help with anything."

TJ narrowed his eyes. "You do that."

Reed walked around the table and lowered his voice. "So is the top of the press box still the best place to see fireworks around here?"

I smiled and spooned another serving of sauce on a pile of pasta. "It is. But you have to have special connections to get up there, Fulton."

"Good to know." His dimple appeared, making me almost drop the ladle again. He picked up a couple of bowls. "What time do I meet you there, Crowley?"

My stomach fluttered at the thought. "Nine-ish?"

"Nine it is."

I ladled my last two bowls and set them out for pickup before heading toward Mom for more pasta.

"Shocking, isn't it?" she said to me as she placed a few bowls on my tray. "I can't believe how well it's going, considering the town's two rivals are working together."

"I know. I never would've predicted it." I slid some of the bowls toward the right so she could add a couple more.

"Chad has been asking about you today." Mom nodded toward the drink table, where he filled cups of lemonade next to his father.

"Mom, that train left the station years ago." *And derailed shortly after I found out he was dating someone from Clairview while we were together.*

"He's got a year of college under his belt though. Maybe he's grown up—"

"Not interested." I grabbed another couple of bowls of pasta from her table and placed them on my tray.

"You're right, sorry," she said. "You wouldn't want to start a new relationship this summer anyway. What with the show and your father finding excuses to move at the end of the season."

I fumbled the tray. "Is there any way we can convince him to stay?"

But before she could answer, Ben cried out in alarm, and the "comradery" went up in smoke.

Chapter Twenty-Four

REED

"It is dangerous to spring to obvious conclusions about baseball or, for that matter, ballplayers. Baseball is not an obvious game." —Roger Kahn

I had no idea how a bowl of pasta ended up on Ben's head.

One minute I was standing near the Browns, who talked to me about their store and about how hard it was to run a small business nowadays, and the next minute, Ben yelled out a string of cuss words.

I whirled around, and there he stood. A pile of spaghetti dripping down his head like Medusa's snakes and sauce all over his shoulders and jersey. But not just any jersey.

His Alex Bregman jersey.

Now, I hated Bregman. Always have—especially after the shit hit the fan surrounding the Astros stealing signs in 2017. But Ben was a loyal fan, and he saved up for months to buy that jersey a year ago. Sauce dripped down his chest like he had been shot.

A couple of the Crowley guys in front of him cackled and pointed.

Dominic, Tom, and Brett weaved around the tables toward Ben, all with fists clenched at their sides except for Dominic, who clutched a basket of rolls.

The guests closest to the scene slowly slid out of their chairs and crept away, leaving behind their half-eaten bowls and salads.

Ben flicked sauce off his shoulder and then grabbed the small pile of spaghetti off his head. He rolled it in between his palms and glared at the Crowley guys, who started to back up.

"Ben," I warned. "Don't do it."

But Ben didn't hear me, or he pretended not to. The clump of spaghetti hit one of the Crowley guys right in his nose. A roll from Dominic nailed the other one right between the eyes.

Mayor Dupont stepped forward with his preppy son, Chad, at his heels. "Now, gentlemen, this is a time-honored tradition here, and I—"

A pile of pasta hit him square in the chest. The sauce splattered onto his face and some of Chad's hair.

TJ appeared next to me and the two of us exchanged a look of "Oh shit" a second before Brett yelled, "Food fight!"

Guests screamed and tripped over their chairs to get out of the line of fire. I checked for Eliza. Her mother, thankfully, hurried her behind the street sign at Scoops. Most of my team crowded behind a table flipped on its side near Ben and threw anything they could get their hands on—rolls, pasta bowls, salad tongs, even the wrapped silverware and plastic cups. The Crowley team huddled around another turned-over table about ten yards away and did the same.

TJ and I took cover under the same table away from the war. We went back and forth yelling at our teammates to stop or to aim better.

"Get out there, Fulton!" TJ smacked my arm. "Your guy started it."

"Like hell he did." I lifted the tablecloth for another look and then dropped it as a wad of pasta flew toward me. It splattered against the plastic a second later. "You get out there and tell your guys to back down, or we'll all be in deep shit."

TJ opened his mouth and then snapped it shut before he ran a hand through his hair. "Okay, what if we both go out there? Maybe they'll stop then."

My eyes narrowed.

Or maybe you're trying to lead me into a trap? "Fine." I put my hand on the bottom of the tablecloth to lift it. "On the count of three. One . . . two . . . three!"

We charged out at the same time and then stopped short.

The good news? The fighting stopped before we had to step in.

The bad news? Our families stepped in first.

And they looked pissed.

Granddad and Coach Crowley stood side by side with their arms crossed, glaring at the mess. Granddad had lettuce leaves on his shoulder, and a wad of spaghetti slid off Coach Crowley's neck.

"What the hell, boys?" Coach Crowley shouted.

Someone cut the loud country music.

Coach Crowley walked around the table to join Granddad and Coach Monaco. He picked the lettuce off Granddad and then turned to TJ. "Care to explain how this started?"

TJ stepped in front of me. "I, uh, I don't know, Uncle Will. I was helping with the salads over there, and then I heard all this shouting—"

"And then Ben had a bowl of spaghetti on his head," I added.

TJ pointed to my team. "But then *those guys* threw a roll right at Andy's eyes."

"Yeah, because *Andy* and that other asshole were laughing at him."

"Dude, there was a pile of pasta on his head. It was pretty funny—"

"Enough!" Granddad and Coach Crowley yelled at the same time. Granddad stepped forward first. "Reed, you're captain of this team. So you're going to stay late after everyone cleans up and make sure there is not a drop of spaghetti or a piece of salad anywhere on this street."

"What?" My ears burned.

TJ chuckled, and then Coach Crowley spoke. "And you, TJ, will help him."

Ha!

Oh . . . wait.

Most of the guests left after that. I had hoped to catch Ben before he left, but he was one of the first to disappear after the fight.

I guess I would've too, if I'd ended up wearing my dinner instead of eating it.

As the sun went down, and despite her parents telling her she could leave whenever she wanted, Eliza hovered and helped us clean up. Her mom warned her about getting sauce on her new "Burr Berries"—whatever the hell those were—but Eliza just groaned and rolled her eyes dramatically.

I had laughed at the whole thing, which earned a suspicious look from her father. He kept a close watch on me for the next thirty minutes. What did I do? Was I not allowed to even laugh at something his daughter did?

Chad My-Golf-Shorts-Are-Too-Short Dupont sauntered up to Eliza as she was leaving, and my eye started twitching. The two of them laughed about something before she playfully pushed him a little.

What the f–

"Fucking sucks," TJ mumbled as he ripped off a plastic tablecloth. More spaghetti dropped to the ground with a wet *thwack*.

"Hey, come on. Wipe those down before you just yank the thing off." I crawled over to the new noodles on the ground and threw one at him.

"I'm trying to get this done quickly so we don't miss the fireworks." He picked the pasta off his shoe and threw it back at me.

Eliza looked my way and tapped her watch.

I checked my phone: 8:45 p.m. Dammit. I looked back at her and mouthed, *I'm sorry*.

She made a pouty face and walked away. Chad hurried after her, and my entire body felt like hot lead.

"I really hope she doesn't get back together with that tool bag," TJ muttered.

Same.

TJ and I didn't finish up until fifteen minutes after the fireworks finale, which I could barely see from where we stood. He left on his motorcycle, and I got in Granddad's old truck and swung by the farm for a few things before I made my way over to Eliza's. I didn't sneak down her driveway on foot this time, but I did drive slowly down it.

With the lights off.

Her house was quiet and mostly dark, but small twinkle lights outlined Eliza's balcony. A couple of lamps were on in her room, and all four of her windows were open. Four windows and a balcony. The kind of stuff you saw in movies, not real life.

Or so I used to think.

For the briefest moment, I thought about ringing the doorbell, shaking her father's hand, and asking him if I could take Eliza out for a little while. He'd grip my hand a bit longer than necessary—like any protective father would—but he'd smile and say, "Sure, Fulton. Have her home before midnight though." And I would, because that would allow me to come back the next evening and the next.

But then I looked down at my spaghetti-stained shorts and jersey and back at Granddad's run-down truck.

Get real, Reed.

I smacked the face of my broken watch to bring it back to life and picked up a couple of small stones before tossing them onto Eliza's balcony and waiting.

A sound like a laptop closing.

The creak of a chair.

Then she appeared through a flutter of thin curtains.

Time slowed.

Her long hair hung loosely around her shoulders in waves. The white lights blurred around her. And for a moment, I forgot to breathe.

"What are you doing here?" she whispered, smiling.

"I'm sorry I missed the fireworks." I shoved my hands in my pocket. "Wanna get out of here?"

"Hell yes." She hurried back into her room and switched off her lights before looping a long rope around one of the balcony's banisters.

"Careful," I warned.

But within a minute, she shimmied down it and kissed me.

"Damn, Crowley." I nodded to the rope and tucked a piece of hair behind her ear. "Sneak out often?"

She smirked. "Maybe."

I drove us back toward the farm, parking near the end of the South Five, where I put down the tailgate and spread out a few blankets that I hoped Nana wouldn't notice were missing. Eliza hopped up and climbed toward the cab, where I joined her.

"Wow," she said, leaning her head on my shoulder. "Look at those stars."

I rubbed my thumb on the back of her hand. "I don't get to see stars like this back home. Too many lights."

"Do you miss it?" she asked. "Home?"

"Home." I sighed. "Not sure that what we have right now is *home*. Not without my dad around, anyway."

"Any word from him?"

I shook my head as a sharp pain swelled in my throat.

"I read somewhere once that home can be a person and not just a place."

"Yeah." I picked her hand up and threaded my fingers through hers. "I always felt a little guilty using that word when it wasn't in the same place as my grandparents though. Like we abandoned them or something."

Eliza got quiet for a moment and then sat up straighter, letting her head fall back against the window. "When Grandma died, it felt like she abandoned me. Which feels stupid to say out loud, because she didn't choose it. But I still felt it."

"I get it." I squeezed her hand. "My dad *chose* to join the military. I'm proud as hell of him, but I still feel like he abandoned us."

"Exactly." She wiped her eyes. "But then I realized Grandma was still here, just not in the way she used to be."

"Like in her connections to the town and the theater?"

"Mhmm."

"I think that's what scares my grandparents the most about this summer." I rubbed the back of my neck. "That if they lose their farm, they'll have nothing left to connect them to this town. Like they'll be erased."

And if they're erased . . .

I couldn't imagine not coming back here to see them.

To see her.

Eliza sat up, closed the space between us, and kissed me. If she listened hard enough, I knew she could hear my heart thrumming.

"Fairfield isn't Fairfield without Crowleys *and* Fultons," she said. "We won't let them lose that farm."

We. I liked the sound of that.

Our foreheads touched, and for the first time all day, my body relaxed.

Maybe it was the starlight.

Or the sound of the corn moving with the wind.

Or the beautiful girl sitting next to me.

But whatever it was, my stupidly optimistic heart decided to believe her.

Chapter Twenty-Five

ELIZA

"The theater was created to tell people the truth about life and the social situation." —Stella Adler

The day after the Fourth of July, I worked in the booth alone after rehearsal. The quiet made it easier to focus, and since I didn't have an ensemble on the stage, I was much less self-conscious about my cues and choices of colors and fades.

As I double-checked act 3, scene 5, my phone buzzed on the table next to the board.

Reed: I'm outside

Reed: Is it cool if I come up?

I hurriedly typed Yes before letting him know to enter through the stage door. Once I saw him enter the auditorium, I waved and called out, telling him how to get up to me.

A few minutes later, he knocked and came into the booth, accidentally kicking the broken-ruler door wedge.

"Don't let it close!" I yelled, jumping out of my seat. I secured the wedge and then looped my arms around his waist.

His hands cupped my face as he kissed me slowly, and I shivered when he nibbled my bottom lip before pulling away. "Why do you have a broken ruler holding the door open?" he asked.

"It sometimes locks from the outside. No one can find the key, and maintenance is kinda stingy during the summers." I kissed him again before plopping back into my chair. "Gotta love old buildings."

"Maybe I could fix it for you?" He ran his hands over the hinges and frame. "It's easy to install a new lock, honestly."

"That's sweet, but Ms. Sparrow was supposed to call the owners earlier this week, so I'm sure someone's on their way to fix it." I hoped.

Frankly, it had been a miracle I hadn't locked myself in here while working alone on my cues.

Reed took the chair next to me in front of the soundboard and moved his hand over one of the knobs.

"Careful!" I warned. "That board is super glitchy."

"I thought you said it was a new one?"

"It is, but I'm beginning to think it's as cursed as the theater is . . ."

"But your grandmother did a ton of stuff here." Reed leaned back in his chair. "I'm sure it's not *that* bad."

I spun to face him. "The fire alarm has gone off twice for no reason, the ghost light randomly turns on and off, that booth door won't stay fixed, and my new board keeps crashing—"

"Fair enough." Reed scooted his chair closer to me. "So what are you working on today?"

"Scene five of act three, where Romeo is leaving Juliet's room after they, um . . . well, after they—"

"Sleep together?" Reed's eyebrows went up, and a smirk played at the corner of his mouth, making me want to kiss his dimple. It didn't help that his hair had that messy, wet, just-showered look again.

Focus, E.

"Right." My neck flushed with heat. "I'm trying to capture the mood right for when Juliet's mother comes in, because there's a big shift a second later when the dad enters and says awful things to her." My stomach squirmed.

I honestly couldn't decide who I hated more in this play: the friar or Juliet's father. One abandons her in a freaking tomb while another says he'd leave her to die in the streets if she didn't obey him. Bleh.

"Can I see?" Reed picked up the script. "I can read the lines while you do the cues, if it helps."

"Actually, that'd help a lot. Thanks." The downside to doing cues alone is that you forgot the natural rhythm of dialogue, which could make it hard to guess the fades.

I pointed to where I wanted to start in the script and backed up a few cues to match the spot. "Whenever you're ready, *Romeo*," I nudged his shoulder and pressed the green "GO" button to start the scene.

Reed cleared his throat and began reading. "'Farewell! / I will omit no opportunity / That may convey my greetings, love, to thee.'"

Wow. Total natural.

"Juliet?" Reed nudged me. "Your line."

Oh, right. "'O, think'st thou we shall ever meet again?'" I clicked the "GO" button again for the slow fade into one of my favorite foreshadowing moments of the play, after Romeo's next line.

"'I doubt it not; and all these woes shall serve / For sweet discourses in our times to come.'"

The ace pitcher reads Shakespeare like a thespian. Damn.

The stage continued to slowly darken except for a softer blue that would be behind Romeo as he descended the balcony. As I read my lines, the only light on the stage came from the follow-spot that would be directly above Juliet, casting a small part of Romeo in shadow. "'O God, I have an ill-divining soul! / Methinks I see thee, now thou art so low, / As one dead in the bottom of a tomb. / Either my eyesight fails or thou lookest pale.'"

Reed shifted in his seat. "'And trust me, love, in my eye so do you. / Dry sorrow drinks our blood. Adieu, adieu!'" He leaned back, making his chair squeak. "Damn."

"I know, right? I love her lines in this scene."

"The lines were great, but I meant the lighting."

My lighting?

He stood and moved closer to the open window overlooking the auditorium. "The sun's coming up but you've got it like it's going down as he leaves. Is that the kind of shadow you're going for in the tomb at the end of the play?"

"Yep."

"Brilliant."

I beamed as warmth fluttered through my entire body.

Wow. He gets me.

"Thanks. Would you like to see what I do with the transition between the mother being alone with Juliet and the father coming in?"

He moved back to his seat. "Absolutely."

A half hour later, I saved my latest work and covered the board before Reed and I walked down to the stage to turn on the ghost light. I used my phone as a flashlight to guide us through the aisles in the dark.

"So I never asked last night, but how were the fireworks?" He leaped onto the stage with ease, something I could've done if I were several inches taller like him. "TJ and I couldn't see from the street well."

"They were okay. Would've been more fun to watch them with you." I plugged in the light and clicked it on. It flickered a bit but stayed lit.

"Did you watch them alone, then?" His voice sounded unnaturally high as he sat down near the ghost light, legs dangling off the front of the stage.

"No." The ghost light in between both of us cast our shadows on the floor. "A couple friends were with me."

Reed got super quiet, his entire body looking like it turned to stone.

"Hey, you good?" I kicked him lightly. "Got any plans for the weekend? You and Ben work things out yet?"

"No. He still won't talk to me." He kept his eyes at his feet. "Granddad's got a couple things he needs help with, and I want to take Dad's old pitching net down from the loft in the barn to get some throwing in before next week's game. You?"

"It's the annual Founder's Day Tea at our house on Sunday, so I'll be busy helping my parents get everything ready." I groaned. I hated the big brunch and how 90 percent of the people who went to it acted like they were better than everyone else in the town—and the county, for that matter. But Dad was big on tradition, and since his parents threw it when they were alive, it was his job to keep it going.

Too bad it couldn't be a barbeque. Tea sandwiches were cold, soggy, and gross.

"A big tea party." Reed chuckled and held out his hand for mine. "Sounds thrilling."

"Oh, there's always high drama at high tea." I threaded my fingers through his and scooted closer to him, letting my head drop against his shoulder. "Would you like to come with me?"

"To the tea party?" He straightened up.

"I mean, I know tea parties are old-fashioned and dumb but if you were there, it wouldn't suck so much." *And I could finally tell my parents about you.*

Not that sneaking around wasn't fun—it just was a bit hard when the entire town knew both of you and your families.

He cleared his throat. "I mean, I have a lot of work to do helping Granddad—"

"It was a stupid idea, never—"

"—but sure, why not."

"Really?"

"Really." He shifted a bit. "But maybe we should ask your dad first?"

Right. "Ask" rather than "tell." Because if Reed showed up unexpectedly as my date, what category storm was I tempting to make landfall?

I sighed. "Maybe we should."

"Does he even know about us, E?"

I shook my head. Guilt dropped into my stomach like a chunk of ice.

"If it's easier, I don't have to go. I understand if you don't want to talk to him about us yet."

"It's not that I don't want to talk to him about us." It was more that I didn't know how to.

My phone buzzed twice in my pocket. I didn't have to read the entire message to know what Mom sent. Based off the confetti bursts on my screen and the all-caps, our team just took the first seed in the Legion League Championship.

Any other summer, I'd be elated being on top.

But now?

"Everything good?" Reed asked, taking my hand.

"Yep." I quickly put my phone out of sight as a horribly sour taste filled my mouth.

What the hell kind of a girlfriend was I?

All summer I had been worried about moving if we lost the stadium, but so what? If we moved, we'd still have our lives. Dad had a ton of money from Grandpa and what he did with the stock market, and he'd sell the hardware store. We'd be in a different place, yes, but we'd be together. Dad even said he would manage a new stadium, so eventually, we'd have baseball back in our lives too.

But Reed's family?

Their farm was so close to foreclosure that one bad harvest could shut them down for good. Reed's father wasn't in a position to help out right now, and his mother worked full-time back home just to keep things "normal" for her only son. So what did that leave them?

Nothing.

Nothing except this season and the chance to win something that could literally save everything they had worked for their entire lives.

Reed unlaced his fingers from mine and rested his hand on my bouncing knee, and that was when the truth pressed down the invisible crown I had been forced to wear since birth.

I *wanted* that stadium so I could live my life the same as I always had, but the Fultons *needed* that stadium to live. To survive.

Suddenly, worrying about the Founder's Day Tea and soggy cucumber sandwiches felt like the stupidest thing ever.

Our theater ghosts apparently had a sense of humor, because the ghost light flickered on and off in agreement.

Chapter Twenty-Six

REED

"A baseball game is simply a nervous breakdown divided into nine innings." —Earl Wilson

We only had a few days till we played the Middletown Pistons for our chance to go against the Crowley dynasty. All I wanted to do was practice, but Coach told us to spend a couple of days away from the field. And Eliza texted me yesterday asking if I could be there with her when she told her dad about us.

I went back and forth for hours before sending my response. Typing and retyping my answer.

Part of me was thrilled to get this entire thing out in the open. I hated sneaking around like a criminal. Hated feeling like I wasn't good enough for her.

But the other part of me, maybe a selfish part, didn't want any more pressure or eyes on me than I already had. I had cracked under the pressure once. Lost total control on the mound. It took me months to get it back, and even now I wasn't sure I had it.

Would making our relationship public take me back to last summer all over again?

How many more chances would I have if I screwed up this season?

And if I didn't screw up, if we won the whole thing, what then? Eliza's family would pack up and move to who knows where. I'd go back home. Would we try the long-distance thing?

Since Ben wasn't around anymore and wouldn't have wanted to hear me vent about all of this anyway, I took a long walk with Mickey through the cornfields and talked to him. Dogs were the best listeners for stuff like this. They didn't judge you or interrupt your ranting. By the time we reached the end of the South Five, my gut told me to fight for what I wanted. To do the honorable thing. It's what Dad would do.

Saturday afternoon brought humid heat under a cloudy sky. I parked on Main Street and walked the rest of the way, eventually making it down the Crowleys' long driveway. Classic rock blasted from the garage, where TJ sat facing his bike near a box of tools. Eliza's Jeep sat nearby next to her BMW. I still couldn't believe she had two cars. What a waste to have one sitting there most of the year. Unused.

No sooner had I reached their fancy flagstone walkway than the front door opened. Eliza stepped out onto the porch in a pair of ripped jeans and a fitted *The Goonies* T-shirt. Her smile hit me like a hammer to the gut, and heat rose up the back of my neck. Any second thoughts I had earlier about doing this melted away faster than Nana's pudding pops on a hot day.

Christ, this girl was something else.

"Thanks for being here." She skipped down the steps and took my hand.

"Of course." I fought the urge to kiss her in plain sight of TJ and who knows who else.

One step at a time, Reed.

"Dad's inside." She sucked in a deep breath. "You ready?"

Is anyone ever ready for this kind of thing? I swallowed hard. "Yeah, let's do this."

As we started walking back up the front porch steps, Mr. Crowley met us at the doorway. He had a pencil stuck behind his ear, and his hair was damp and messy, the way mine looked after a shower.

"Eliza." His gaze traveled from Eliza to me and then back to her before moving slowly down to our joined hands. "What's . . . going on here?"

Her hand started sweating in mine. I squeezed it to remind her I wasn't going anywhere.

"Daddy, I'd like to invite Reed to the Founder's Day Tea party tomorrow." Her voice squeaked with the last word.

"Is that so?" Mr. Crowley moved forward and descended a couple of steps before stopping. "And when did this"—he pulled the pencil out from behind his ear and pointed to the two of us and then to our hands—"begin, exactly?"

At the carnival, when we almost broke a wall in the house of mirrors while having the hottest make-out session. "A few weeks ago." I stood up straighter. "With your permission, sir, I'd, um, like to come with Eliza to your party." My stomach knotted, but my chest felt lighter at the same time.

No turning back now.

"Doesn't this seem a little silly?" he asked.

My shoulders tensed. "Why would it be—"

"You're only here for the summer, Reed." Mr. Crowley walked down the rest of the stairs and stood next to me, now of equal height. He looked at Eliza. "What happens after that?"

The doubt came back like a slushie sliding down my throat.

"We'll figure that out at the end of the summer." Eliza squeezed my hand and smiled up at me.

"Exactly." I smiled back at her, but a tiny part of me wished she had said, *Long distance. Haven't you heard of it?*

Mr. Crowley tucked the pencil back behind his ear and crossed his arms. "Do you have something dressy-casual to wear, Mr. Fulton?"

What the hell is dressy-casual? A tie over a T-shirt?

"I'll make sure he does, Dad," Eliza said.

He pursed his lips. "Then I guess we'll see you tomorrow. Eleven thirty."

Eliza let go of my hand, wrapped her arms around her dad's neck, and said, "Thank you, thank you, thank you," while he stared at me with laser eyes over her small shoulders. She then turned back to me. "Come on, I'll take you shopping for a new shirt. And a new battery for your broken watch."

Shopping? "I should be getting back to the farm—"

"I promise it'll be superfast. Let me just grab my wallet and keys." She hurried up the steps and disappeared through the front door. Which left Mr. Crowley and me alone in the most uncomfortable silence I had ever experienced, other than the time I had to sit outside of a dressing room when I was ten while Mom helped Nana find new bras.

I cleared my throat. "Congrats on getting to the championship, sir."

"Thank you." He drummed his fingers on his forearms. "Is your team ready to play the Pistons?"

"I think so."

"That's a big game. And then the championship?" He made a clicking noise with his tongue. "Pressure like that can really get in some people's heads."

Translation: "some people," like me.

"I've got my head in the right place, *sir*."

"Let's hope so."

What the hell did that mean?

"How's the farm doing this year?" he asked.

"Fine." My jaw ticked. "It looks like Granddad will have a good crop this year."

"That's good to hear." He raised an eyebrow. "I know they need a good season. Must be hard not having that consistent paycheck. And being behind on payments and such . . ."

How did he know about that?

The front door banged open. Eliza tucked her wallet under her arm as she threaded her hair through her Yankees hat. "All right, let's go." She gave her dad a quick peck on the cheek before taking my hand and tugging me toward the driveway.

"Be back in a couple of hours, Eliza," Mr. Crowley's voice warned. "We've got a lot of setting up still to do."

"You got it, Dad," she said.

"Fulton?" TJ lifted his head from under his bike and sat up. "What the hell are you doing here?"

"I just asked Dad if he could come to the Founder's Day party tomorrow with me." Eliza unlocked the Jeep and tossed her wallet in the back seat. "We're going shopping. Wanna come?"

"Ha. Hard pass." TJ stood and glanced back and forth between us. "He really said you could come, Fulton?"

I shrugged. "More or less."

"But why would you actually *want* to?" He flipped his hat around. "I'd give anything not to go."

I chuckled and nodded toward Eliza. "I'm going for her."

A slow smirk spread onto his face as he grabbed a drip pan. "Isn't that sweet."

Eliza opened the driver's-side door of her Jeep. "Shut up, TJ."

"Heard you hit the shit out of that pitcher last night." I handed him a wrench he didn't ask for but that I knew he needed for the drain plug. My version of a peace offering for hitting him with a pitch and for the mess we had to clean up at the Fourth celebration.

He took the wrench and nodded. His version of . . . acceptance? "They had no depth in their bullpen." He let the oil slowly spill out into a drip pan. "It got worse the more the game went on."

I grabbed a rag from the top of a toolbox and tossed it to TJ. What would Granddad say if he knew I changed a tire with one Crowley earlier this summer and now I was helping another change out the oil?

"You pitching against Middletown this week?" He wiped his hands on the rag before tucking it into his back pocket.

"Nah. Coach wants to save my arm for the championship."

TJ smirked. "*If* you go."

"*When* we go." I chucked another rag at him. "I've got a two-seamer with your name on it, Crowley."

"Bet."

"All right, all right." Eliza beeped the horn and stuck her head out the window. "Let's go, mister. You need a new shirt."

My eye started twitching. "I did bring some decent clothes from back home, Eliza."

"Okay, but what's 'decent' to you?" She rested her chin on her forearm. "Is it a button-up?"

"Yes." I squinched my eyes shut but the left one kept twitching away.

"What color?"

Twitch. "Navy-ish?"

"A dark color in the dead of summer?" She shook her head. "White would be better."

Twitch. White would also stain super easily, but people like her probably didn't worry about stains since they could just up and buy a replacement whenever they needed to. "Okay," I mumbled.

"Come on, it'll be fun." She brightened. "I'll treat us to ice cream after I replace the watch too."

Twitch. Twitch. Twitch. "I thought we were getting a new battery, not a new watch." I banged my fist on its face until it blinked back to life.

See? Works just fine.

My phone buzzed, and my stomach dropped when I saw who texted me.

Ben: Got a sec?

Ben: Need to talk to you about something.

"Reed?" Eliza called from the driver's side. "Come on."

I sent Ben a quick message back saying I'd call him later and then walked around the Jeep and opened the passenger-side door. "I can treat us to ice cream."

It's not like I can't afford a couple of freaking cones.

Chapter Twenty-Seven

ELIZA

"No legacy is so rich as honesty."
—William Shakespeare, *All's Well That Ends Well*

Sunday morning came quickly, and our driveway filled with cars for the Founder's Day Tea. I sighed and leaned my forehead against one of my bedroom windows as I watched the guests parade down the driveway to our backyard.

Reed was officially late and hadn't texted me all morning.

What if he didn't come? Maybe I overdid it with the shirt and watch battery? But he did seem to like the shirt and he had smiled—sort of—at his watch with a new battery . . .

Then again, judging from the over-the-top outfits strolling down the driveway and around back, maybe it wasn't enough? Since when had a tea party turned into a derby race?

I didn't remember everyone and everything being so superficial when Grandma and Grandpa had been here to help host it. The townspeople of Fairfield had looked one another in the eye and called each other by their first names, not their last. They'd asked questions about the "family" and not chitchatted about their high-paying jobs. I missed that kind of Fairfield.

But then a familiar old truck pulled up.

I threw open my balcony door and hurried out to the railing, squinting for a better look. Reed stepped out from under the shadow of the trees, and my heart drummed inside my chest at the way the sunlight made his dark hair glow amber.

I flew back into my room and raced down the hallway and stairs. By the time I opened the front door, he stood on the top step of our porch. He wore khakis, the shirt I bought him, and a light blue tie. "Where'd you get that?" I asked, pointing to the tie.

"I bought it after you dropped me off at my truck. Like it?" He smiled, and something hummed and zipped through me from head to toe.

"It looks great."

"You look beautiful," he said, stepping closer.

"Thank you." I tugged at the skinny belt around my sunflower dress. "What'd your nana think about you coming here?"

He ran a hand through his hair. "She, um, doesn't know yet. She and Granddad had a bit of a fight this morning. Wasn't the right time."

"Oh."

"*Wasn't the right time*"?

I hadn't thought it was the right time to tell Dad, but I still did. When would the right time be for Reed?

Chill out, Eliza. Stop jumping to conclusions.

Reed held out the crook of his elbow, and I looped my arm through it before leading him down the steps toward the back of the house. "I'm glad you're here."

He stopped at the gate to the backyard and looked down at our arms. "Are you sure this is okay? I mean, we don't have to walk in, like—"

"It's absolutely okay." I stretched up onto my tiptoes and kissed his cheek. "Dad did give his blessing." *Sort of.*

I opened the gate and walked with Reed next to the rose-bushes until he stopped short again. "Whoa," he said, scanning the party. "This is . . ."

"Over-the-top." I smoothed out the bottom of my dress. "I know."

Our yard had a huge white striped tent in the middle, with twenty or so tables with small vases of pink and white roses on each. Dad hired a band from Raleigh to play cheesy elevator jazz music under our gazebo. Dozens of people milled about the grounds, many of them stopping to talk to my parents, who stood near our garden pond filled with different species of goldfish. Bright green lily pads with deep purple flowers dotted the water.

A waiter walked by and offered Reed and me drinks in tall

champagne flutes filled with natural strawberry lemonade my mother had ordered from the Brew. A fresh sprig of mint sat on top of each drink.

"Champagne glasses?" Reed asked, lifting his for a better look. "I thought this was a tea party."

I shrugged. "Grandma always had tea, but Dad loves an excuse to call in the expensive party rentals from Clairview." I hated how it made us look extra snobby. We had a perfectly good place downtown we could've used, but I'd be lying if I said I didn't love the lemonade.

Reed offered his arm, and I took it gratefully as we strolled toward the white tent. Gazes followed our footsteps, but with Reed next to me, I could handle them all.

"E!" Lauryn waved to me from next to one of the tent poles, where she stood with TJ, who shoved an entire cucumber sandwich into his mouth and grimaced as he swallowed it down.

I waved back and leaned in closer to Reed. "You cool if we go over there?"

"I'd much rather be near those two than the rest of these people. Just don't tell TJ I said that," he whispered.

I laughed.

Lauryn gave a small clap as we walked up. "Wow. You look great, Reed."

"Thanks," he said.

“Nice tie,” TJ mumbled. The collar of his button-up was open.

“Thanks.” Reed tugged on it. “I hate ties.”

“Me too. Tossed mine under one of those tables thirty minutes ago.” He stepped closer to us. “So at what point can we sneak away from this shitsh—”

“Who’s your friend, Eliza?” an overly sweet Southern voice asked behind us.

Well, hell.

Chapter Twenty-Eight

REED

"You're saying I should hop over that fence and pickle the Beast?" —Benny "the Jet" Rodriguez, *The Sandlot*

Shit. I hated that voice.

Eliza and I spun around. My stomach lurched as I came face-to-face with none other than Viola "Greedy" Gratton. Of course she was here. She'd probably get enough dirt on people today to last her through at least Thanksgiving.

Maybe that was why these women wore such big hats at these things? Easier to spy on one another. Hide their beady, judgmental eyes.

TJ hummed a dramatic "dun-dun-dun" before Lauryn elbowed him in the ribs. Eliza stuck out her hand and said, "Hello, Ms. Gratton. So nice to see you."

Damn. That almost sounded sincere. She was good.

"Eliza Crowley." Ms. Gratton gave her hand a little squeeze.

"I so miss seeing you at our book club gatherings, but I hear you've been . . . busy." Her eyes narrowed and gave me a once-over like I was some kind of prized meat in the butcher-shop window. Or more like the kind of meat about to expire.

Eliza gestured to me. "This is—"

"Reed Fulton." Ms. Gratton stuck out her lace-covered hand. "It's been a long time, honey."

Does the lace keep her snake venom away or will it still soak through her skin? "It has." I shook her hand firmly. "Last time I saw you I think I was eight or maybe nine years old."

Ms. Gratton's fake smile turned into a thin line. "That's right. That was the summer I lost my prized petunias."

Sweet tea sprayed out of TJ's mouth like a broken fountain. "Dude, that was you?"

"Oh my God, TJ. Do you have *any* self-control?" Lauryn pressed a napkin to his face.

I fought my own laugh as I spoke to Ms. Gratton. "I'm truly sorry about that, ma'am."

Sorry your little yipping dog stopped me before I could go after your roses too.

Almost ten years ago, I found Nana aggressively weeding in one of her flower beds and had asked her what was wrong. She had told me Viola Gratton bullied the town council into voting the Fultons out of their stand at the farmer's market because of "past discrepancies." It was the first and only time I had ever heard Nana say the word "horseshit." I had never been prouder and more pissed at the same time in all my life, so I got on my bike and the rest was history.

Ms. Gratton cleared her throat. "Yes, well, flowers grow back, I suppose. Mr. Mosely's head, however, could not."

"Mr. Mosely?" I asked.

"My poor garden gnome." She took a sip from her champagne flute. "Less than a month after your *accident* with my flowers, someone decapitated him."

TJ snorted into his glass as Ms. Gratton grabbed some funky-looking hors d'oeuvres from the tray of the closest waiter.

I turned my head and whispered to him, "You?"

"I would never, Fulton," he mumbled in a slow Southern drawl.

Ha! Nice.

Eliza stepped forward. "You do have the prettiest flowers in town, Ms. Gratton."

Probably fertilizes them with the blood of her enemies.

Ms. Gratton beamed. "Thank you, dear." She waved over another waiter and grabbed a new glass from his tray. "Now, your daddy tells me that you're doing theater this summer. What part are you?"

"I'm not on the stage. I'm in charge of lighting design," Eliza said.

"Oh." Ms. Gratton frowned. "I thought he meant you were *in* the play. What a pity."

"She *is* in the play." I took Eliza's hand. "Eliza's amazing with the lighting."

"It's true," Lauryn added. "Without her, the mood would be entirely different." She smiled and nodded at me before we continued facing off against our shared nemesis.

"Did you ever perform on the stage, Ms. Gratton?" Eliza asked.

"Me? On the stage?" Ms. Gratton's shrill laugh made my skin crawl. "Heavens, no, dear. In my time, that was reserved for the more . . . free-spirited kinds. The ones who blew whichever way the wind took them, or to whomever it took them. Ones like your grandmother, Eliza."

My free hand tensed. God, I wish I had a baseball right about now. It always chilled me out.

Nana loved Eliza's grandmother, and while I only knew her mostly in passing, I'd be damned if I was going to let this viper say shit at her party. "I heard Marguerite Crowley was incredible on the stage," I said.

Eliza beamed at me and mouthed a silent *Thank you.*

"Oh, she was, Mr. Fulton. She was." Ms. Gratton took a sip of her drink. "Pity Eliza didn't follow in her footsteps."

Jesus Christ, this woman had no chill.

Lauryn stepped away from TJ and flanked the other side of Eliza like a protective mama bear. "The real pity would be if Eliza *had* followed in her footsteps. We need someone strong like her in the booth," she said.

"Oh, of course." Ms. Gratton tipped her glass to Lauryn and then waved someone over from behind us.

"I hear you're quite the pitcher, Mr. Fulton," she said.

Great. Now it's my turn.

"Eh, he's okay," TJ mumbled before grabbing a forgotten cookie from the nearest table and shoving it into his mouth.

I forced a small smile. "I'm doing all right. Thank you." My phone buzzed a couple of times in my back pocket. I turned away and snuck a quick look.

Brett: Have you seen Ben?

Brett: He didn't come to the house again last night.

Fuck. I totally forgot to call him back. And what the hell does Brett mean by "again"?

I tried responding, but Eliza pulled me back toward the conversation. "Reed, Ms. Gratton was just asking about this season."

"Yes. I'm wonderin' how someone as young as you is handlin' all the pressure?" Ms. Gratton flicked a piece of her fake blond hair behind her shoulder. "What with what happened last year at that showcase . . ."

"Not to mention with everything your grandparents have invested into this tournament." Chad Dupont appeared at Ms. Gratton's side dressed in a light gray suit.

Who wears a suit in the dead of summer, anyway?

"I thought my dad told me you couldn't come?" Eliza asked him.

"Change of plans." He winked at her, and I definitely wanted a baseball now. But not to calm me down.

"I take it a day at a time," I replied to Ms. Gratton's meddling. My jaw felt so tight, it hurt to say the words. "Do you play, *Chad*?"

He laughed, and my fingers itched. "No. I play golf and water polo."

TJ snorted. "Of course you do."

Chad's smug face turned to stone. "Did you say something, TJ?"

TJ stood straighter and for one wonderful moment, I thought I'd get to see Chad Dupont get his ass kicked, but sadly Ms. Gratton stepped in. "Oh, I do *love* baseball. America's pastime, right boys?" She clicked her tongue. "What I don't love are surprises. I'm a fan of tradition, you see."

Now it was Eliza's turn to squeeze my hand.

"I'm not sure I follow you," I said.

"Fairfield has always had *one* team. One team for our small town to be proud of. One team that has always represented the *best* interests in Fairfield." Ms. Gratton took a step closer to me. Her heavy perfume made my nose itch. "What will happen to our great town if new management takes over? What kinds of people may move here then, I wonder?"

"*What kinds of people*"? "I think my family would do a

damn good job at the helm, *ma'am*." Several people near us stopped talking. An older couple gasped.

What?

Did I speak too loudly?

Were you not supposed to curse at these things?

Eliza released my hand and leaned in closer to Ms. Gratton. "What he meant to say was—"

"Exactly what I said." I downed the rest of my glass and slammed it on the empty cookie plate. "Now, if you'll excuse me, I think I forgot something in my truck."

Screw this. And screw all these fancy-ass people with their fancy hats and fancy drinks.

I stepped around Ms. Gratton and stormed toward the gate that led to the front yard, but a strong hand grabbed my elbow.

"Enjoying yourself, Reed?" Mr. Crowley held a shorter glass with something that smelled a lot stronger than lemonade.

"Absolutely." I stared past him toward my escape. Only ten feet away. So close to freedom. "I just wanted to grab something from my truck."

Like one fucking moment of peace and quiet, for starters.

But Mr. Crowley put a heavy arm around my shoulder.

"Before you head that way, I'd love to introduce you to the governor."

"I'm sorry, did you say the governor? She's here?" Was the president swinging by too?

"She and the senator are by the band. Come with me." He

started steering me toward the small group near the musicians, and every part of me began to sweat. I didn't come here to rub elbows with the fucking governor and a bunch of politicians. Come to think of it, why the hell did I come here?

"Reed!" Eliza appeared at my side. "Dad, can I steal him for a moment?"

Yes. Please steal me away. Now.

"Don't you want to introduce him to our friends?" Mr. Crowley took a drink and nodded toward the band.

Eliza made a face. "They're not our *friends*, Dad. They just show up every year because you donate to their campaigns."

"Money is always the best influence, honey," he said.

"Funny." I stood up straighter. "I thought honor was."

Eliza grabbed my hand and started pulling me away. "We're just going to take a break from the party for a bit. Come on, Reed."

No argument here. A break from all this sounds great right about now.

Chapter Twenty-Nine

ELIZA

"I want you to try and remember what it was like to have been very young. And particularly the days when you were first in love [. . .] Will you remember that, please?"

—Thornton Wilder, *Our Town*

Reed didn't say a word as I led him away from the party and into the woods that eventually ended at the small gravel parking lot of Bud & Bloom, our local florist. I motioned for him to go up the ladder of my brother Robbie's old treehouse and followed him, sitting so our legs touched and dangled off the edge. The treehouse's roof blew off in a storm a few years ago, but the floor, railings, and ladder were still sturdy enough.

"I shouldn't have worn the damn tie." He yanked the knot till the tie hung loosely. "I looked like an idiot."

"You look great." I placed a hand on his shoulder, but he shrugged it off.

"Everyone else was in a suit."

"Why should you care about what everyone else wears?"

"Good point. I never used to . . . till recently," he muttered.

"Recently"?

I opened my mouth and then shut it quickly. Something was seriously stirring inside of him. I had never seen him so tense before, even on the mound.

After a long moment of silence, Reed finally spoke. "She's not wrong, you know. Ms. Gratton, I mean."

"Not wrong about what?" I asked.

"About it being a lot of pressure." He rolled an acorn back and forth. "It has been hard to keep it together."

I placed my hand on his leg. "But your team is undefeated. You're all playing so well—"

"We've gotten lucky more than once. We almost lost the last game."

"But even if you had, you'd still probably make it to the championship. You still will. It's just one more game."

"A championship I *have to* win." He leaned his forehead against the railing, keeping his eyes toward the noise from the party. "If I don't . . ."

"Your grandparents lose some of their sales. I know—"

"Forty percent isn't 'some,' Eliza. That's almost half. They'll lose the farm."

"I know." Hollowness settled into my gut. "And if we lose, we'll have to move. It sucks either way."

"What?"

My empty stomach turned sour. "A new town my senior year. I won't know anyone. Wherever I go, the theater department won't put a new girl in the booth. And everything I worked for will be for nothing—"

"Moving is hard. I get it." He flicked the acorn into the brush below. "But your family will still be together. You'll still have your money. You guys will be okay. Mine may lose everything, Eliza. Everything."

"I know." My palms started sweating.

"You just can't understand what people like us go through."

"'People like us'?"

He sighed. "My family. Farmers. You just . . . you don't understand what it's like to live paycheck to paycheck or harvest to harvest."

That's true.

But I had seen it with others like Lauryn or the Browns. How it wore on them, made them look tired and sad. Lauryn gave up a lot of her earnings when she first started making jewelry just so she and her mom could pay the bills or fill up the tank for the car they shared. And once, while getting a haircut, I overheard Mrs. Brown, two chairs away from me, speaking about their thrift store and how they'd need to take out a second mortgage just to keep their house. I didn't even know you could do that—take out a second mortgage. That must've felt so scary.

Something sharp pinched in my heart as I turned toward him. "So why don't you tell me about it?"

"It's not something I can explain. You've been a Crowley your whole life." He looked toward the treetops and then to my wrist. "Your watch probably cost twice as much as the down payment on my granddad's truck."

I tucked my arm under the folds of my dress. "Grandpa left it for me in his will."

"You have two cars."

"I didn't ask for the BMW. I told you—"

"I know."

But do you believe me?

The silence and tension between us for the next few minutes was so thick I could've cut it with one of Mom's spiky heels.

"Why don't we just get out of here?" I finally asked, blinking away the burning feeling in my eyes. "Far away from Greedy Gratton, the fancy lemonade, all of it."

"And go where?" His voice cracked. "We can't outrun this, Eliza."

"This"?

The burning in my eyes turned to tears. "We can try."

"You've got rehearsal tonight."

"I'll skip."

He ran a hand over his face. "You and I both know you can't do that. And I wouldn't want you to. Not for me."

I brought my legs up and let my dress spill around them like a blanket, wishing I could hide under the light fabric and wake up to all of this just being a bad dream.

"I should get going." Reed stood. "I promised Granddad I'd help him work on the B Field so we'd stop rolling our damn ankles before the championship."

"I can talk to my dad about letting you guys use the main field for your practices," I said.

He made a face. "Your dad will never let that happen. They've got a championship to get ready for too."

But I can still try.

"I just think . . ." He ran his hands over his khakis. "Maybe we both have too much going on right now. I'm throwing slower than usual. I've been late to a few practices because I've been with—"

"I've been late a couple times too, you know." I scooted back. "Maybe if you got a new battery for that watch sooner—"

"It belonged to my dad, Eliza, just like these." He pulled at the chain around his neck. "I would think someone who wants to spend every waking minute in a broken-down old theater because her grandmother did would get that?"

Dizziness washed over me. "It's old, but it's not broken."

"Exactly." He dropped his head. "I don't need you to buy me a new watch, Eliza—"

"I don't want to buy you a new one—"

"You can't fix everything . . . every problem I have. This is bigger than a radio on my bike or bee stings from the creek or a fancy new shirt."

Is that what he thinks of me? That I'm just some rich girl looking for charity cases to fix?

The hollowness returned but instead of staying in my gut, it moved directly to my heart.

"I'm sorry. But I"—Reed took a deep breath in and then released it—"I think we need to take a break. At least until my season and your show are over. It . . . maybe it'll help both of us focus on what's important."

"What's important"?

I wanted to shake him.

Smack him.

Kiss him and tell him that *he* was important to me. That I didn't want to fix a damn thing about him. That it was okay to want both him and the theater.

But maybe none of that mattered.

Because maybe *I* wasn't important enough to him.

"Look, you've got a really important opening night coming up." Reed straightened himself. "And I—"

"—have a championship to win." I stood and faced him. Ms. Sparrow's words swirled around me with the humid passing breeze.

They need a Doolittle in that booth.

She was right. We did.

And if this was my last summer working with her or in that theater, then I'd have to give it my all.

Which meant I couldn't give my all to the boy standing across from me. Suddenly, everything inside of me started to hurt.

"It's like your dad said . . ." Reed sniffed. "I mean, it was probably just going to be a summer thing anyway, right?"

"Right. Just a summer thing." I turned away so he couldn't see the tears falling down my cheeks. "And now you don't have to worry about finding the 'right time' to tell your grandparents."

He took a step back. "Right."

Everything around me changed to white noise, a loud static filled with blurred and shadowed answers.

Reed headed down the ladder, skipping the last three rungs and landing with a soft *thump* on the leaf-covered ground. He started walking away and then turned around. "Break a leg, Crowley. I know you'll do great."

My chest ached so much that I could barely breathe. I waited until Reed disappeared through the edge of the woods before I sank back down onto the worn planks of the treehouse and cried until I ran out of tears.

Chapter Thirty

REED

"It ain't over till it's over." —Yogi Berra

Dad used to tell me that giving up baseball was one of the hardest things he ever did. That yes, he felt the call to serve our country, that he was damn proud to answer it, but that the pull of the game still held strong. Like gravity. He couldn't ever let it go.

I assumed baseball was my gravity too. I was wrong. Giving up Eliza Crowley proved that.

Five days. Four practices. Sixty-two pitches thrown. Three rounds of running poles. Two rounds of PFPs. And all of them done in a daze because I had lost my center.

Because *I* was the idiot who suggested taking a break. Who quoted her own dad and said it was "just a summer thing."

But she didn't argue against it.

Maybe she had taken me to the treehouse to end it, and I beat her to it?

Coach Monaco clapped loudly and snapped my attention back to the game. "One, two, three. That's all it takes, boys. Three outs, and we're in the championship. Let's go!"

Our guys rushed by me to the field. I cleared my throat as Ben tightened one of his leg guards. "Hey, man, I'm sorry I forgot to call you back. A lot of shit went down this weekend."

"It's fine." Ben kept his eyes down as he finished strapping on his gear.

"Let's catch up after the game though. Okay?" I stepped toward him.

"Yeah. Maybe," he said before he left for home plate.

The B Field sandlot stands were packed tonight, and those who couldn't have a seat in the bleachers came prepared with bag chairs near the third- and first-base lines. We were ahead 6–4 in the ninth. It had been a fast game with no errors from either side. Cameron pitched most of it and was relieved by Tom in the bottom of the seventh.

"Fulton." Coach Monaco patted the top of the dugout fence. "Why don't you stand up here with me?"

"Okay, Coach." I rose and stood between him and Cameron. Nana and Granddad waved to me from behind home plate. I smiled, but my stomach soured when the top of the Pistons lineup strolled up to take his stance in front of Ben.

"It would be the top of the lineup right now," Cameron muttered.

Coach spat a couple of sunflower shells over the fence. "Tom can handle it."

I hope so.

The first batter crowded more of the plate this time than last. Then again, I would too, if I were 0–2 in at bats tonight. We were lucky though. Both of those outs could've easily been home runs if Nick hadn't snatched them from above the fence like Aaron Judge.

Tom must've noticed the change in the guy's stance because he pitched a brushback. The batter twisted backward out of the box. Another inch and he would've taken that ball right in his elbow.

It was a risky pitch but a good one. Sometimes you gotta shake the batter a little before bringing the heat.

And that's what Tom did.

Three pitches later—two fastballs, one slider—the guy sulked back to his dugout.

"Two to go!" I yelled. "Let's go, Tom!"

Cameron leaned in closer. "I've been meaning to talk to you." He spat a sunflower seed. "About Ben."

"Now's not a good time." The last thing I wanted to do right now was receive a guilt trip about Ben and how everything had gone down.

The next batter strutted toward the plate. His cheek bulged with some kind of chew, and he stuck out his chest before he took a couple of practice swings.

Shit. I gulped.

This steroid dude already had one home run this game.

"But something's wrong with him. With Ben." Cameron nudged my elbow. "He's been angrier than usual—"

"We had a fight a little while ago." I patted his arm. "But it'll be okay."

Maybe telling myself that enough would make it true?

Tom threw a perfect curveball for the first pitch. The slap of the ball into the glove gave me goosebumps. The ump's fist rose into the air. "Strike!"

The next two pitches were straight down the middle, but thankfully, the big guy swung over both. He chucked the bat as he stomped off the field.

Two down.

One to go.

One batter now stood between us and the championship.

Between us and the Crowleys—

"He's been drinking a lot though," Cameron blurted.

"Wait. What?" I clutched Cameron's arm.

Coach clapped his hands again as the batter fouled off the first pitch. "Did you see that changeup?" he asked me enthusiastically before looking back to the mound. "Two more, Tom!"

I leaned closer to Cameron so Coach wouldn't hear. "How is he getting it? Who's buying it for him?"

The ball made a loud *thwack* as it hit Ben's glove. "Strike!" the ump yelled.

"I dunno." Cameron spat out another sunflower seed. "But I heard him talking to Brett during our pregame warmups about how much he hates it here. Then he started going on and on about how much of a loser his dad is. And he started talking about Erin again . . ."

Double shit.

Ben's dad was the one ghost he couldn't shake after Erin broke his heart, so I didn't let him out of my sight for months. I knew if I did, he'd spiral. And now he was.

And it was all my fault.

Tom set up slowly for the third pitch, brought up his knee, and released.

Zip.

Drop.

Swing.

"Strike three!" the ump's voice boomed. "You're out!"

The dugout emptied, but I still held strong to Cameron's arm. "Keep an eye on him, okay? Make sure Brett does too." My heart raced. And not from the win.

"That's the other thing. Brett says he rarely comes there anymore. It's like he's totally checked out." He frowned before I let him go and walked to the mound, where the others were jumping up and down in a trance.

"Totally checked out"?

Fuck, this was bad.

This was really, really bad.

My head buzzed with so many questions and fears that the announcer's voice sounded muddied and garbled. "And the Fulton Hawks beat the Middletown Pistons 6–4! They're heading to the Legion League Championship!"

I had eyes on Ben as we lined up and shook hands with the Pistons.

And during our post-game team meeting behind the dugout.

But I lost him when Granddad and Nana pulled me aside in the parking lot to congratulate me.

My texts went unanswered.

My calls to him went straight to voicemail.

I'd be damned if I'd let him hit rock bottom again.

So the boys and I got together and decided to split up and search the town, with me taking the northern side to search the library, the Methodist church, the gas station, and the Lyric.

Chapter Thirty-One

ELIZA

"The good die young but not always. The wicked prevail but not consistently. I am confused by life, and I feel safe within the confines of the theater." –Helen Hayes

Ever since Reed walked away from the treehouse, I filled my every spare moment with working at the Lyric. If I buried myself in my cues, busied myself with helping Cara and some of the others with finishing touches on the sets and costumes, I could convince myself it didn't hurt as much.

And sure, the pain of losing Reed may have lessened, but it didn't go away. Like a bad cut trying to heal itself, every time I saw something that reminded me of him—the train station overlooking his cornfields, Jenny's Diner, or the elementary school where he had pitched to me—the wound opened, bled and stung and ached all over again. No bandage could fix this kind of hurt.

I had walked around the empty fairgrounds, hoping it would

give me some kind of symbolic closure, but each passing humid breeze took me back to that smug smile he gave me when I kicked his ass in our basketball shoot-out and the dizziness of our meetup in the house of mirrors.

Even tonight, after I almost tripped on a bucket of rags and turned off the ghost light to work on cues, I swore I saw his shadow move across the stage. Probably just inhaled too many fumes from the latest coat of stain that Mr. Newcomb added this afternoon.

I fixed about thirty cues and set several new ones in the two hours I sat alone in the booth. Reading the script aloud for timing helped with the fade-ins, but it still wasn't as effective as having someone reading with me.

God, I missed him.

My phone buzzed from the table next to me where the soundboard sat. The thin scar from Reed opened again as I read TJ's text about how the Fulton Hawks won their game tonight. Reed's team would be playing ours in the championship next week. A game that would not only change my life but his as well.

If Grandma were faced with the same decision as me, which would she have chosen?

You know which one, Eliza.

As much as she was a family woman, she would have always picked those in need first.

Crap.

The Fultons needed this. They needed it so much more than we did.

I inserted my flash drive into the board and saved my latest batch of cues. A small light flickered near stage left, and then something that sounded like footsteps dragged themselves across the stage.

"Hello?" I called into the darkness.

No answer.

Should've kept that ghost light on.

The flash drive stopped blinking, so I removed it and powered down the board. A loud *CREAK* sounded from below, making me jump out of my chair.

What the hell? "Hello?"

Silence.

There's no such thing as ghosts. There's no such thing as ghosts . . .

My hands shook as I draped the board with its cover.

I grabbed an emergency flashlight from one of the shelves next to me and turned it on. Moving it slowly from stage left to stage right, I yelped and dropped it as soon as the beam illuminated a dark figure and face I knew well.

"Ben?" I called. "What are you doing here?"

He raised a hand above his eyebrows and squinted into the beam of light I'd thrown on his face. "Jusssst want to see wha' tha' big deaaaaal is mmhere, Erin."

Erin? Who's Erin? "Are you drunk?"

He laughed and stumbled a bit to the side. "Maaaaybe." A brown paper bag wrapped around some kind of bottle hung loosely at his side before he dropped it onto the stage and put a cigarette to his lips.

"You can't smoke in here!" I yelled. Smoking hadn't been allowed in this theater since the '70s. Not to mention, he was dangerously close to the newly stained sets and the bucket of rags that Mr. Newcomb's crew forgot to take outside.

A second later, a small spark glowed and lit Ben's cigarette. But he must've burned his finger in the process because he cursed and then tripped over the ghost light cord.

"Watch out!" I moved to turn on the house lights so he could see better, but it was too late.

Ben fell.

The cigarette flew out of his fingers and into the bucket of rags, which exploded, some of the flames leaping onto Ben's pullover. He jumped up and cried out, waving his arm wildly around as he stumbled backward toward Juliet's balcony.

Her freshly stained balcony.

"Ben! Stop!" I leaned out of the booth's window just as his burning sleeve made contact with the set piece. Bright orange flames climbed the terrace, igniting it like a twenty-foot torch. A second later, the flames licked the midcurtain and spread across its valance to the other side of the stage.

Oh my God, oh my God.

Ben ran downstage and leaped off it just as another set piece, the entrance of the tomb, burst into flames.

Why wasn't the alarm sounding yet?

And why the hell weren't the sprinklers working?

I backed up but tripped over the dropped flashlight. My shoulder rammed into the door to the booth, shoving it closed. Half of the new ruler I had used to prop it open now lay splintered inside with me.

No!

I scrambled to my feet, the heat from the auditorium fire already burning the back of my neck, and shook the doorknob.

It didn't budge.

Shit, shit, shit . . .

Smoke started creeping into the booth. I pulled my shirt up over my nose and mouth and kept yanking the door until my arms went numb.

"Help! Somebody, help me!" My throat tightened and my heart raced as I spun around the room for something, anything, to use to break down the damn door. But everything looked so blurry.

I swallowed a scream and gripped the back of the closest chair for a moment, trying to slow my breathing down, regain my balance, and focus, but it didn't help.

How long have I already been up here? How long can I last before the smoke becomes too much . . . or the flames . . .

Cold tears spilled onto my warm cheeks.

I wasn't ready for this. I didn't want to—

The fire alarm finally rang throughout the building, and the sprinklers over the auditorium seats sputtered and sprayed. But there weren't any sprinklers on the stage.

I fumbled with my phone and dialed 911.

The operator picked up on the first ring. "911, what's your emergency?"

"I . . ." My hand shook so hard I had to use my other to steady it. "I'm on the second floor of the Lyric Theater in Fairfield. In the light booth. The door is jammed; there's a fire in here. There's a lot of smoke . . ." A coughing fit rattled through my chest. "There's smoke everywhere. I'm stuck!"

"Okay, honey. Stay on the phone with me while help comes. Have you tried breaking down the door?"

"Of course I have!" I yelled and put the phone on speaker while I tried kicking the jammed thing again. It didn't budge.

I pounded my fist against the door again and again before sinking to the ground. I couldn't even cry because it felt like thousands of needles were stabbing my eyes over and over.

A voice called from the end of the hallway. "Eliza? Eliza, are you in there?"

Reed?

"Reed! I'm here!" I jumped to my feet and rattled the knob. "I'm locked in!"

The 911 operator's voice came through the phone again. "Ma'am? Are you okay? Has help arrived?"

I hung up as Reed tried opening the door. "I'm gonna go grab something. Hold on!"

I didn't know what he was doing here, but at that moment I didn't care. I crouched down on the floor to wait, but an old reflector spotlight pushed into the corner behind the soundboard gave me a better idea. After yanking some chords out of the wall and scratching my cheek with one of them, I tugged the fixture toward me.

Jesus, this weighs a ton.

I stood and brought the light above my head with shaky hands and slammed it down onto the doorknob, making two of the screws fall to the floor.

Okay. I can do this.

I grunted and lifted the warm metal above my head before yelling, bringing it down with twice as much force on the spot where the doorknob met the frame.

The knob clattered to the ground.

Yes!

I dropped the light and flung open the door. Reed stood there with a metal stanchion from the lobby held above his head, his mouth opened in shock.

"You're here," I said before I had a coughing fit.

He dropped the stanchion and stepped forward, wrapping

his arms tightly around me and resting his chin on the top of my head. "Thank God you're okay."

Something crashed from below in the auditorium, and Reed pulled away.

"We gotta get out of here." He tugged my arm and pulled me down the hallway and then the stairs as they filled with smoke mixed with the warm sprays of the sprinkler water.

What felt like only seconds later, I collapsed onto the grass near the sidewalk outside of the Lyric, coughing so hard I wasn't sure I could stop.

Reed ran his hands over my arms and legs before lightly touching my cheek. I winced at the sharp sting.

"Are you hurt?" he asked, panting, his eyes frantic.

I shook my head and pressed my hand against my chest. God, my lungs felt thinner than tissue paper. "Ben . . . Ben's in there," I gasped.

"Ben?" Reed coughed into his elbow. "Are you sure?"

I nodded.

Reed stared at the burning building for a moment and then pressed his forehead against mine. "Stay safe," he whispered.

And before I could stop him, he sprinted back into the building just as the fire trucks and a police car pulled up.

"Reed, no!" I crawled toward the building as he disappeared into the smoke-filled doorway, the windows of the main floor now glowing with fire.

Come back, come back, come back.

A fireman hurried over to me, but I pointed toward the theater. "There are two boys in there. Hurry!"

The fireman spoke into a radio clipped to his chest and then hurried inside the building with another. I slowly got to my feet, but then my knees shook and everything started spinning.

Someone gripped my elbow and guided me back to the ground. My eyes stayed glued on the theater as the flames continued to spread.

Please, please. Where are you?

The theater wasn't that big. What was taking him so long?

Whoever crouched next to me spoke, but all I heard were the sirens coupled with my pounding heart.

A window popped, and glass rained down to the flowerbeds below. More smoke poured out of the building before billowing higher and higher into the sky as two ambulances drove up.

Come on. Come on.

Why couldn't they find him? Where—

Finally, the two firemen who had gone into the building came out, one carrying Reed draped over his shoulders and the other carrying Ben.

Oh God.

Four EMTs hurried over with two gurneys as the boys were lowered to the ground, where they didn't move.

No, no, no.

I tried to stand again, but another EMT appeared at my side. She held my wrist and timed my pulse with her watch while I stared at Ben and Reed being wheeled into an ambulance. Reed's hand hung loosely to his side.

No, God no. Not him. Please, not him.

"You're lucky." The EMT took off her stethoscope and shined a bright light into my eyes. "A few more minutes and we'd have had to take you in too. I'd like to clean that cut before we let you go though."

"But— Re— What's going to happen to him?" I pointed toward the ambulance.

"They're taking both boys to the hospital. Probably had some bad smoke inhalation." She took out a kit and began blotting something that stung onto my cheek. "Don't you worry. I'm sure they'll be okay."

A loud *BOOM* came from the theater and shook the ground. Like something out of a movie, the roof of the Lyric collapsed. Flames shot skyward like rockets. A crowd had gathered nearby, all of them pointing and yelling and filming the destruction of one of the oldest buildings in town.

One of the best connections I had left to my grandmother.

Gone.

The ambulance's sirens started up before it sped away toward Clairview, and my head fell into my hands.

Inside that bus lay the boy who had done nothing all summer except try to save his family's legacy. The same boy who just risked his life to save mine. I'd never forgive myself if he wasn't okay.

Chapter Thirty-Two

REED

"I'd wake up at night with the smell of the ballpark in my nose, the cool of the grass on my feet . . . the thrill of the grass." —Shoeless Joe Jackson, *Field of Dreams*

My father, dressed in uniform, walked with me toward the empty, familiar diamond of the sandlot. Thunder rumbled in the distance, and a cool, damp breeze drifted over the infield.

A single baseball lay on the mound surrounded by dead grass and dry dirt.

Dad picked up the ball and smiled at it. "You know what I loved the best about pitching, son?"

"What?" I asked.

He pressed the ball into my hand. "The control and power it gave me. It was the one place in the world I felt like I had any control over my life, over what happened to me."

I rolled the ball back and forth.

"But that didn't stop me from taking risks." Dad faced me and put both of his big hands on my shoulders. "Don't be afraid of the things you can't control. Baseball brings it all in balance, but to do so, it has to have something else to balance with. Don't let it be the only thing you love and fight for."

"Reed," a voice from far away floated through my head, and the ballpark and my father disappeared. A soft hand brushed my cheek.

"Reed," it said again. Closer now. Clearer. "Come on, honey. Wake up now."

I tried to speak, but clawlike fingers raked themselves down my throat. Something heavy sat on my chest, and a sharp, searing pain burned on my upper-left arm.

I opened my eyes and quickly closed them.

Too bright.

A steady beeping sound came from my right. And the same soft touch that brushed my cheek now squeezed my hand. "Turn off one of those light switches, Louis," the voice said.

Nana?

I opened my eyes again, and this time, two familiar figures blurred into focus, like heat waves on a paved road in the dead of summer.

"Wh-where am I . . . ?" Jagged spikes caught my voice. Bandages covered my left arm above my elbow.

"You're at the hospital, dear." Nana leaned closer to me and patted my hand. "You've been out of it for almost twelve hours. They took you off oxygen just a couple hours ago."

Granddad rubbed my shoulder. "You gave us quite the scare."

"Your mother is here too." Nana kissed my forehead. "She got in early this morning but stepped out to take a phone call."

Granddad poured water into a small, pink cup and handed it to me. I winced as the IV tugged on my skin but gulped the entire cup down. Water never tasted so good.

"What about Eliza?" I tried sitting up. Damn, my chest hurt. "Is she okay?"

"She's okay." Nana gave her famous warning glare to Granddad before speaking to me again. "Just a bad scratch on her cheek."

Thank God.

"And Ben?" I asked. I had found him collapsed near the stage with singed clothes and tried to drag him out, but there was too much smoke. I must've passed out because the next thing I saw was a fireman standing over me. And then I must've blacked out again.

Granddad and Nana exchanged another look. She smoothed the thin, itchy blanket by my leg. "He's in the ICU. The police have been outside his room for the last couple of hours—"

"The police?" *Shit, Ben. What the hell did you do?*

Nana cleared her throat. "We believe they'll charge him with fourth-degree arson."

"Basically, it means he was acting reckless when he set fire to the Lyric," Granddad added. "But judging by the damage to the building . . ."

"How bad was it?" Based on their faces, though, I already knew the answer.

"Total loss, honey." Nana squeezed my leg.

I sank back into my pillow. "*Total loss*"? That theater had been around for decades. Had helped so many families. And what about Eliza's grandmother? She had passed away years ago, but the tradition she'd been a part of had still stood. Her legacy had lived on.

Till now . . .

"Eliza Crowley sat outside your room for hours before finally going home," Granddad said, his voice tense.

She was here?

"Got something to tell us, Reed?"

"It's a long story," I said.

Granddad crossed his arms.

I sighed. "We were together for a little while, but now we're not." The deep ache in my heart after leaving her in the treehouse almost a week ago resurfaced. And everything suddenly felt very cold. "It's . . . it's over, Granddad."

He huffed. "It should've never begun."

Yeah, I tried to tell myself the same thing. Didn't work.

Nana hushed him and moved around the bed to pour me another glass of water. "A girl sits outside your room for hours, cries as her father practically has to drag her out of here . . ." She handed me the cup. "Doesn't sound like something that's over to me."

Granddad mumbled under his breath and moved toward the window. "Honestly, Joyce, how can you encourage—"

"Oh, get over yourself, Louis," Nana snapped. "I don't need to *encourage* anything. You can't fight what's meant to be."

But if it were meant to be, why does it have to be so damn hard?

Mom appeared in the doorway. I smiled and was about to say hi but stopped.

Her eyes were bloodshot and puffy, and the hand that held her cell phone trembled at her side.

"Susan?" Nana stood. "Susan, what's wrong?"

Mom didn't speak. She stared at me, blinking slowly before stepping into the room and closer to my bed.

"Mom?" I sat up straighter.

She sucked in a sharp breath. "Your father . . . There's been an accident."

No. Please, no. Not now. Not ever.

Nana gasped. Granddad hurried over to the bed and put his arm around her. "What do you mean, 'an accident'?"

Mom wiped her eyes. "It was an IED. His unit went down in the attack. They . . ." She swallowed hard. "Not all of them made it."

"But Dad?" My voice cracked. "What about Dad?"

Mom put her phone on my bed and took my hand. “They’re not sure. They’re still identifying the bod”—she sniffed—“the bodies. Three were taken in for injuries.”

“Well, that settles it, then. He’s one of those three. I’m sure of it,” Granddad said. “Patrick’s strong . . . strongest person I know. He’ll be fine.” He patted Nana’s shoulder. “He has to be.”

Please.

Please let him be.

Chapter Thirty-Three

ELIZA

"And though she be but little, she is fierce."
—William Shakespeare, *A Midsummer Night's Dream*

I almost turned around when I reached a red light at the corner of Maple and Main Streets across from the courthouse. It had only been a day since the inferno—to which I'd had a front-row seat—that swallowed my dream. My grandmother's legacy.

Maybe it was too soon to go back?

Reed was still in the hospital. His nana called my mom to let me know he'd be released tomorrow or the following day. I should've been elated at the fact that he was okay, that his family had called mine like it was the most normal thing in the world, and yet guilt hadn't stopped churning through my stomach. It should've been me in that hospital. If I had noticed that spotlight in the booth a few minutes sooner, I would've run into him *outside* of the theater. Not in the hallway, surrounded by smoke.

Someone beeped their horn twice behind me. The light had

changed to green. I reluctantly pulled forward and parked in the Methodist church lot. Yellow caution tape blocked the parking for the Lyric. Or what used to be the Lyric.

Lauryn waited for me in front of a line of trees that separated the church property from the theater and gave a half wave as I got out of the Jeep.

"Are you sure you're okay to be here?" After hugging me tightly, she stared at the cut on my cheek, held together with two butterfly bandages. "Everyone would understand if you didn't come to this right now."

"I need to be here. It"—my voice caught in my throat—"it was my home too."

My grandmother's.

She nodded and took my hand. "Ready?"

No. "Yes."

We walked through the trees and stopped short.

Oh, Grandma. Thank God you're not here to see this.

It was much worse than I'd thought.

The fire department saved some of the building, but the town would have to tear down what was left and completely start over if there was ever a hope of having the theater up and running again.

Lauryn's hand tensed in mine. "It's . . . it's like a-a—"

"Nightmare," I said.

Hollowed-out windows, crumbling bricks, naked drywall frames. Piles upon piles of rubble covered in soot and ash.

Singed fabric from a few remaining seats flapped in the wind like flags that had gone through a war. And lost.

I wanted to curl up into a ball right there on the sidewalk and wait for someone to kick me into a gutter.

Gone.

Everything . . . so much work and sweat and tears.

Gone.

All of my grandmother's work. Her pride. Her joy.

Gone.

Several cast and crew members crept around the rubble, turning over pieces of stone and wood with their shoes as if they were looking for something, anything, that might have survived.

But my feet were glued to the sidewalk next to Lauryn.

I could pretend to be strong like my father, my mother, my brother. But my Crowley heart wasn't a phoenix. It wouldn't rise from these ashes. At least, not the heart I knew.

Ms. Sparrow passed us, squeezing my shoulder as she did, and stepped under the caution tape. The cast stood still, and no one spoke as she moved among the piles of debris. She bent down near what used to be the stage-right alcove that led to the dressing rooms and pulled something flat and speckled out of the rubble.

Her clipboard.

As bad as I felt, I couldn't imagine what must've been going through her head right now. How could you even begin to calm the nerves of over thirty people who stared at you like you were their last hope?

"Let's all step away from this mess. Maybe under those oaks." She pointed to the cluster of trees that Lauryn and I had just walked through.

We sank down into the warm grass and dead leaves with the others and waited for Ms. Sparrow to speak again.

"First." She tucked her dirty clipboard under her arm. "I wanted to say thank you for meeting me here. I wish it were under different circumstances—"

Jack, aka Mercutio, raised his hand. "Is the show canceled?"

Ms. Sparrow pushed her glasses farther up her nose. "We've lost all our sets, all our costumes and props. I don't see how anyone could expect us to still have a show. I . . . I'm so sorry, everyone."

Murmurs and cursing drifted over the crowd.

I wiped away tears as I looked back toward the rubble. Some of those costumes were as old as my grandmother. Some she made, and they had been preserved in a glass case near the old popcorn machine in the lobby. *Oklahoma*, *Guys and Dolls*, *Hamlet*, and countless renditions of *A Christmas Carol*—their sets were repurposed each year to save money. That theater and everything in it had survived for over eighty years only to be brought down by a drunken fool.

Cara rose to her knees. "So that's it? There's nothing we can do?"

"I'm afraid so." Ms. Sparrow clutched her clipboard against her chest the way I used to hold Penny, my childhood teddy bear, when I was scared of thunderstorms. "It's too late. We can't put on a show when we don't have a theater or a venue."

I snapped the twig I held in my hands.

All of this was so unfair.

We had worked so hard to continue the treasured tradition of what would've been a phenomenal summer show, and now it was all for nothing. No matter what I had tried to do beforehand, in the end, nothing could've stopped that fire.

Or Ben stumbling about on the stage with a cigarette.

Or Reed being a stubborn hero and going back in the burning building for him after coming to help me.

I took the small piece of the remaining twig and sketched a stage in the dirt while reciting the order of the catwalk lights in my head to calm me down. *R1, R2, R3, E1, E2, E3 . . . chained together in groups of three . . .*

What would Grandma do if she were here right now? How would she fight this?

She'd probably fundraise, but even as well-loved as she was, she'd never have raised enough money to rebuild an entire theater in time for a production just a couple of weeks away.

I rubbed my fingers over the looping text of my baseball tattoo and smiled.

So what else, Grandma? Other than literally putting out the flames yourself, because that was the kind of woman you were?

I dropped the twig next to the rough dirt outline of the stage and then moved a few small stones and acorns into arcs around it like an amphitheater.

Wait. Amphitheater!

Clairview!

My hand shot into the air. "What about Clairview?"

The cast quieted so quickly it was as if someone had pressed a mute button.

"What about it?" Cara asked.

"They have an amphitheater." I stood, my mouth dry. "I was there a couple weeks ago. It needs a little love, but it's still standing. It's got a roof over the stage too."

"No one's used that stage in years." Raul kept his eyes on his phone as he spoke. "It's probably a walking death trap."

"It's not. I stood on that stage." *Danced on it.* My heart squeezed. "We can use it." I stepped around a few people to get closer to Ms. Sparrow. "It won't be easy, and we may not have enough time to pull it off, but . . . maybe if we push our opening night back one week, we can do it."

Ms. Sparrow smiled, and her eyes glistened.

"What about sets?" one of the techies asked.

"Um . . ." I picked at the end of my shirt. "Maybe we don't need them. Shakespeare didn't, right? If we really want height with scenes like the balcony, we can use a ladder and dress it up with some fake vines. I've seen that done before."

"And with costumes," Lauryn chimed in, "we go minimal

too. Matching colors like we had planned, but simpler. I saw a ballet production of *Romeo and Juliet* once where the families wore matching leotards."

Bradley, aka Mr. Capulet, sniggered. "Trust me. You do not want to see me in a leotard."

The group giggled.

"Okay, so what about lighting?" Cara asked, an eyebrow arched up.

Oh. Good question.

Even minimal for that would be pricey.

"The sun doesn't set until, what, eight thirty–ish now?" I asked. "If we do a seven thirty curtain, we'll have some natural light left. But like I said, the stage has a roof over it, and there's a ton of trees providing shadows, so we'd still need a couple of light trees, truss squares, a lamp bar, and at least one spot."

Everyone started speaking at once, and they sounded split down the middle. Some smiled and talked excitedly, but others kept frowning and throwing their hands up like they wanted to surrender and go home.

"Look, guys." I walked toward the middle of the group and crouched down, remembering what Dad had said once: *The best way to get your team to hear you is to get down to their level.* I drew the stage in Clairview in the dirt and small U shapes where the audience would sit. The cast and crew pressed in closer.

"There aren't walls on this stage, so we'll need some drapes or curtains to hide the cast," I said. "Or we can do it like some of the newer productions and have the cast on the stage the entire time, but watching and interacting with what goes on. I saw a great musical called *Bright Star* that did that and—"

"*Hamilton* does that too!" Lauryn squealed.

"Yes, they do." I winked at her and then went back to my drawing. "The one thing I'm not sure about is sound. How could we mic people and run that—"

"I think I can take care of it." Ms. Sparrow crouched down near us. "I have a friend at UNC who owes me a favor."

And there you go.

Jack raised his hand. "Not to be a buzzkill, but how do we pay for the new lights and costumes?"

Right. Money.

Crud.

Hadn't gotten that far.

"What about one of those GoFundMe things?" Cara asked. "We can promote the hell out of it on social media too."

"Oh!" Katie's head popped up out of the group. "I've got the best idea for a TikTok for it."

I straightened up and did my best James Earl Jones impression: "'People will come, Ray. People will definitely come.'"

But everyone blinked at me in silence.

Well, Reed would've gotten it. "What do you think, Ms. Sparrow? Can you run it by the Clairview Parks and Rec?"

"I already made the phone call while you were making the

game plan." She stood, beaming. "We've got the amphitheater at Clairview booked for opening night in two weeks!"

Everyone jumped up and went back and forth between hugging, crying, and cheering.

Ms. Sparrow pulled me aside and gave me a hug. "Now that, my dear, was a Doolittle moment."

A couple of days later, the cast, crew, and some parent and town volunteers helped us move lumber, fabric, and old props from the high school to the Clairview Amphitheater. It looked worse than I had remembered but nothing that some good weeding, painting, and maybe a couple dozen prayers couldn't fix.

I hoped.

Lauryn had gotten the GoFundMe up and running hours after our meeting at the Lyric, and we'd already raised about a thousand dollars so far. It was great, but it still wouldn't be enough for what we really needed for lighting and costuming.

The sounds of circular saws and hammers on nails echoed through the tall trees that framed the stadium-style seating in the grass as Lauryn and I pulled up. My door opened before I could do it myself, and TJ leaned against it. Even though TJ bothered the snot out of me 99 percent of the time, I was relieved to see him. "What are you doing here?"

"Your mom thought you might need an extra hand." He smiled.

"Watch out world, TJ Crowley is turning into a softy," Lauryn said as she moved around to the back of my Jeep for her sketchbook and fabric she had picked up from town.

"Only for some people," TJ added, taking the fabric from her.

The three of us made two trips back and forth from the Jeep to the stage to get the rest of the boxes.

"This place *is* pretty sweet." TJ set a box down near the front row. "Didn't they used to do a Shakespeare in the Park kinda thing here?"

"Yep. Ren Faire too." I wiped my hands on my shorts. "Grandma performed here a few times."

Lauryn sighed. "I would've killed to see that."

Same.

Lauryn opened her sketchbook and motioned for us to come closer. "Okay, so I've got some ideas to run by the parent volunteers and costuming people." She pointed to her latest designs. "Since the costumes are going to be pretty simple now, I'm thinking Montagues and Capulets can wear family-specific headpieces . . . Maybe Paris could wear the Capulet one at Juliet's funeral and when he fights Romeo at the end."

"Are those silver and gold?" TJ asked.

She nodded. "Silver leaves for the Montagues and golden flames or sunbursts for the Capulets. What do you think?"

TJ nudged her. "I think they're fire."

"Seriously, Teej?"

"Crap. Sorry." He winced and patted her shoulder. "Too soon. I know."

But Lauryn's eyes lit up, and I couldn't help but smirk at the two of them.

Ms. Sparrow hurried over. "Thank you so much for being here." She shook TJ's hand. "What's the latest with the lighting?"

"Everything should be here in a couple of days," I said. "I had to rush order so we'd have enough time to get it all hooked up. We could really use someone to move that follow spot, though, since it won't be able to be hooked up to this kind of board."

Ms. Sparrow nodded. "I've got someone in mind. Now that we're working with fewer mics, you can train Hazel."

I forced a smile.

Train someone?

When would I have time for that?

Mom suddenly appeared next to us with carryout trays filled with coffee, her big sunglasses propped on her brown-and-silver pixie-cut hair. "Thought you guys might need some fuel." She handed one to Ms. Sparrow, who thanked her before scurrying away toward Mr. Newcomb and other volunteers behind the stage.

"Reed was discharged last night." Mom flicked something off my shoulder. "Mrs. Fulton called me this morning and said he was doing fine but was still a little sore. He's waiting for the doctor's okay to play in the championship."

"But isn't that game in a couple days?" I asked. "How will he be okay by then?"

Mom handed me a coffee. "Your father had the game moved out two weeks. But that puts it on the same night as your opening night. I'm sorry."

Hold up. "Dad moved the game?"

"He did."

My heart filled with warmth, and my head spun with a thousand questions. "He moved it so Reed could pitch?"

"He said a championship team deserved to have their ace on the mound." She steered me away from the group, stopping near a pile of lumber and a big tractor. "So can you tell me about him now? Reed, that is?"

"Um . . ." I picked at the lid of my cup. Damp, tall weeds rubbed against my ankles. "It doesn't matter anymore."

"Why's that?" She leaned against one of the wheels and put her free hand in the pocket of her beige jumper.

"Because it's over between us." I took a long sip of the hot coffee and moved next to her. "We just didn't time it right."

"Timing is an easy excuse." Mom brushed a piece of a leaf off my shoulder. "You make it work when you really want it to."

I huffed. "So what, now you're okay with the Fultons?"

Maybe I hit my head during the fire and didn't remember doing it?

"I'll be the first to admit that I may have misjudged them." She drummed her fingers on her cup. "But I saw how Reed stood tall at Angelo's about the reservations, and how he worked with your cousin after the food fight that he didn't start on the Fourth . . ." She laughed lightly. "But do you know what really stood out to me?"

I shook my head and blinked back the tears I could feel coming.

"It was the way he looked at you at our Founder's Day Tea. He was a fish out of water, but when he looked at you, his entire face changed. Like you kept him centered. And you looked at him the same way, sweetie." She lifted my chin a little.

"You make it sound so easy." My throat squeezed. "But how could we have made it work, Mom, when we both want to win? In the end, one of us will lose."

"I never said it would be easy. The best things never are." She searched my eyes. "Do you care about him?"

I opened my mouth to answer and then snapped it shut. Saying it out loud would only make the scars open again, would only make all of this hurt even more than it already did.

"Just because you want to win doesn't mean you have to want the other one to lose." Mom stepped closer to me and placed a hand on my shoulder. "You're both equally passionate about something. What's wrong with that?"

I shook my head. "But I . . . I wouldn't even know where to start. I want to thank him for what happened at the theater, but everything I typed up in a text sounded so stu—"

"My daughter is braver than just sending a text." She smiled.

"Besides, his nana told me you were the first person he asked about when he came to in the hospital."

I was?

A tiny flutter of hope bubbled inside me before I tucked it away. "But what if we lose, Mom?"

It suddenly hit me that if we did, it wasn't just about us moving away from Fairfield. I'd be moving away from the one place I had in common with Reed. And if he lost, and his grandparents also lost their farm, it would be the same for him.

Fairfield wasn't just my home or his.

It was ours.

"You can spend a lifetime going over every what-if, but in the end, what is meant to happen will happen." She let go of my shoulder and slid her sunglasses back on. "I wish I could tell you what to say to Reed, but I've learned two important lessons so far in my life. One: You need to remember that people can surprise you . . ." She nodded toward the parking lot. Dad waved at us from the back of his truck, where he and two of his assistant coaches unloaded weed eaters and backed up a tractor from his trailer.

Wait. Had he come here to help instead of having practice?

The tears I held back finally fell onto my cheeks.

"And two . . ." Mom kissed my forehead. "Sometimes you just gotta take a leap of faith."

Chapter Thirty-Four

REED

"It's hard to beat a person who never gives up." —Babe Ruth

I drummed my hands nervously on the steering wheel of my truck. The morning sun burned brightly in a sky without clouds, and the wind moved just enough to keep the humidity at bay. Would've been a great day for baseball.

After being discharged yesterday, Mom and I went back to the farm, where Nana insisted on cooking a meal fit for Thanksgiving, because "hospital food was just plain embarrassing." Nana wasn't wrong—the food was disgusting—but I knew the real reason for all the fuss.

Nana cooked when she was worried. And she had a right to be.

We still hadn't received any word about Dad since Mom first heard from his base three days ago. At this point, even if the news was bad, I'd rather hear something than nothing. The silence was suffocating.

I gripped the tags under my shirt and stared at the hospital doors, out of which a nurse wheeled a young woman as a car pulled up. The clock changed in the truck to 10:00 a.m. I had sat in the hospital parking lot for almost thirty minutes. That was long enough.

No more putting this off, Reed.

I closed the driver's-side door and pushed my shirt sleeve up a little higher so it wouldn't rub the bandages still on my bicep. The doctor said the burn was healing quickly, but that I needed to take it easy for a few days.

Right.

I had a championship to prepare for but, sure, I could "take it easy."

After signing in as a visitor and pressing a sticker onto my shirt, the nurse directed me to the second floor, where I would find Ben. Apparently, he was moved out of the ICU last night.

A familiar-looking deputy stood guard outside of his room. "Reed Fulton," he said with a smile as I walked up. "Haven't seen you in years. How's your granddad doing?"

"He's doing good, Mr. . . ." My mind went totally blank.

"Ferguson. Russ Ferguson, remember? I went to high school with your dad."

Russ! Yes! "Good to see you." I shook his hand and peered around him. Ben lay on a bed with his eyes closed. He had bandages on both of his hands. "How's he doing?" I asked.

"He was banged up pretty bad and has some second-degree

burns from where the accelerant caught fire on his clothes. Lotta smoke inhalation." He crossed his arms. "You know he's being charged with arson, right?"

"Fourth degree?"

"Yep."

"Can I go in there?" I asked.

Russ frowned. "'Fraid not. He's eighteen. Only his lawyer and family are allowed in there."

Family. I used to be that to him.

"Has his mom been here yet?"

He nodded. "Yesterday. But she had to leave for some kind of meeting."

I scoffed. "Always working."

"She in realty?"

"No, home health care."

Russ scratched the stubble on his chin. "Said she had a meeting with a realtor."

Realtor? Why would Ms. Talbot need to meet with a realtor? Unless . . .

"Look." My chest tightened, and I rubbed the heel of my hand against it. "I'm the only real family he's got right now. And we haven't spoken in days. Can you give me, like, five minutes? Please."

"I don't know—"

"Please." I looked into the room again. "There's something I gotta say to him."

Russ checked the time on his watch. "Five minutes. No more."

"Thank you."

Russ quietly closed the door behind me. I grabbed a chair and pulled it up next to Ben's bed.

His eyes flickered open. "Hey." His voice was scratchy.

"Hey." I poured him a cup of water. He drank it all in one long gulp. "How are you feeling?"

He wiped his mouth with one of his bandaged hands. "Like hell. You?"

"Same." I took the cup back and set it on the table. Everything I rehearsed in the truck, all the calm questions and phrases, felt silly now. I wanted to hit him, shake him, scream at him for being such an idiot.

"Reed." Ben pressed a button that raised the back of his bed up a little. "I'm so, so sorry. Is Eliza okay? Are you okay?"

"We're okay." Anger burned behind my eyes. "But it could've been a lot worse."

"I know. Christ, I'm so sorry." He let his head fall back against the pillow. "I don't even know why I went there. One minute Eliza told me about not smoking, and the next my arm was on fire . . ."

"When I got to you, you were passed out on the floor. I tried to get you out, but there was too much smoke."

"You're the one who came to get me?" He lifted his head off the pillow. Eyes wide.

"The guys and I split up and looked for you all over town." I took off my hat. "I had just left the library gardens when I smelled smoke and saw it coming out of the theater."

I spun the chair around and sat on it backward. "I was inside the lobby when I heard Eliza screaming for help."

Memories from that evening flashed in front of me, like someone was clicking too fast through one of those old slide-show reels.

The smoke.

The heat.

Her voice. The way it made my heart beat so wildly, I thought I'd have a stroke before my adrenaline kicked into overdrive.

"After we ran out of there, she told me she saw you inside too." I ran my thumb over the palm of my hand and wished I had a baseball to hold. Something to channel all the emotions running through my head. "So I went back."

I poured him another cup of water, and he drank it. Slower this time.

An announcement for the pharmacy sounded in the hallway.

"I can't believe you went back into a burning building for me." Ben's voice had turned quiet.

"Yeah, well, that's what friends do."

He took another sip. "Even when they're not speaking to each other?"

I twisted my hat in my hands. "Even then."

"I wish . . ." He let his head fall back against the pillow and stared at the ceiling for a moment. "I wish I could finish this season. Play one final game with you."

"*One final game*"? "We'll have spring ball back home, Ben."

"I'm not going back home after this summer."

"Wha—"

The door flew open. Officer Ferguson tapped his watch. "Three minutes, Fulton."

"Got it." I waved him off before scooting closer to Ben's side. "What do you mean you're not going back home?"

Ben finally looked at me. His face was pained. "Mom got a new job. She's already found an apartment outside of Charlotte. We move after this season ends."

"What?" Cold filled my core as my heart raced. "But that's . . . that's—"

"I found out a couple weeks ago. Right after I left your grandparents. Wanted to tell you but"—he ran his bandaged hands over his blanket—"wasn't sure you'd care."

Seriously?

"You've been my best friend for years." I sat up straighter. "Give me a little more credit than that."

He sighed and stared past me for a moment. "I don't want to start over, but maybe it's for the best."

"What do you mean?"

"I've burned so many bridges back home. Some literally." He

chuckled. "Might be good to have a fresh start where no one knows me. Get away from the memories . . ."

I knew he meant his dad. And Erin. But I still couldn't believe what I was hearing. What this meant. Ben, the guy who had caught for me in every major game I had ever played, who helped me out of some of the darkest pits I had ever experienced, was leaving me.

First Dad.

Then Eliza.

Now Ben.

Who would be next?

"My lawyer came when Mom was here. Said he thinks he can get charges dropped to a probation. Community service or something like that." Ben put the cup down on the small table.

"Well, that'll be one way to get to know your new town." I forced a smile.

"Yeah." He smiled back. "Heard they moved the championship."

I stood up and walked toward his window. "Granddad said Coach Crowley did that so I could pitch."

"Wow." Ben brought his bed up straighter. "Guess those Crowleys are more unpredictable than I gave them credit for."

Tell me about it.

The clock ticked several times and filled the silence.

The door opened again, and Officer Ferguson pointed to his watch. "Time's up, Fulton."

"Just another minute, please?" I asked.

He rolled his eyes but stepped back out.

Ben cleared his throat. "Look, what I said about Eliza. Calling her a princess and comparing her to Erin—"

"Ben, we don't—"

"Just let me finish, okay?" He stared at his IV tube for a moment before continuing. "I know you and her go way back, and maybe this thing you've got going on is, um, great, but promise me you won't throw this season away now." He swallowed, and his face scrunched up in pain when he did. "That championship, it means something big to your family. And you worked your ass off this summer to get this far."

I rubbed the back of my neck and leaned against the window. "I know."

"Good." He let his head fall back against the pillows. "Then go win the damn thing. Everything else will work itself out."

The door opened, and Officer Ferguson nodded toward the hallway. "Time's really up, Fulton."

I patted Ben's knee. "I'll see you around. Rest up."

"Good luck in the championship," he said.

My eyes stung as I turned to leave.

"Reed?" Ben called out, stopping me.

"Yeah?" I turned around.

"Tell Eliza I'm sorry. I know it doesn't make up for anything, but"—he picked at the edge of his blanket—"I'm sorry for everything."

I nodded and tugged on my hat before hurrying through the rest of the hospital. Fresh air never tasted or felt so good.

I ripped off my visitor sticker, chucked it into the trash can, and kicked it.

My fault.

All of this was my fault. Had I not broken the pact, Ben wouldn't have left the farm. Had I responded to his text before that damn tea party, he wouldn't have spiraled the way he did. I could've helped him through it. We would've gotten through it. Together. Like we always did. He never would've gone into that theater.

Shit.

I was just as guilty of starting that damned fire as he was.

I trudged back to my truck and didn't see the Jeep parked a few spots over from mine until I unlocked my door.

"Hey," Eliza said. "Your nana told me I'd find you here. I hope that's okay."

"*Okay*"?

It was more than okay. It would always be more than okay.

Small flyaways framed her face, and she had a smudge of green paint on her cheek. I shoved my hands into my pockets to keep myself from reaching out to wipe it off. To play it cool despite the way my heart hammered inside my chest.

"H-how are you?"

"I'm okay." She nodded to my arm. "Does that hurt?"

"This? Nah." I pointed to the bandages. "Not much anymore."

Her shoulders relaxed. "Good."

I stepped around the hood of my truck and started moving toward her. But she took a step back.

Oh.

Something sharp like a chisel pierced my heart.

"I wanted to come here to thank you." She rubbed her thumb against her palm. "Thank you for coming into the theater to save me."

I leaned against my passenger door. "If I remember correctly, you didn't need saving."

"True." She smiled and fumbled with her keys.

Say something, idiot.

Tell her you miss her.

Tell her you were wrong about taking a break.

Tell her you could do both. Baseball and be with her. Even if you weren't sure in the moment that it was possible.

"I . . . um, I gotta go." Her eyes searched my face and settled on my mouth for just a second before moving back to my eyes. "I have rehearsal."

"At Clairview, right?" I pushed off the truck. "Nana said the whole town's talkin' about how you came up with the idea to have it at the old amphitheater."

"Well, I wouldn't have thought of it had I . . . had we not . . ." Her cheeks flushed pink. "I should go." She opened her door.

"Eliza?"

"Yes?" She looked at me expectantly.

Now's your chance. Fix this.

I took a step closer to her Jeep, but the magazine on her dashboard with the title *Philadelphia High School for the Creative and Performing Arts* made me stop short. She was already looking at other high schools. Already planning the what-if-we-lose scenario for her family.

But Philadelphia? How many hours away was that from North Carolina? And how could I expect her to want to be with me right now when she had so much on her own plate?

The pieces of my broken heart dropped to my feet. The least I could do was help her keep her head in the game and focus on her big night. She didn't need to worry about me or mine.

I swallowed hard and forced a smile. "I just wanted to say . . . break a leg, Crowley."

A tear fell onto Eliza's cheek. Fuck, it killed me not to wipe it away. Not to hold her.

"Thank you," she said before wiping it away herself. "Good luck out there, Fulton."

A moment later, she started her Jeep and drove away.

I got back into my truck and sat there with the engine idling.

Ben was moving. I wouldn't play ball with him again. Eliza was already planning on moving. Still no word on Dad.

I shook my head and put the truck in drive. The air circled through the open windows as I made my way back to the farm. To the family who needed me to win. Who were counting on me to save everything they held dear.

As much as I wanted and needed to be with Eliza, my focus had to be on baseball. I couldn't control most of the things happening right now. But the one thing I could control was myself and keeping my head on straight for the championship.

I promised Granddad I'd give it my all.

And a Fulton never backed out of a promise.

Chapter Thirty-Five

ELIZA

"We all must do theater, to find out who we are, and to discover who we could become." —Augusto Boal

Being that close to Reed in the hospital parking lot was one of the hardest things I had ever done. Not touching him, not letting him hold me or kiss me . . .

I went there, waited for a half hour, because I wanted to apologize. Because I missed him. Because I stupidly listened to Mom and thought I needed to "take a leap." But the pain he failed to hide brought me back to reality.

His best friend was being charged with arson. Mrs. Fulton told Mom that Mr. Fulton's unit was attacked and that they still hadn't received word on his condition. Reed didn't need anything else to worry about going into that championship.

So in those quick minutes, I had backed down from my "Get Reed back" plan and decided instead to spend every day of the next week pouring all of myself into getting the play ready in its new location.

Tech Week, aka Hell Week, officially arrived and, naturally, it came during the hottest week on record.

God, what I wouldn't give for air-conditioning.

I took a long swig of water from my fourth bottle of the day while Carl, my "favorite" light guy, finished inspecting my job of hooking up our new trees and fixtures. He explained the complexity of DMX cables while he looked over everything, and my head spun.

Can you Google Translate an electrician?

"Okay." He rubbed the sweaty stubble on his chin. "We've got good news and bad news."

Great. I groaned. "Bad news first, please."

He tucked his clipboard under his armpit. "Bad news: You've got a faulty fixture for your stage left."

"But how is that possible?" They'd just come in a couple of days ago and were working fine until yesterday. I chucked my bottle into the nearby trash can.

"Nice shot." Carl pulled a Red Sox hat from his back pocket and tugged it on.

Ugh. He would be a BoSox fan.

"Sometimes, these lights are like . . . like sleeper cells from a spy movie." He rubbed his nose. "You don't know they're bad until *BAM!* They start stabbing you in the middle of the night."

Super. "So what do I do?"

"We're going to run it from a splitter so it can't affect any of the other lights. Kinda like a virus. Gotta keep it from spreading and infecting." He made a few notes on his clipboard.

I rubbed my sunburned neck. "Okay. It'll run from its own board, but can I still sync that up to my main one?"

"Yep. And don't forget: With that older model of a board, you gotta do any chase sequences or big effects manually if they're not already preprogrammed."

"Right. Thanks."

"But now for the good news! The flickering spot you called us about? It's just a bad cable." He pointed to the output. "Go ahead and shake that one right there. Go on."

I blew on my fingers—Dad did that once before jumping my Jeep and swore it helped—and wiggled the cable to the spot. Sure enough, the bulb flickered. "The kit we bought came with extra cables," I said. "We can use one of those, right?"

"Right."

I let out a breath. "Change a cable, add a splitter, set the rest of my cues, and get Hazel caught up on the follow spot. Totally doable." *If I had weeks and not days.*

"About that splitter." Carl tapped his clipboard. "It is going to cost a little more than what the website says."

So much for optimism. "How much more?" I'd sell one of my kidneys if I had to so I could get this crap done. It's not like I needed both.

Ms. Sparrow appeared at my side and placed her hand on my

shoulder. “Money is no longer a problem. Just get our girl what she needs.”

Say what?

“You got it.” Carl gave a small salute and hurried over to the back of his truck.

“What do you mean, ‘Money is no longer a problem?’” I grabbed two bottles from the cooler near my and Katie’s table and offered one to Ms. Sparrow.

She grinned. “We received a donation of fifteen hundred dollars yesterday.”

Water sprayed out of my mouth. “Wh-what? From who?”

She pulled her bright yellow framed sunglasses down to the tip of her nose. “From your father.”

I drove over to Crowley Park on my lunch break and marched straight onto the field. “Dad?” I called.

TJ flipped up his mask from behind home plate and yelled toward the outfield. “Hey, Coach! You’ve got a visitor!”

Dad said something to Caleb and Asher, two of his outfielders whom he also coached at our high school, and then jogged over to where I stood by the dugout. “Hey. Don’t you have rehearsal today?”

“Yeah, I do . . .” I bounced back and forth on my feet. “But this is my lunch break.”

"Oh." He took off his hat to wipe his forehead. "Is everything okay? Did you need something?"

I crashed into him and wrapped my arms around his neck, hugging him tighter than I had in years. This was the dad I had been waiting for, the one I had missed for so, so long.

He squeezed me tightly before pulling away. "What was that for?"

"For moving the championship so Reed could play. For bringing your coaches to help get the amphitheater ready, and for"—tears fell down my cheeks—"for donating that money. Dad, I—I don't know what to say—"

"You've already said it." His eyes turned misty, and he pulled me into another hug, patting my head the way he used to in junior dance rehearsals when I'd had a horrible performance. "I'm so sorry it took me this long to get here. I won't make that mistake again, Eliza Jean. I promise."

Later that week, I woke up to back-to-back texts and selfies from Lauryn at the salon. She had bags under her eyes, but her hair was already looking awesome.

Lauryn: This crown braid is taking FOREVER

Lauryn: And Mom's driving me crazy

Another picture downloaded of Lauryn's mom photobombing her selfie, holding up two cups of coffee behind her.

Me: Your hair looks AMAZING!

Me: And at least she brought coffee!

Lauryn: Those cups are both hers ☹

Lauryn: She said no caffeine for me today because it'll dry up my throat

Lauryn: I'm in hell Eliza. The thresholds of HELL.

I cackled. A knock came from my bedroom door before it opened. Mom stood in the hallway holding a tray of her famous bacon-cheddar scones and a cup of steaming hot coffee. "Happy opening night . . . day!"

"Thanks, Mom." I threw off my covers and stretched. "That smells amazing."

She set the tray on my desk and plopped down at the end of my bed. "You feel ready?"

"Kind of."

I finished all the cues two days ago but had only seen them once with a run-through. Normally, I'd have a few days of tweaking the finished show, but there was nothing normal about this setup. I planned to get there early and adjust what I could, which would be tricky enough with the sunlight overhead.

"I'm proud of you either way." Mom patted my legs. "I can't wait to see it."

"You're coming?" I crossed my room and grabbed a scone before sinking into my desk chair. "What about Dad's game? The championship?"

"He knows, and he understands." She smiled. "Besides, he's not the only one who has a championship tonight. I want to support yours too."

Gratitude washed over me. "Mom, don't make me cry before nine a.m."

She winked and kissed my head before heading out the door. "Have you spoken with Reed at all this week?"

I shook my head and slumped against the back of my chair. "Like you said, we've all got our own championships tonight. He needs to focus on his."

Never mind the dozen texts I'd typed out and erased without sending.

I wasn't sure how or when it had happened, but he had become my person. The one I wanted and needed to tell things to. Even if it was something random like how I caught Viola Gratton fussing at the mailman the other day for not letting her "help" him hand out other people's mail. (Reed would've had the same thought as me: The woman never stops snooping.) Or how Chad threw a tantrum in the middle of the street over a parking ticket. (Reed would've loved that.)

But I couldn't tell him.

I spun my chair around and ran my hand over the small pile of performing arts high school pamphlets I'd printed off from the library. Honestly, all of them were amazing and probably better than Fairfield High, but would there be a place for me at any of them?

"Hey." Mom tapped on the door, bringing me out of my mixed-up thoughts. "Just don't forget you need to have your head in your big night too. You can't control what happens at that ball game, but you've worked too hard to let tonight happen without giving it your all." She gave me her infamous "You hear me?" look and closed the door.

I grabbed the coffee Mom brought me and then stepped out onto my balcony. The air smelled like freshly cut grass, and the sun already burned brightly above the tall oaks lining our driveway. The forecast called for a warm day but with low humidity and a clear night.

It would be a beautiful evening for a baseball game.

And an even more beautiful one for an opening night under the stars.

Mom was right. I couldn't change the course of events that led to the Legion League Championship, but I could change my own future and do Grandma Marguerite proud by lighting the shit out of *Romeo and Juliet* tonight.

Who knew where I'd end up next year? But I sure as hell wasn't about to let that uncertainty keep me from doing my job.

A Crowley always finished what she started.

Chapter Thirty-Six

REED

"I'm not going to play because I can. I'm going to play because I deserve it." —Greg Maddux

As we finished our side shuffles with arm crossovers, the lights of Crowley Park burned brightly, despite the faint gray color of the sky. After some slow forward lunges, half of us moved on to twenty-yard sprints while the rest did more static stretching. Tom, Cameron, and I stood near the dugout and used our J-Bands to loosen up our shoulders.

Even with thirty minutes until opening pitch, the stands were packed. Energy and excitement buzzed through the air.

"Reed!" Granddad leaned against the railing of the seats behind our dugout, where Nana and Mom would soon join him.

I stepped closer to him. "Yeah?"

"I wanted to wish you luck." He lowered his voice a little. "And to give you one last piece of advice."

"Granddad, I gotta finish warming up so I can get to the bullpen." I coiled up my J-Band.

"I know, I know." He put his hands up. "But I've been meaning to tell it to you all season, and now I finally remembered."

"Okay." I crossed my arms. "Shoot."

"You're not untouchable."

Uh . . . "That's your advice?"

"Not all of it." He smiled. "You can try to be as controlled as possible, but you can't control every hit that comes at you. You're not untouchable. Pitching is the riskiest part of this sport. Once you accept that, you'll be the best pitcher you can be."

Something small warmed my heart. "Thanks, Granddad."

"Don't thank me. Thank your father."

"What?"

He stood up straighter. "Your father used to say that."

I clutched the tags underneath my jersey as the warmth in my chest tightened like a fist.

Damn, I'd give anything for him to be here.

Granddad sat down behind the dugout, and I jogged toward the outfield where the Crowley Cardinals played catch and finished some stretches. Before heading toward the bullpen, I walked up to someone I needed to speak to.

"Coach?" I asked.

Mr. Crowley turned around with his clipboard in hand and tucked a pencil behind his ear. "Mr. Fulton. Healed up okay?"

"Yes, sir." I patted my arm where a smaller bandage still lay. "Ready to play."

"Good."

I extended a hand. "Thank you for moving this game out a couple weeks. I"—my throat grew thick—"I really appreciate it."

"After how well you played this season, you deserved it." He shook my hand firmly.

"Good luck, sir."

"And to you."

If someone told me several weeks ago that I'd shake that man's hand before the championship game, I would've never believed them.

I warmed up well with Cameron in the bullpen. Troy would be behind the plate for us tonight since Ben was officially off the team. Troy was a damned good catcher and had a great arm, but I had only thrown with him a few times. It took a long time to build up a rhythm between a catcher and a pitcher. I hoped he was ready.

Coach Roeper told us to join the team for the national anthem. As Cameron and I jogged toward the first-base line, Mom and Nana waved from behind the dugout before they both shouted, "Good luck!"

I took off my hat and waved it at them, beaming.

A barbershop quartet from town began the national anthem, and I bounced back and forth on my feet. Dad always said that my games should be for me. That if I worked hard, I shouldn't feel guilty about wanting the win. Wherever he was, I wanted him to know that I played the best I could this summer—not only for me, but mostly for him and for Granddad.

The anthem ended. And after a few power fives, Cameron and I ran back to the bullpen as Tom took the mound first.

Here we go.

The game flew by, and both teams had definitely come to win.

Brett doubled to deep right center in the bottom of the second and brought Dominic and Alejandro in to give us the first points of the game.

But then the Cardinals rallied in the next inning after TJ homered with two runners already on base.

Nick singled to left center in the bottom of the fourth, bringing Troy barreling into TJ as he slid into home. A couple of batters later, Brett brought Nick in with a shallow single to center and gave us the lead again.

When I had taken the mound in the top of the fifth, one of the Cardinal outfielders, Asher, hit the shit out of my curveball and drove in Matt—who got on base thanks to a very generous and very bullshit ball-four call. Asher didn't stay on base long though. He tried stealing second a few moments later but never made it.

Dominic tagged him out a second after he hit the dirt to slide.

Never underestimate the cannon of an arm Troy has from behind the plate.

Another Crowley Cardinal hit a lucky blooper off my changeup just over Dominic a moment later, but I got the next guy to hit a grounder into a double play. The score stayed tied 4–4.

The sixth inning was a blur. Both teams had three up and three down, with the only hit coming from Alejandro, who popped up and gave TJ an easy catch behind the plate.

But finally, in the bottom of the seventh, a miracle happened. David, our third baseman, who hadn't hit well most of the season, popped a sacrifice fly to right field that brought home Nick. Our bench emptied with cheers.

We were now up 5–4.

Two innings left.

If we could hold them off for just a bit longer, the game would be ours.

As I took the mound a moment later, I snuck a quick look into the stands at my grandparents and Mom. The three of them smiled and waved, and for the first time in days, the tension in my shoulders and neck lifted away.

They were here for me. And they'd be here for me no matter what happened tonight.

Pitching was risky as hell, yes, but damn, I loved it.

Granddad was right. I was the most exposed guy on this

field. I wasn't untouchable. And it didn't matter that I towered over the guys at the plate. Or how fast my two-seamer was.

What mattered was my love of the game.

If I remembered that, no matter the outcome, I could walk away from this game with my head held high.

Chapter Thirty-Seven

ELIZA

"But screw your courage to the sticking place, and we'll not fail." –William Shakespeare, *Macbeth*

Groups of fireflies milled about near the tree line, as if they wanted a front-row seat for the show. If I listened carefully enough, the chirping of tiny tree frogs down by the river mingled with the low whirr of energy pulsing around me from the audience.

Sure, the amphitheater didn't have air conditioning or velvet seats or a top-of-the-line sound and lighting system, but performing Shakespeare here, outside, felt pretty darn magical. If I closed my eyes long enough, I was transported to the Globe. Maybe it was the night air or the tension of the tragedy about to unfold, but this performance felt like it would be our best yet.

I thought we had lost everything over a week ago with the fire, but really, we gained something more than I ever could've imagined.

We had become a family.

I cupped my left hand around the mouthpiece of my headset. "The audience seem overly quiet to you, Cara?"

Silence filled the receiver for a long minute before she replied in a whisper, "Well, it *is* a tragedy. And it's not like they don't know what's about to go down."

"True," Katie chimed in from next to me on the soundboard.

I leaned back in my chair and clicked my next cue, slowly bringing the lights down on stages right and left. The sun had set not too long ago, so Hazel's spotlight could finally stand out, highlighting all the attention on Romeo and Juliet in the tomb. Romeo had just died by poison, and Juliet was about to wake up.

Lauryn killed it in her rehearsals this week but hadn't delivered believable crying, which she needed for this final scene. I crossed my toes and held my breath.

You can do this, Lauryn.

Her eyes fluttered open. Even from this distance, her grief was so palpable that my own throat tightened. I could barely breathe as she tried to shake her (now dead) husband awake.

Suddenly, the Friar's voice boomed as he fled the scene. "'I dare no longer stay.'"

Ugh. Truly one of my least favorite characters in any play. A "man of God" abandons a young, just-came-out-of-a-coma girl, leaving her alone with her dead husband in the middle of a freaking tomb surrounded by her other dead relatives, including her cousin, who's still freshly decomposing, and yet everyone calls Paris or Tybalt the bad guy? Please.

Lauryn's body collapsed in grief over Romeo's on the floor of the stage, the lavender in her hair sparkling under the single spotlight as her Capulet headpiece clattered to the floor.

I gasped.

Whether or not she meant for it to fall off, it was the most powerful moment yet.

Ms. Sparrow's idea, to have Romeo die on the floor instead of on Juliet's stone slab like so many other versions, added a totally different level of emotion. The two of them isolated, in the dark, with this lighting, was almost too painful to watch.

Lauryn found the dagger and held it up, the blade glittering, her eyes more golden than brown. She mumbled something wordless as if to call forth its power.

Chills draped over me like a cold blanket from my shoulders to my ankles as her cheeks glistened with tears.

"Oh, Lauryn," I whispered as I hit my next cue.

Her voice trembled with emotion, but her projection effortlessly carried over the amphitheater. "'O, happy dagger, / This is thy sheath. There rust, and let me die.'" She brought the blade down swiftly and "stabbed" herself, the audience members simultaneously sucking in a deep breath.

Crushed it.

My heart pounded as the families entered the tomb a moment later and crumpled around the two lovers' bodies, my fingers trembling with the final cues. The fade-out on this "new" program on my laptop was super tricky. I had to hit "Enter" at just the right moment and hope the Prince would keep his pacing the same as he did during rehearsals, which was a 50/50 chance, since most actors sped up during the live performances.

"You got this," Hazel's voice came through my headpiece as she slowly zeroed out her spotlight.

The Prince began his final phrase, and with shaky fingers, I pressed my last cue, which would momentarily outline the lovers before a final blackout.

The faint blue of a silhouette appeared and started fading.

Three.

Two.

One.

Blackout.

I threw my fist into the air before high-fiving Katie as the audience rose to their feet with applause and cheers.

After I brought up all the light trees on the stage for bows, Hazel almost bowled me over. "That was awesome!"

"Thank you!" I squealed. "I couldn't have done this without you. Your timing and hits were perfect."

She beamed and hugged me quickly before hurrying off down the main aisle toward the stage.

We had to take our troupe out of the theater, it's true, but you could never take the "theater" out of our troupe.

Five minutes of happy dancing with Katie later, I powered down my laptop and started packing up the gear in the tubs Ms. Sparrow had brought over from the high school. The sound techies were already winding up some of the cords as well and carefully placing their new mics back in their padded cases. We would load the tubs and cords into one of our rental vans for overnight storage before unpacking it all again for tomorrow night.

"Eliza!" Lauryn crashed into me, still wearing her funeral gown. "I CAN'T BELIEVE WE DID IT."

"Oh my God, I know, right?" I fixed one of the pieces of lace on her shoulder. "You were phenomenal. Seriously. The best I have ever seen you perform."

"Really? Even better than Dorothy two years ago?"

"Totally. You kicked Dorothy's ass right back to Oz." I laughed and started singing the theme from *The Wiz*.

She hugged me again and then reached into her bag. "I have something for you."

She pulled out a breathtakingly beautiful crown no one had worn in the performance. Its band was golden with flames like the Capulet headpiece but woven around the flames were dozens of tiny silver leaves from the Montague design.

"I thought you, more than anyone else, needed to have a

crown that represented both families." She gently placed it on my head. "Perfect."

I ran my fingers over it and beamed. "I love it. Thank you."

"Hey, Crowley." Cara hurried over, headphones draped around her neck, and extended her hand. "Way to go."

I shook it. "You too."

"Promise me you'll take good care of this program for me next summer, okay?" she asked.

My throat tightened. "I promise," I said. *If I'm still here.*

Ms. Sparrow weaved her way through the crowd toward us with someone I didn't recognize. She gave Lauryn a hug and whispered something into her ear before she hugged me. "That was outstanding. It took my breath away. You may be a Crowley, but you've got the heart and soul of a Doolittle. Your grandmother would've been so proud of you."

I blinked away tears. "Thank you." Wherever she was, I hoped she saw it.

Ms. Sparrow gestured to the tall woman next to her. "Eliza, Lauryn, I'd like introduce you to my fiancée, Morgan Adams."

"You're engaged?" Lauryn clapped and bounced on her toes. "Congrats!"

"Yes, congratulations!" I added.

"Thank you," Ms. Adams replied. "But I think *you two* deserve the congratulations after that stellar performance."

Ms. Sparrow nodded. "Morgan is the head of the UNC theater department, girls."

Wait. THAT Morgan Adams?

Lauryn stared, speechless, while I offered my hand to Ms. Adams, praying it wasn't sweaty. "It's an honor to meet you, Ms. Adams. I caught your productions of *The Crucible* and *A Raisin in the Sun* last year—amazing."

"Thank you." She shook my hand. "Charlotte has been singing your praises to me all summer. I couldn't get her to talk about anything else . . . other than flower arrangements." Her eyes twinkled.

Really?

"You had to reconfigure everything you did at the Lyric onto a new board and in less than two weeks, right?"

"Right." My cheeks burned.

"That's impressive—especially for a high school student. The simplicity of your choices was outstanding. I especially loved your use of lanterns on the stage as well. Brilliant." Ms. Adams beamed.

A million words rattled around in my brain, but all I could manage was a semi-coherent "Thank you."

Ms. Adams pulled out two small cards from her purse and handed one to me and the other to Lauryn. "I assume you ladies have heard of our new internship opportunity for next summer?"

"Internship?" Lauryn asked, her eyes sparkling.

"Yes." Ms. Adams winked at me. "It's a great way to get your foot in the door with our department before the fall semester begins. While you don't have to be a committed UNC student to apply, I do hope you two will consider our program as you make your choices this year. We could use innovative minds like yours in our department."

"Innovative minds"?

Ms. Sparrow put her hand on my shoulder. "I'll make sure they both get the forms turned in on time, Morgan."

"We will!" Lauryn blurted before Ms. Adams and Ms. Sparrow left hand in hand a moment later.

Did that really just happen?

Mom hurried up to us with tearstained cheeks, looking as giddy as I felt. "Eliza, that was incredible. You have a real talent for setting the mood. I mean, my *God*, with the wedding, Mercutio's death, and that final silhouette before the blackout . . . I think I held my breath the entire time."

I hugged her tightly. "Same. I'm still struggling to catch my breath."

"You're going to struggle a bit longer, then," Lauryn chimed in. She held out her phone, which was open to the Crowley Park Facebook page.

The Fulton Hawks were up 5–4 with one inning left to play.

Holy crap.

Reed was doing it. He finally found his rhythm.

Pride, and something much stronger that I hadn't found the courage to admit to myself yet, bloomed in my heart, daring me to take a chance.

"I gotta go." I grabbed my keys and wallet from between the sound and light boards.

"Now?" Mom asked. "Why?"

"Because sometimes you just have to leap first and think later, right?"

She grinned and took my keys. "I'll drive."

Chapter Thirty-Eight

REED

"Follow your heart, kid, and you'll never go wrong."
—Babe Ruth, *The Sandlot*

Dad would've loved to see this game. To watch me finally settle into myself and just play the game I loved. My two-seamer finally sank the way I had always wanted it to. Its speed never slowed. And the Crowley Cardinals couldn't touch it.

Our guys were hyped to take the plate in the bottom of the eighth, and they showed it. After two back-to-back singles, the crowd started chanting, "Rally! Rally!" But in the end, we couldn't follow through. Our third batter was caught looking, and our fourth tried to bunt but mishit. He practically rolled it directly toward third and gave the Cardinals an easy double play.

By the top of the ninth, we still held them with a narrow lead of 5–4. Before we took the field, Coach Monaco called us into a huddle inside the dugout.

"I need you boys to take a second and look around." Coach Monaco took off his hat and leaned forward on his knee.

I glanced at the guys standing with me and swallowed over the sharp ache in my throat. Ben should be here. We should've had one more game together. But I still had these guys. My brothers from back home, who gave up their summer to follow me to Fairfield. Who agreed to play for my family, knowing how much was on the line for us. I doubted I'd ever have the right words to truly thank them.

"No one thought we'd make it this far," Coach added. "Especially not that team over there." He pointed to the Crowley dugout, where they were huddled up as well.

"But we did. We're here. And it's because every single one of you played with your heart." He stood up straighter. "I need you to remember this moment. Remember how you feel when you take that field under those lights. Because in the end, it doesn't matter how good you are. That doesn't win championships."

He paused and tapped the spot of chest over his heart. "This does."

Everyone nodded. Our quiet dugout now hummed with energy.

Coach Monaco moved off the stairs and motioned to the field. "Now get out there and finish this."

The crowd cheered as we entered the field. The Cardinals followed a second later.

We just had to hold them for this final at bat. If we kept them from getting any runs, the game would be ours.

I picked up the rosin bag, and something bright reflected from behind the press box. I squinted to get a better look. For the briefest, most foolish second, I swore I saw Eliza's silhouette. The same outline and stance she'd had the first time we played her father's team. When she broke through my attempt to block out the fans.

Funny how I had hated the way she did that. How I thought she was the reason I couldn't get or keep my head in the game this season.

But it took losing her for the truth to finally pummel me: The only one who was responsible for how I threw this season was me. It had always been and would always be me.

The pressure didn't have to be a distraction. It could be a purpose. Something to throw for and not battle against.

I closed my eyes for a moment and pictured her standing in front of me again. Her hand pressing the baseball into my glove.

No one owns that mound but you.

No one owns the mound but me.

The tension in the air at Crowley Park was palpable when the first batter took the plate. That same on-edge tingle I sometimes felt right before a major thunderstorm, from my neck to my knees. The batter spat close to Troy, who then flipped him off quickly so the ump wouldn't see. I laughed into my glove.

A second later, Troy asked for the heat, and I brought it.

It was a risky throw, but he made a good call. The idiot on the plate had a shit-ton of chew in his mouth and was too busy pushing it around to focus.

Four pitches later, I got him. Lucky bastard got a piece of a good slider but missed the following one.

The next batter got a piece of my curveball, but Nick was ready in left field and made an amazing sliding catch to give us our second out.

I rolled my shoulders and took in a deep breath.

One more.

One.

More.

So naturally, it would come down to a Fulton pitching against a Crowley.

TJ dropped a white doughnut ring off his bat before he took the plate. He was on fire tonight, 4–4.

I kept my chin low, brought up my knee, and released a freakin' beautiful slider.

TJ swung and missed.

The ump held up a fist and yelled, "Strike!"

Troy gave the next call, a curveball. It should've been an easy throw compared to my slider. It should've swooped down as it crossed the plate. But this one didn't.

The pitch went high and tight. Had TJ not jumped out of the box, he would've needed new teeth.

"Ball!" the ump called. And then he stared at me a bit too

long before brushing away the dirt on home plate. Translation: *Watch it, pitcher.*

The boys banged the top of the fence and jumped up and down in the dugout while I faced the outfield and lifted my gaze to the dark night sky. Dad's tags grew heavy on my chest.

I almost hit a batter. Again.

What if I nailed TJ with this next pitch? What if I fuckin' blew this shot like I did last summer?

The stands, the lights, the fancy scoreboard pushed against me from all sides.

Blinding.

Heavy.

Suffocating.

But then the wind changed, and the moon broke through the clouds. The weight lifted. Dad's words that Granddad had shared with me before the game found their way to me again: *Every pitch is a risk.*

And some risks just had to be taken.

I slowly turned back around toward home plate, and my team quieted.

Troy gave the signal for the pitch I needed to throw, the one I had worked on all summer. My two-seamer.

I nodded and exhaled into my glove as my fingers found the right position.

Control. Keep control.

I stared down TJ.

This one is for you, Dad.

Wound up.

It's not about speed. It's about late movement. You've got this.

Released.

CRACK!

TJ made contact but too far under. The ball popped way up high above my head. I waved off the infielders and yelled, "I got it!" as TJ jogged to first.

The ball dropped.

Please.

And dropped.

You can't miss this.

And dropped . . .

You need–

Right into my glove.

The umpire yelled, "You're out!" The crowd erupted into cheers, and my team charged me on the mound.

We won! *Holy shit, I can't believe we did it.*

Brett and Dominic hoisted me onto their shoulders as the rest of the boys tossed their hats into the night air. Out of the corner of my eye, I caught TJ walking slowly around the bases and taking off his batting gloves.

The boys lowered me back to the dirt, and I jogged over to him. "Hey, TJ. You had a hell of a game."

He stopped. "You too. That last pitch was nasty. Two-seamer?"

I nodded.

"You *did* say you'd save it for me." He reached his hand out and I shook it.

"Maybe we'll get to play each other again sometime," I said.

"Yeah, maybe." He peered around his shoulder, and his smile grew wider. "Uh, Reed, I think you have a visitor."

When did the stadium grow so quiet? Like someone flipped a mute switch?

The crowd between me and home plate parted down the middle. Granddad, Nana, and Mom stood at the end of the long line, all of them beaming. Mom's hands were in front of her face. Her cheeks were wet with tears.

Someone stepped out from behind home plate, and everything slowed down. He stood as tall as I remembered, taller, and wore camouflage with tall brown boots laced up to his shins. His right arm was crossed over his chest in a sling, but his familiar golden-yellow and forest-green insignia still rested above his heart. The corners of his mouth drew into a slow smile.

I knew that smile. That same smile had greeted me from the dugout when I finished my first inning on the mound ten years ago. Had waited for me by the mailbox after I took off my training wheels. And had lifted me off the ground when I crashed into that mailbox on my way home.

Dad.

I dropped my glove and sprinted toward him. I had never

run so fast in my entire life. Seconds later, my hat flew off, and I threw my arms around his neck and buried my face in his shoulder.

He was real.

He was here.

And he was okay.

Thank God.

"Dad," I whispered against the cold buttons of his uniform. "Dad, you came back."

He pressed his cheek onto the top of my head. "Of course I did." His voice cracked. "I missed you so much, son."

Missed you more.

I pulled back and wiped my eyes. "But how . . . ?"

"After my unit went down, it was pretty bad. I was really lucky to be one of the ones who made it through alive. All I thought about was you, your mother. And that got me through." He took off his hat.

The stadium's explosive clapping made us both jump as the scoreboard changed to a live feed of our reunion with a banner caption underneath it that said, "Welcome Home, Sergeant Major Fulton."

Dad waved his hat in the air and mouthed a silent *Thank you* to them before turning back to me. "They released me a few days ago. I debriefed most of the day yesterday and got here just in time. Your fastball . . . two-seamer?"

I smirked. "You saw that?"

"I saw it all." He pulled me into another hug. "Great game, kid."

We stayed like that for a while or for what felt like forever. Blurs of movement shifted around us, but I didn't move. Wouldn't move. Because part of me still worried if I did, he would vanish, and all of this would be nothing but a dream.

But then he ruffled my hair. And he didn't disappear.

He was finally home.

"Thank you, Reed, for winning back what should've always been ours," he said.

Ours.

A rock dropped into my stomach. We won. Which meant Eliza's family lost. The stadium now belonged to the Fultons.

"Um, Reed?" Dad asked.

So the Crowleys would move away from Fairfield, from us, and start a new life. Eliza would go to one of those amazing schools for the arts.

I checked the time on the scoreboard. Could I drive to Clairview right now and catch the curtain call? Convince her that maybe we—

"Reed." Dad patted my shoulder and pointed toward the Crowley dugout.

—could still make it work?

Eliza Crowley crossed the field and came toward me. My stomach dropped more in that moment than it had in the house of mirrors.

She was here. And she was smiling.

Smiling?

Wait. She couldn't be. She probably hated me right now.

Breathe, Reed. Chill.

Dad picked up my glove and backed away to leave the two of us alone.

Or as alone as you could be in the middle of a ballpark.

Under blindingly bright lights.

With a few hundred people surrounding you.

She pulled my hat from behind her and handed it to me. "Lost your crown twice and now your hat." She shook her head. "What are we going to do with you?"

I tugged the hat onto my head and flicked the silver and gold crown on hers. "Maybe I'll just take yours?"

She laughed, and everything in me ignited. God, I had missed that sound.

But it wouldn't change what had happened here tonight. What would happen because of tonight. "Eliza, about the game. I'm—I'm so sorry—"

She held up her hand. "You came here to win back that stadium for your family, Reed. You made a promise to your granddad, to your nana, and you kept that promise."

"But I wouldn't have made that promise had I known it would make you uproot your whole life."

"Yes, you would have." She brushed something off my shoulder. "And so would I, had I been in your shoes. Because family is everything to us."

I snuck a quick look at mine: My dad, who had his arm around my mom. Proud Granddad and Nana, who looked around the stadium with tears in their eyes.

Family *was* everything.

But so was she.

I took a step closer to her. "I . . . I must've typed out a dozen texts to you over the last week. I tried to convince myself that the reason I didn't send any of them was because I wanted you to focus on your Tech Week and kick ass tonight, which I'm sure you did."

She smiled.

"But that wasn't why I stayed quiet." I rubbed the back of my neck.

"So why did you?" She bit her lip as she looked up at me, and my heart squeezed.

"Because I wasn't ready to admit the truth." I sighed. "I lied, Eliza. Everything I said at the treehouse was a lie. What I said about the championship, about focusing . . . I used it all as an excuse."

"An excuse for what?"

I reached out and took her hand, rubbing my finger over her small wrist tattoo. "For feeling like I wasn't good enough for you. For thinking you deserved better."

She took her free hand and cupped the side of my face. Warmth spread over every inch of me at her touch. "I don't think there's anyone better than you, Reed."

I leaned into her hand.

"Then again, you did steal my toys when we were kids." She raised an eyebrow.

"I returned them. Well, most of them." I smiled. "Besides, you melted two of my best Transformers. Don't think I've forgotten that."

"How about a truce, then?" She took my baseball hat off and lifted her crown before placing it on my head.

I bent down and let my forehead press against hers. "Does this mean you won't knock it off of me?"

"Not on purpose." She smiled, and her eyes turned misty under the floodlights. "Reed, I'm sorry I thought for even a second that my family losing the stadium would be worse or even equal to the loss yours would face. Fairfield isn't Fairfield unless the Fultons are here."

"It isn't Fairfield without the Crowleys either."

"Reed—"

"Hold on. I've gotta get all this out." I swallowed hard. "You are the top of the lineup with a full count when the bases are loaded in the bottom of the ninth. I used to be afraid of that kind of game, of those kinds of risks, but I'm not anymore." My heart pounded so loudly, I thought my jersey might move with it.

"I love that you call me on my bullshit, that you know how to hit the hell out of my curveball and that you can throw some heat. I love that no matter where you end up, you're going to shine brighter than anyone because you're the one holding the light. And I know long distance will be hard. But I don't care." I paused and stepped back so I could see all of her. "I want to be with you. I *need* to be with you. You're what keeps me grounded when everything else tries to knock me down."

A tear fell onto her cheek, and I brushed it away. "There's no crying in baseball, Crowley."

"Are you going to kiss her or make us wait all night?" someone yelled from the stands. Both teams were near each other now. Most of them with their phones out and pointed at us. Of course.

"A Crowley and Fulton standoff." She laughed and wiped her eyes. "How predictable of us."

"I can think of something that would be unpredictable." I took her hand.

She raised an eyebrow. "Is that so?"

I grinned. "Will you hit me if I kiss you?"

"No." She dropped my hand and slid both of hers around my neck as she rose up on her toes. "But I will if you don't."

It didn't matter that the entire town watched us or that neither of us knew what came next or that the ground tilted when she kissed me.

Eliza Crowley was my gravity. The constant that stayed with me when everything else blurred or faded into shadow.

She *was* the no-hitter. The two-seamer I so desperately needed but never thought I'd get. Never thought I deserved.

The game hadn't been perfect between us, but, hey, baseball—love—was far from perfect.

Chapter Thirty-Nine

ELIZA

"The fault [. . .] is not in our stars, but in ourselves."
—William Shakespeare, *Julius Caesar*

One week later, on a Friday morning, I woke up to the sun beaming into my room and the noise of a lawnmower across the street. Two bouquets of flowers perched on my desk side by side—daisies from Reed and lilies from Dad. Both had come to the Saturday night show the day after the championship and opening night.

They had sat together.

And through some act of God—or who am I kidding, maybe the juju of Andrew Lloyd Webber—I didn't miss any cues, despite peeking at the back of their heads more than I did the stage. How could I not?

Reed and I had spent every moment we could together over the last several days. He introduced me to his nana's eccentric chickens, and his granddad even gave me an official tour of their farm. We had survived a Fulton-Crowley luncheon at Angelo's despite a heated moment about—you guessed it—baseball. And Reed had survived a family dinner—even when TJ made a smart-ass comment about the Yankees buying championships. At that point in the evening, though, Reed didn't have to say much. Dad had put TJ in his place in a matter of seconds, like he always did when TJ said that.

I just wished I could've slowed it all down.

Reed's family was due to go back home today.

And in three days, we'd be visiting Arlington and then Philly to look at some houses and performing arts schools.

I knew summer couldn't last forever, that Reed and I were going to see each other regardless of how many miles we had between us, but that didn't make today's goodbye any easier to swallow.

Dad yelled from downstairs, "Eliza, you up?"

"Yep!" I called, stretching.

"I made breakfast and a fresh pot of coffee. Interested?"

"Coffee" is always the magic word. "Be right down!"

I threw on a pair of old denim cutoffs and my favorite Aaron Judge jersey before skipping down every other stair and stopping short when I got to the kitchen doorway.

Bagels, muffins, fresh fruit, and two steaming mugs of coffee covered the table in front of our bay window. With the morning light streaming in and catching the steam and bits of dust in the air, the room seemed dreamy, almost magical.

"Did Mom set this up before she went to the store?"

"Nope. This"—he gestured with open arms to the bounty—"was all me."

I eyed him suspiciously as I plopped into a chair.

"Well, I set up the silverware." He stabbed a couple of melon pieces and dropped them onto his plate. "And I did pick up the bagels and muffins."

I laughed. "Thanks, Dad." After careful consideration, I went with my favorite, an everything bagel smothered in cream cheese. Perfection.

He sat down and took a long drink of his coffee. "I spoke to Ms. Sparrow and her fiancée as they came out of the bank yesterday. Looks like they'll get approved for the loan."

"That's great!" After our Sunday night final performance, Ms. Sparrow tearfully accepted our bouquet on the stage then surprised all of us with an announcement that she and Ms. Adams would be buying the Lyric and hoped to start the rebuild this fall. There wasn't a dry eye in that amphitheater.

"Meeting up with Reed again today?" Dad asked.

I nodded. "At the stadium, I think."

"He leaves soon, right?"

The bagel turned scratchy as it slid down my throat. "Tomorrow."

Thanks for reminding me.

"Wow." He picked up a muffin and unwrapped it. "Doesn't feel like it's been two and a half months since the start of the season. So much has changed."

Understatement of the year.

"So I know you're busy getting that application and essay for the UNC internship completed, but I was wondering if you'd help me out with a little . . . project." He set his mug down, cupping his hands around it.

"What kind of project?" I popped a piece of cantaloupe in my mouth.

"We need to think of a new name for the stadium."

"Shouldn't that be the Fultons' concern now?"

"Yes." He paused and pursed his lips. "And ours."

The fruit caught in my throat. "Wait. What do you mean—"

"I've agreed to co-own it with the Fultons."

My fork clattered against my plate. "Seriously?"

"Seriously." He smiled. "Truth is, it's a hell of a lot of work for one person to run alone, especially when you have another business to keep up. Makes sense to have two people—or two families—run it."

"So that's it?" I leaned back in my chair. "After decades of fighting, you guys are just going to work together now?"

"I thought the big lunch we had at Angelo's the other day went well." He broke off a piece of his muffin and ate it. "I mean, I know I got a little carried away when Louis made the comment about pro baseball not needing so many games per season, but come on. We got along fine for the rest of the afternoon."

I guess he was choosing to forget the part where they also argued about whether baseball managers should be able to challenge calls, or the part where they argued about the correct way to boil hot dogs in concession stands, or about whether stadiums should use a prerecorded version of the national anthem.

"Have a little faith, Eliza." Dad stole a grape from my plate. "People can surprise you."

I leaned forward as hope welled up inside of me, squeezing my heart. "So . . . so this means we're not moving? No trip to Arlington or Philly this week?"

"Not unless *you* want to take a look at those schools. I want to do what's best for you too. Even if that means moving."

I sprang out of the chair and fell against him. My voice was muffled against his polo. "Thank you."

"No, thank you." He hugged me tightly.

I pulled away. "For what?"

"For reminding me that I don't need to run away from my ghosts. I should honor them by staying and helping protect what they built." He clasped his hands in front of him as I sat back down. "Watching you work in the theater, seeing the same joy on your face that I used to see on hers . . . it keeps your grandmother alive. Keeps her closer to here." He tapped his chest. "I needed that."

I rubbed my fingers over my tattoo.

Me too.

"I'll always keep the light on for her, Dad," I said. "Don't you worry."

The grass glistened with the morning dew in the outfield of Crowley Park, or now Fulton Park. Crowley-Fulton Park? Fulton-Crowley Park?

Reed sat on the rubber of the pitcher's mound with his long legs pulled against his chest. The sun burned brightly above him, silhouetting his hair and shoulders. I couldn't wait to tell him that we weren't moving.

But it didn't change the fact that he'd still be leaving. Tomorrow.

As if he felt me staring, he turned around and smiled. "Hey."

"Hey." I crossed the red dirt of the first-base line and sat next to him, intertwining my fingers with his. "Did you hear the news about my dad and your granddad?"

He chuckled and scratched the back of his neck. "Yeah, I heard it. Can't believe they're going to work together."

"I know, right?" I leaned against his shoulder. "I'm so going to take videos and send them to you when they start arguing."

"Or maybe I'll send them to you."

Send them to me? Why would he be sending them to me?

Unless . . .

"Dad's retiring from the army." He faced me. "And he and Mom want to move back here." He paused, but I couldn't speak. My brain was going a hundred miles a minute, and my mouth apparently couldn't catch up.

"*He's* going to be the one to work with your dad," Reed continued, smiling. "And he wants to be around to learn the ropes of the farm for when Granddad finally retires—"

I cupped his face with my hands and kissed him so deeply that a prop box full of bulbs crashing onto a hardwood floor wouldn't have fazed me.

"I was hoping you'd be happy about it." He laughed softly and ran his fingers down my jaw, making the warm rays of the summer sun prickle against his cool touch.

Happy?

I was elated.

Ecstatic.

Relieved.

Until I remembered . . .

"You do realize that my dad coaches the high school team. He'll be your coach this spring," I said.

"I'm looking forward to it." He bopped my nose. "I need a good coach for my senior year."

The sunlight reflected off the silver chain that disappeared under his baseball tee. I ran my fingers over the grooves of it.

"I've been meaning to ask you about this all summer. What's on the necklace?"

He lifted the chain over his head and laid a set of dog tags in my hand.

I read the text engraved on one: "Always near, never far."

"My father had them made for me before his last deployment. Said they'd bring me luck." He looked around at the stadium and released a deep breath. "Guess he was right."

Guess he was.

He stood and then pulled me to my feet. "So I've been thinking about that time we played ball in Clairview."

I smirked and slipped his necklace back over his head.

"The one where I hit the hell out of your changeup? And then your fastball?"

"Yep, that time." He laughed and nodded toward home plate, where a bat and a bucket of balls sat. "You up for a rematch?"

"Are *you*?" I bounced back and forth on my feet. "I *am* wearing my lucky jersey today. It never fails me."

He flicked my hat and then picked up his from the mound, tugging it on. "We'll see about that."

I hurried behind home plate and threw him a few balls before taking my stance inside the box. "Don't go easy on me, Fulton."

He smiled. "Wouldn't dream of it, Crowley."

Acknowledgments

This book is the product of a decade's worth of work, and as such, there have been many wonderful people over the years who helped it find its way into your hands and onto your shelves.

First and foremost, thank you, God, for standing by me and reminding me to trust in your timing. I don't deserve your grace and your blessings, but I am so grateful for them.

Thank you to the OG Twitter writing community who supported me and guided me many years ago (and even today) when I was neck-deep in the query trenches and pitch contests. Ernie Chiara, Jenny Howe, Jeanne Renee, Joy McCullough, Miranda Asebedo, Sonia Hartl, Erin Hahn, Erin Craig, Jennifer Iacopelli, Samantha Joyce, Heather Powell, Lindsay Landgraf Hess, Starla DeKruyf, Erica George, Beth Ellyn Summer, Kara McDowell, and Jackie Yeager, I'm so thankful for your kindness and support over the years.

To the early readers of this story: Susan Bishop Crispell, Heather Cashman, Nikki Lenz, Emily Matheis, Tammy Oja, Jenny Howe, and Allison Epperly Chambers, thank you for your time and input with the early versions of Fairfield and its characters!

Speaking of input, a special thanks goes to Katie Kingman, Katy Brooke, and Jacy Sellers. You three have stood by me the longest and have gotten me through so many ups and downs of this journey. From the bottom of my heart, thank you, my dear friends.

Sending this book off into the hands of people I've admired for a long time was so surreal, and I'm so honored and grateful that these incredibly talented and kindhearted authors blurbed my debut: Charlene Thomas, Jennifer Iacopelli, Kara McDowell, Emily Wibberley and Austin Siegemund-Broka, Erin Hahn, Sarah Henning, and the great Hambino, Patrick Renna.

To my Rosebud Family: You are the brothers and sisters I never expected and am so very thankful to have in my corner. I love you all and hope I can continue to make you proud.

Ann Rose, my fearless leader and incredible agent: You are and have been a lighthouse for me for several years, guiding me home when I want to drift away and protecting me from the rocks and voices that seek to pull me under. *Thank you* will never feel like enough for all that you've done for me, but know that I will continue to work my ass off for you to show my gratitude.

To my editor, Dana Leydig, thank you so much for not only giving me the opportunity to revise and resubmit this story years ago but also for your unwavering faith in it. I love that you see this story in the same movie scenes, GIFs, and musicals that I do. You have been a dream editor to work with, and I am beyond honored that you "bet on it" with Eliza and Reed.

To everyone at Penguin Young Readers: I owe you a dozen fried Oreos for the great care and dedication you gave my debut. The way you brought this book to life is pure magic.

Speaking of magic, my cover is the most beautiful cover I've ever seen, and that's thanks to illustrator Steve Scott and designer Kaitlin Yang. You guys truly knocked it out of the park.

To my parents, Sue and Tom, your unconditional love and encouragement make you the kind of parents any author strives to write and any character dreams of having. To my brother, Nick, thanks for letting me pick your brain about baseball and for humoring my love/hate relationship with our Yankees.

For my husband and best friend, David: This book would simply not exist without you. Your patience, persistence, and unconditional love and support moved me ever forward when I often wanted to stand still or throw in the towel. I love you more than words can say.

Tommy and Andy, may my journey teach you two important things: *Never* give up, and you are never too old to chase a new dream. I love you both bigger than the universe.

Thank you, Miller family, for your constant support and love throughout this journey.

Lastly, to the true inspiration for this story: Grandma Mutzi and Pop-Pop, thank you for introducing me to the magical world of theater many years ago and for always pushing me to embrace my artistic and musical side. And to Grandma Monaco, thank you for showing me the importance of hard work (and for always having a Yankees game on in the kitchen).